ALEXANDREA WEIS

This is a work of fiction. Names, characters, places, and incidents are products of the author's imagination or are used fictitiously and are not to be construed as real. Any resemblance to actual events, locations, organizations, or persons, living or dead, is entirely coincidental.

Copyright © Alexandrea Weis 2014
First Edition Alexandrea Weis November 2, 2014

Licensing Notes

All rights reserved. No part of this book may be used or reproduced in any manner whatsoever without written permission, except in the case of brief quotations embodied in articles and reviews.

Book Cover: Bookfabulous Designs
Editors: Maxine Bringenberg, Melissa Ringsted

Chapter 1

A swirl of cigarette smoke gathered about the darkened entrance of Owen's Bar, hovering in the air like a ghost waiting for a divine wind to move it along. When the thick, wooden door of the establishment opened, the smoke cloud parted. In walked a slender brunette with alabaster skin, pink lips, and cheekbones so well-carved that they seemed chiseled by a master's hand. Her lean body, shapely legs, and slender hips sauntered into the dank bar. Dressed in jeans and a white tank top, she turned a few heads of the men gathered about the worn walnut bar across the room. She glided like a dancer as she moved amid the paltry array of dark wooden tables set about the dirty stone floor. Her deep green bedroom eyes flashed with recognition when they settled on two young women, their heads together, at a table not far from the entrance.

"Madison," a yellow-haired girl in pigtails called.

"Hey guys," the brunette greeted as she stood by the table, gaping wide-eyed at her friends. "What did I miss?"

A round-faced redhead with curls and thick lips smiled up at her. "Madison Barnett, you're late. We've already done a round of tequila shots. You need to catch up."

The blonde narrowed her blue eyes on Madison, smirking with delight. "I warned you, girl. We're gonna get shitfaced tonight."

"Sorry." Grimacing in apology, Madison removed the small black purse from about her shoulder and eased into her seat at the table. "I got held up with old man Pellerin."

"And how did the old coot act?" the bouncy redhead inquired.

"He was sweet, Lizzie, and don't call him an old coot. He told me if I ever wanted a job with his architecture firm, I had one."

The blonde reached for a half-empty glass of beer. "Come on, Mads, you know you hated working for him. You told me the other day that he was creepy."

Madison glanced over at the blonde, her green eyes clouded with misgivings. "I know, Charlie, but he was really sweet today. He even got me a cake and had a nice little sendoff with everyone from the office."

Charlie raised her glass to Madison in a celebratory toast. "Luckily, you're done with Pellerin, Everly, and Walters. Tomorrow you start working for Parr and Associates, the biggest residential architectural firm in Dallas. You've hit the big time, kid."

Madison ran her fingers along the gouged surface of the wooden table, her full lips turned downward. "Not the big time, Charlie. I'm not working for a firm that builds skyscrapers, only houses for rich people."

Lizzie patted her hand reassuringly. "Hey, you're only twenty-six. You'll get there. First, the houses for the snooty people, and then the skyscrapers. Baby steps there, girlie."

"Hey," Charlie shouted as she banged her beer glass on the table, "don't go and get all depressed on me, Mads. We're here to celebrate! Your new job and my wedding." She waved her hand, summoning a barmaid who was resting her elbows against the wooden bar. "It's not every day I get married, or my roommate gets such a cushy job. We need to top this night off with some serious drinking."

"Absolutely." Madison smiled brightly and slapped her hand on the table, banishing her unhappy thoughts. "But we can't get too wasted. I start my new job tomorrow."

Charlie nodded. "Agreed. I've got my last dress fitting at eight, so we have to make sure we're in bed by three at the earliest."

"Charlie," Madison scolded with a caustic gaze, "you're going to be Nelson's wife in three weeks. Don't you think you should start cutting back on the late nights?"

The barmaid came up to the table. "What'll it be ladies, another round of beers?"

Charlie gave a wobbly shake of her head, already appearing lit. "Three tequila shots and another round of beers, please."

The barmaid grinned, happy for the business. "You got it."

As she walked away, Charlie rolled her blue eyes. "I'm not dead...I mean married yet, Mads. I've got to get it out of my system before I make that march down the aisle."

Madison shook her head, angrily pressing her lips together. "If you feel that way, why marry Nelson?"

"I love him," Charlie avowed. "I'm just terrified of marriage. You know, sleeping with the same guy for the rest of my life seems so boring."

"I don't know," Lizzie piped in. "It would be kinda cool not having to go out on any more dates, have those awkward first times in bed with someone...you can just be yourself with a guy."

"Hey, don't knock those awkward first times in bed," Charlie countered. "They're some of the best memories I have of my sex life."

"Not me." Lizzie grimaced. "I remember the first time I did it, I was in high school and it really sucked. Took me a few times to get comfortable with sex. I always thought it was going to be like it is in the movies, you know?"

"Yeah, me too." Charlie slapped back in her chair, the spark dimming in her eyes. "When I lost my virginity, I was sixteen and he was a senior on the football team. What I remember was how much it hurt."

"Mine was with a guy in my high school chemistry class." Lizzie shrugged. "I remember being disappointed it didn't last longer...or he didn't last longer." Giggling, she reached for her beer.

"What about you?" Charlie turned to Madison. "You never told me about your first time." She rolled her eyes again with incredulity. "Let me guess...you and the prom king on the night of your senior prom. I bet he rented some expensive hotel room and everything."

Lizzie and Charlie snickered as Madison ran her hands nervously up and down her bare arms. "No, ah, it wasn't like that."

Looking over her glass at Madison, Lizzie took a sip of her beer. "So, spill it. What was your first time like?"

Madison sat back in her chair, debating on how much she should disclose to her friends. "I was in college, and I didn't really know him. It was just the one time."

"What did you do…pick him up in bar?" Charlie's smug look gave Madison pause.

The barmaid returned to the table, saving her from having to come up with an answer right away. "Twenty-six even, ladies," she stated, removing the drinks one by one from her black tray.

Madison eagerly reached for her purse. She searched for her wallet while avoiding the inquisitive stare of her roommate. After handing the money to the barmaid, she picked up her glass of beer, looking for a distraction.

"Are you going to tell us?" Charlie insisted.

After taking a swig of courage, Madison put the glass on the table and nodded her head. "I was nineteen. Everyone I knew had done it, and I figured it was time I did something about it. I felt so embarrassed to tell any of my college friends that I was still a virgin. I remember pretending that I had slept with guys, but the truth was I had never wanted to do it with anyone until…."

"Who was he?" Lizzie asked, leaning into the table.

Madison skittishly smiled while searching for the words. Christ, did she want to do this? She had never told the story before, but now with her friends…was she ready to talk about him? Breathing in the essence of beer and stale smoke in the air, she rallied her nerve. "It was spring. I had just failed my first midterm in my Introduction to Architectural Design class and I needed to get out. I was feeling really low and I remembered there was this bar around the UT Arlington dorms that everyone talked about being great for hookups. So I got dressed up and headed out. I never told anyone where I was going, not even my roommate. Looking back, it was really a stupid thing to do."

"Wait, you lost your virginity to some guy you picked up in a bar? For real?" Charlie angled closer to the table, her blue eyes ablaze with interest. "You're always so picky about men. You never want to go out with anyone I set you up with."

"That's because the guys you set me up with are scary, Charlie."

"Doug the paralegal was not scary," Charlie argued.

Madison rolled her eyes, mimicking her friend. "He was married."

"Separated," Charlie protested. "And so what if he wasn't technically divorced. I thought you two—"

"Would you let her get back to the story?" Lizzie cut in. She turned her doe-like, amber eyes to Madison. "So what happened with you and the guy in the bar?"

"Skylar's, that's what it was called. Inside there were a lot of business types hanging out…you know, guys in suits. Some girls, but more men. I went to the bar and had a seat on this torn, red leather stool. I remember that stool…funny, huh? Anyway, it didn't take long for a few guys to hit on me, buy me drinks and stuff."

Lizzie snorted. "You must have been some real eye candy. Men love to watch you."

"It's because she was a dancer," Charlie inserted. "Men love watching dancers."

Lizzie slapped Charlie's hand. "Let her get back to the story."

"Well," Madison went on, "none of the guys that talked to me really hung around for long. They just talked and left. I guess I had been there about an hour, and was a little buzzed from drinking vodka, when this guy came up to me." She closed her eyes as her thoughts went back to that night. "He was really good-looking, handsome with thick, dark wavy hair, small gray eyes. I think he was in his late twenties." She opened her eyes. "He was slender, but built, like he worked out. I remember he had on this dark blue sweater, a real nice one, and he smelled…." She sighed. "Really good. His face was kinda rugged, with a wide jaw and thick brow, which made him seem really intense. The first time I looked into his eyes it was like pow."

"Whoa," Charlie breathed. "What did he say when you first met?"

"Hello," Madison replied. "He just said 'hello,' and had a seat next to me."

"What, no pick up line?" Lizzie questioned.

Madison shook her head. "No, no lines. In fact, the whole night he never used one line on me. I remember he told me he liked to cut right to the chase. He thought 'games were better suited for cards, not people,' his words."

"Sexy. Did you get his name?" Lizzie fidgeted in her seat, enthralled.

"He said his friends called him Harry, so I called him Harry. I told him my name was Mary." Madison sipped her beer as a myriad of lustful memories came back to her. She could see him sitting beside her, still feel his hand on hers, smell his musky skin, and…she regained control and went on with her story. "We spent about an hour at the bar talking. Well, we didn't talk per se, he just asked questions and I talked. He asked me a lot of questions."

"What kind of questions?" Charlie intruded.

"Where I was from, what I was studying in school. He knew a lot about architecture and was pretty smart. I think he talked about how hard architecture school was, but I'm not sure if he mentioned going to one. He wanted to know about my family, what I liked to do outside of school…stuff like that."

"Get to the good part." Lizzie moved her chair closer to Madison. "Did he take you to his place?"

Madison played with her beer glass in her hands, fighting that rush of unease. "He drove me in his Porsche to his apartment. More like a penthouse really. It had this wall of windows with a great view of the UT campus. I remember he had a bar." She cocked her head, lost in her memories. "Really nice paintings on the wall. He told me the name of the painter, but I've forgotten."

"Sounds nice." Charlie grinned. "He must have been rich to have a place like that."

"I don't think we ever talked about his family. I don't know if he was rich, but he seemed sophisticated. Like he knew a lot of things." Madison shrugged and rested her arms on the table, getting comfortable. "He led me into his apartment, turned on a song named 'Feelin' Good.' I remember asking him about it. He told me it was by his favorite singer, Nina Simone."

"Is that the song you always play? You know, I'm feeeliiinnn' goooood," Charlie sang out. "I hear it coming from your bedroom sometimes."

"Yes, but I listen to the Michael Bublé version."

"Oh, I love him," Lizzie squealed.

"So you play that song for him, don't you?" Charlie probed. "You're dreaming of being with him again."

Madison nodded. "I always wonder what it would be like if he was there with me. Sometimes I daydream about dancing for him, and...." She rubbed her arms, feeling she had said too much. "Silly, huh?"

"I think it's romantic," Lizzie giggled. "You and Harry have a song."

"Enough about the song," Charlie clamored. "What happened next?"

"He wanted me to sober up a bit before, so he made me some coffee in his kitchen. I was sipping on the coffee and we were standing in the kitchen talking when I slipped or got dizzy…I'm not sure. He went to grab me, and I spilled some coffee on his nice sweater. I was mortified and kept apologizing, but he just laughed at me." She smiled, lost in her thoughts. "He had this great laugh. Deep, soulful; the kind that vibrates inside your bones. The one thing I clearly remember about that night was his laugh."

"And then what happened?" Lizzie inserted.

Madison was awakened from her memories. "I grabbed for some paper towels and started wiping his sweater. I must have looked like a total idiot. He took the paper towels from my hands and kissed me."

"Good kisser?" Charlie posed with a hopeful lilt in her voice.

Madison nodded, blushing. "Really good. The kind you don't want to stop kissing."

Lizzie's grip on her glass of beer tightened. "Then what?"

Madison lowered her eyes to the table. "He took my hand and led me from the kitchen to the master bedroom. When we got to the door, I think I had a mini-panic attack. I was so nervous…never having done it before. He put his arm around me, kissed my cheek, and gently eased me into the room." She raised her head. "After that, I wasn't quite as nervous."

Charlie's blue eyes grew round. "And the sex? How was it?"

"He was very gentle." Madison shrugged her shoulders. "I thought it was going to hurt more, but he went really slow. I'm not sure if he knew I was…. He made me feel comfortable, or as comfortable as I could feel in that situation."

"Jesus." Lizzie reached for a shot glass in the middle of the table. "He must have been really good." She knocked back the small glass of tequila.

Charlie nudged Madison's hand on the table. "But what exactly happened? How did he do it?"

Madison's jaw dropped. "What do you mean 'how did he do it'? You're kidding, right?"

"No, Mads, I'm talking about before he took off your clothes. How did he seduce you? You know, what kind of moves did he put on you? Or did you two just get right to it?"

"Oh that." Madison became silent for a few seconds. "Yeah, well, he, ah, danced with me. After we stepped into the bedroom, he took my hand and held me close. I don't know how long we swayed like that to the music, but he made me feel special."

"Special?" Charlie laughed. "What about the morning after? How did you feel then?"

Madison slumped in her chair, tucking her hair behind her ear. "There wasn't a morning after. When he fell asleep, I snuck out of his apartment and walked back to campus."

Lizzie stared at her. "You snuck out? Honestly, you didn't want to hang around and find out more about him?"

"No. I was so relieved to have finally done it, I just wanted to get out of there and avoid the whole morning after thing."

"Damn," Lizzie extolled with admiration in her eyes. "You're a lot braver than me. I always wanted to meet some hot guy in a bar, but with all the crap out there these days, I'd be terrified to have him touch me unless he was encased in rubber."

"Please tell me you used protection," Charlie groaned as she reached for her shot glass.

"We used protection. He had condoms."

"Ever wonder what happened to him?" Lizzie pestered.

"Sure," Madison reluctantly disclosed. "He was a really nice guy. I kind of wish I could meet someone like him today. You know…handsome, sophisticated, articulate, someone who made me feel—"

"Special?" Charlie interjected.

Madison nodded to the three-carat diamond on Charlie's left hand. "You've got Nelson. You're lucky you don't have to go out in the world and find a man anymore."

Charlie pushed the last shot glass of tequila across the table toward Madison. "You'll find someone…you just have to hit a few more bars."

Lizzie snorted with laughter while Madison smirked at her roommate. Picking up the shot glass, Madison toasted her friends.

"To meeting men in bars," she proclaimed.

Lizzie lifted her beer glass and Charlie did the same. "To meeting your Harry in a bar," Lizzie declared. "I'd kill to find a man like that."

They each gulped back their drinks, and after Madison put her empty shot glass down on the table she shook her head.

"I should really be pretty angry with Harry."

"Angry? Why?" Charlie asked.

"He ruined me for other guys."

Lizzie tittered with a high-pitched laugh. "What are you talking about?"

Madison ran her finger over the rim of her empty shot glass. "Every guy since then has never quite lived up to him. I mean, I know it was a one-night stand and all, but no guy has ever seemed as smooth or as charming, or—"

"Good in bed," Charlie cut in.

Madison swept her long brown hair about her shoulder, snickering. "Yeah, that too."

"Just be thankful you've had that," Lizzie advised. "I've been at this dating game for damn near ten years and I've never met anyone like your Harry. I was beginning to think men like that only existed in romance novels."

"Did you ever want to go back to his place and find out more about him?" Charlie's blue eyes contemplated Madison's perfect profile.

"Thought about it…but I doubt he would remember who I was." Madison glanced around the half-empty bar. "No, if we met up again, it would ruin my memories of that night. I'd probably discover he's just like every other asshole out there."

"Yeah, but what an asshole," Lizzie imparted with a giggle.

"I don't know." Charlie leaned forward. "Might be nice to know if the two of you could make it or not."

Madison shook her head. "A man like that would never look at me."

"Why not?" Charlie challenged. "He certainly liked what he saw in the bar."

"Charlie, a guy like that wants one of those ultra-chic women; the kind that leave high heel marks in their back, max out their credit cards, wears a size zero, and can suck the cap off a fire hydrant."

Lizzie began snorting loudly with laughter.

Charlie ignored Lizzie and glared at her friend. "Why do you always do this, Mads? You never think you're good enough for anyone." Charlie waved her hand up and down Madison's figure. "You can have any guy you want, but you always end up with losers."

Madison reached for her glass of beer. "Losers? Like who?"

"Oh God," Lizzie chimed in. "Can we ever forget the foghorn, Elliot? The guy's laugh could clear a room faster than a rabid raccoon in church on Sunday."

"That's mean, Lizzie," Charlie scolded. "It wasn't his laugh that drove people crazy, it was that obnoxious habit he had of sucking air through his teeth." Charlie imitated the sound, drawing the attention of a few nearby tables. "He wasn't the worst. Remember Sid, the furniture repair guy?"

"He restored furniture, not repaired," Madison corrected with a smirk.

"Was he the one who always smelled like salami?" Lizzie queried.

Charlie shook her head. "That was the guy who worked in Rocco's Deli." She glanced over at Madison. "Wasn't his name Rocco, too?"

"Stop it, both of you," Madison chided. "Elliot was a sweet guy. Sid was very nice to me, and his name was Ronnie, not Rocco. And he didn't smell like salami…at least not all the time."

Charlie shook her head, reaching for her beer. "Honestly, Mads, you have great guys asking you out, but you only date men who are less than what you deserve."

"Maybe I don't deserve a great guy."

"Where is that coming from? Of course you do. We all do." Charlie motioned between the three women. "The problem with being female is we're raised in a society that constantly tells us how to act, what to be, and what we deserve, but that's not the reality. We're different, but not any less equal to men. We should—"

"Oh great. Here she goes again," Lizzie interrupted.

"Good thing she's marrying a civil rights attorney," Madison commented. "Now she has someone to listen to all of her rants."

"Very funny. And I don't rant. I'm a law student; we debate," Charlie professed, smirking. "But think about it, where would our sex be if people didn't rant?"

Lizzie stretched for her beer, frowning with boredom. "Probably still sweeping out caves, right?"

"When I'm gone, Mads," Charlie went on, "you'll need someone to watch out for your interests. I swear there are days when I think if I'm not around to protect you, you'll end up in the arms of some psychotic asshole."

"I'll be fine, Charlie."

"I hope so." Charlie eyed her suspiciously. "Just use your head in the future, all right? Don't go out to any bars and pick up strange men hoping to find that Harry again. Promise me."

"Why not?" Lizzie countered. "Seems to me that was the one time she found herself a great guy."

"Perhaps," Charlie agreed with a slight nod of her head. "But lightning never strikes twice. You lucked out the first time, kid." She took a sip of her beer.

"I know." Feeling depressed by her situation, Madison raised her beer to her lips. "Just wish I could get that lucky again."

***

Pushing the door of their fifth floor apartment open, Madison giggled as Charlie followed her inside. When Charlie flipped on the lights, the small living room—piled high with boxes—glared back at them.

Madison gazed about the bare white walls and sighed. "It's going to be empty without you, Charlie."

"You'll love not having me around, Mads. No more waiting for the bathroom, listening to my alternative music selections, and—"

"No more listening to you and Nelson going at it," Madison jumped in.

Charlie furrowed her sleek white brow. "Were we that noisy?"

"Are you kidding me? The neighbors even complained."

Charlie snickered and breezed into the apartment. "Well, you can have the privacy now to bring a guy home and disturb the neighbors with him." She casually tossed her purse on top of the boxes stacked on the plush green sofa.

"You know, it's funny." Madison shut the door and turned the deadbolt. "Of all the guys you brought here, I never thought you would end up with Nelson. He seemed so…mild-mannered."

"Mild-mannered?" Charlie leered back at her. "Hardly. How a man appears to be vertically is never how he acts horizontally."

Madison lowered her eyes to the floor. "Oh," was all she could manage to say.

"I think you're the same way, Mads. I think this," Charlie waved her hand down the length of Madison's figure, "sweet little girl routine hides the assertive woman beneath. After all, a woman who is as shy as you would never have gone to a bar and just picked up a guy."

Madison moved toward the kitchen. "I was young and stupid. You said so yourself."

"You were also brave, and I think you need to start tapping into that side of you, especially now."

Madison placed her black purse on the breakfast bar that divided the kitchen from the living room. "What are you talking about?"

"Mads, you start working at a renowned architectural firm tomorrow. You're going to have to fight to prove yourself. I know how those places are. I've been clerking in Nelson's firm for a year now and companies like that are pretty ruthless. You're a woman, a very pretty woman who is going to be a magnet for men who are going to make your life a living hell." Charlie came up to her. "You need to promise me that you will stand up for yourself in this job. Working for old man Pellerin is nothing compared to the place you're going. You need to watch out and don't trust anyone."

"Stop worrying so much about me." Madison pointed at Charlie. "You're the one getting married. Shouldn't we be concerned about you?"

"Perhaps you're right; I'm the one heading into the shark-infested waters of marriage."

"Don't let Nelson hear you say that."

"Actually, it's more like, 'don't let Nelson's mother hear me say that.'" Charlie rolled her shoulders forward. "Here I am warning you about standing up at your job, and I can't even stand up to my future mother-in-law."

"You caved on the teal bridesmaids' dresses, didn't you?"

Dejected, Charlie slowly nodded her head. "She hounded me until I gave in. I swore I would never have teal as a color in my wedding, and here I am with teal and chocolate all over everything from the sanctuary to the floral arrangements. My bridal party is going to look like day old bruises."

"Must be love then, eh?" Madison joked. "Only love would get you to push your principles to the side."

"Love and an insistent mother of the groom," Charlie snickered. "I swear, if my mother was alive, I wouldn't be in this mess. I kind of wish she were here to help plan everything. Sometimes I think Nelson's mother is stepping in because I have no mother."

"Your mom is with you, Charlie. I know she would have been so proud."

"Yeah, I know." Charlie shook off her sullen mood. "I wish I'd met Caroline Peevy when Nelson and I were first going out. I might have bolted right then and there." She turned toward a hallway off to the side of the living room. "There's another lesson for you, Mads. Meet the mother-in-law before you take the ring."

Madison highly doubted she would ever be plagued with such a dilemma as a mother-in-law. She had long ago put any notions of marriage and children out of her head, determined to be a successful architect and not a wife and mother. She did not envy Charlie in the slightest. In fact, Madison was relieved it was not her. "Life is an investment," her late grandfather had always told her. She needed to invest wisely and stay focused on her goals, no matter the cost.

Chapter 2

Parr and Associates was located in the Renaissance Tower in downtown Dallas. A fifty-six story modernist skyscraper, the sleek glass and steel structure gleamed in the early morning sunlight that peeked out from behind the fall clouds blanketing the sky.

Reaching for the brass door handles that marked one of the glass entrances to the building, Madison took in a deep breath. The butterflies that had been swarming in her belly all morning only seemed to get worse as she neared the sleek, silver elevator doors which were to take her to her new home away from home.

After stepping inside the crowded elevator, she pushed the lighted button on the console for the thirty-third floor and eased her way to the back. She was brushing her hand down the front of her smart blue pinstripe dress when a tall man in a gray suit eased up next to her. Out of the corner of her eye, she could see his dark brown wavy hair and determined profile. She didn't want to stare, but found herself admiring the curve of his square jaw and the cut of his cheekbones along his clean-shaven face. When he turned to her, she immediately lowered her eyes. The butterflies in her stomach were in a full blown fury now, and she swallowed back the burning taste of embarrassment in her mouth.

As she stood there, eyes riveted to the elevator floor, she could feel his gaze on her. She knew it, sensed him drinking in her profile. Terrified, she fought every impulse to look up at him, and when the elevator doors closed, the car shot upward and jostled her to the side, making her brush against him.

"Sorry," she whispered, keeping her focus fixed on the ugly brown tiles on the elevator floor.

"Think nothing of it."

It was a soft, seductive, deep kind of voice that a woman would want to hear from the pillow next to her in bed.

She could detect the slightest whiff of his cologne; spicy, but with a hint of muskiness. Not enough to overwhelm the nose, like so many other men's fragrances, but just enough to tantalize the senses. With her curiosity getting the better of her, Madison tried to edge her eyes slowly upward, hoping to catch a glimpse of him. Unfortunately, the elevator came to a halt, the doors opened, and a rush of people began to push for the exit.

Glancing at the lighted console, Madison determined they had stopped on the twentieth floor. The man beside her shuffled forward and she thought he was going to exit the elevator, but instead he took a step closer to her.

Madison's heart raced as the elevator doors closed again and the car shot upward.

"First day?" his velvety voice inquired.

She bit her lower lip and nodded her head. Raising her eyes ever so slightly, she concentrated on his freshly-shaved chin. "How could you tell?"

His thin lips curled into a maddening smile. "You look absolutely terrified."

Madison fought to get ahold of her emotions. If he could see it, imagine what her employer would think. She had to appear self-assured and ready to take up her new responsibilities.

"I'm just nervous," she shyly admitted.

The edge of his jacket brushed against her shoulder. "There's nothing to be nervous about."

His words sent an unsettling chill throughout her body. There was something about the way he had said it—the tone of his voice, the inflection—that reminded her of someone she could not place. Intrigued by the stranger, she was just about to raise her head to him when the elevator car once again jerked to a stop. When her eyes shifted to the lighted panel, she saw they had come to a stop on the thirty-second floor.

The man beside her made a move toward the doors, and came to a stop right in front of her. Madison ogled his thick, wide shoulders, the way his suit jacket hugged his trim waist, and then her eyes drifted down to his round backside.

Someone cleared their throat in the elevator and she instantly thought she had been caught staring at the guy's ass. A flush of warmth spread across her cheeks and she clutched her purse to her side as her eyes once again plummeted to the elevator floor. The group of people, including her stranger, moved out the elevator door, and for an instant, Madison felt a twinge of disappointment that she had not gotten a better look at the man. Luckily, just as the elevator doors closed, she caught a glimpse of him, standing just outside of the doors, staring back at her.

The jolt that hit her body was overwhelming. His face was more than she expected; rugged, good-looking with gray eyes, a wide forehead, and chiseled features that would have made him the object of any woman's fantasy. His trim figure appeared tone and lean behind the fabric of his suit, and as he grinned back at her, he eased his hand into his trouser pocket before dipping his head.

When the elevator doors finally closed, Madison thought her knees were going to give out.

What in the hell is wrong with me?

By the time she was able to regain her composure, the elevator doors opened onto the thirty-third floor. Gripping her purse, she forced all thoughts of the devastatingly handsome stranger from her mind. She had a job to do.

Making her way along the pale beige hallway, she stopped in front of a glass entrance to Parr and Associates. The two front doors were trimmed in dark wood and covered with the company logo of a black rooftop which covered the name of the firm written in red. Easing her hand around the sleek wood handle, Madison glanced once more down the hall toward the elevators, hoping for…. She pulled the door open and stepped inside.

The reception area was done in alternating shades of brown and beige, with a burgundy Oriental rug covering a dark green stone floor. On the walls were various framed pictures of famous houses, probably designed by the firm over the years. Some were well-known landmarks to many who resided in the Dallas area; others had graced the front covers of various architectural magazines or won prizes for their unique presentation.

Approaching a cherry-stained reception desk with a dour-looking receptionist, Madison remembered her posture, squared her shoulders, and put on her best smile.

"Hello. I'm Madison Barnett, one of the new architects."

The ashen brunette forced a smile to her wan lips. "You're early. I like it. Welcome, Madison. I'm Sam, Sam Copper. I run the front desk." The plump receptionist stood from her high backed chair. "Glad to see we have a woman joining our ranks. I'll show you to your office. You'll be sharing it with the other architect Mr. Parr hired. Another man." She rolled her tired brown eyes.

"But Mr. Parr didn't hire me," Madison injected. "I met with Mr. Worthy."

Sam came around the desk. "Mr. Worthy is Mr. Parr's right hand man. Trust me, Mr. Parr has the final say in every person who works here."

Madison waited as Sam opened a pair of dark-paneled doors. "I hope I get to meet Mr. Parr sometime soon. He's quite a legend in architectural circles."

"Old man Parr was the legend. He retired from the firm a few years ago. His son, Hayden, runs Parr and Associates now."

"I didn't realize that," Madison confessed.

"Yeah, Hayden's been real instrumental in getting Parr and Associates some media exposure over the years. He's into social networking and PR."

Madison hurried through the doors and the faint aroma of freshly brewed coffee tempted her nose. "Does Mr. Parr make it a habit to meet with new employees after he hires them and not before?"

Sam motioned down the dark-paneled hallway to her left. "I don't know why he never met with you. I know he met with your new office mate, Adam, however."

Madison rubbed her hands together as she followed Sam down the hallway. This wasn't good. This wasn't good at all. "Now I'm kind of worried about meeting him. What if he doesn't like me?"

Sam turned to her and placed a motherly hand on her arm. "Don't be nervous, dear. He'll love you. Mr. Parr is a pretty nice man to work for. Sure he has his shouting days and his days where you had better stay clear of him, but he also goes to a lot of social functions around the city, and usually makes sure his employees get invited. It's one of the perks of the job...we get into all the best events." She turned away. "Before he separated from his wife, Mrs. Parr used to make a point of stopping by the office and meeting all the new employees." She winked at Madison. "Probably why he never hired any women architects before you."

Madison was taken aback. "His wife didn't like him hiring women?"

Sam stopped before an office door with a bright brass handle. "Ellen Parr was kind of the jealous type, but when you meet Mr. Parr you'll see why." She pushed the door open.

Madison followed her into the small office. There was not much to it, just beige walls decorated with only one picture of a house the firm must have designed, one long window that overlooked the Dallas skyline, two pine desks with high backed chairs, and one small dark wooden table in the corner with a telephone, printer, and several stacks of design books piled behind it.

"This is your office," Sam stated. "Your cohort in crime hasn't arrived yet, so feel free to grab the best desk and make it yours."

Madison eyed a desk right by the window. "What did you say his name was?"

"Adam Turnbull." Sam nodded to the desks in the room. "There's an orientation schedule on your computer. Mr. Worthy wants each of you to spend some time in the different departments on this floor and on thirty-two."

Madison spun around to Sam. "Thirty-two? I thought this was the only floor the firm was on."

Sam stepped back outside the door. "The official offices for all the architects are on thirty-three, but accounting, advertising, and the administrative offices are on thirty-two." Sam smiled at Madison and put her hand on the door. "I hope you like it here, Madison."

After Sam had closed the door, Madison went to the desk by the window and put her purse down on the smooth wood. Her hands glided over the surface of the desktop computer and she smiled. Ever since the day she had taken a seat in her first architectural design course, she had been enthralled with designing buildings. Every time she sat behind a computer and pulled up the computer assisted design program, her imagination kicked into overdrive. Aching to be used, the blank computer screen seemed to call to her, begging to bring to life all the designs she had swirling about in her head. Glancing to the wide window beside her, she marveled at the rooftops of the nearby skyscrapers. Flashing red and white lights momentarily mesmerized her with their beauty against the cloudy, white sky. When the office door behind her opened, she struggled to turn away.

"I guess you've already staked out the best desk, eh?"

His voice was deep, alluring, but did not match the lanky body of the man who stood in the doorway. He had dark red hair, lots of freckles, and friendly green eyes. His nose was slightly crooked, his face long and sullen, but his wide smile had the warmth and mischief of an adorable little boy.

"Sorry," he mumbled, easing into the room. Slung over his shoulder was a blue backpack that made the jacket of his dark suit rise up his left side. "I'm Adam Turnbull. The lady at the reception desk told me to come on inside." He motioned to the desk next to hers. "I guess I'll take that one."

Madison shook herself from her stupor. "I'm Madison, Madison Barnett. Good to meet you, Adam." She waited until he stood before his desk, and then held out her hand.

Smiling, he gave her hand a slight tug. "So, we're gonna be office mates." He went to his desk and dropped his backpack on it with a thud. "You don't have any disgusting habits like slurping coffee or liking pastrami sandwiches, do you?"

Madison nervously clasped her hands in front of her. "No, ah, I've never eaten pastrami."

Adam's green eyes swept up and down her figure. Madison could see the hunger in them, and took a cautious step back. The last thing she needed was to get involved with a co-worker.

"Glad to hear it." Adam rested his hip against his desk and folded his arms over his narrow chest, eyeing her face. "Where did you go to school?"

"UT Arlington," Madison told him. "What about you?"

"Tulane."

"Wow, New Orleans. I bet that was a fun place to go to school."

"And to grow up. I'm from the Big Easy."

Madison searched for a friendly question, afraid of the silence. "Was Parr and Associates your first choice?"

Adam raised his red eyebrows and frowned, reminding Madison of a petulant child. "Nah, I wanted to get on with Taylor and Buckholt in New Orleans. They do a lot of restoration jobs in that city—I even did my internship there—but they didn't have a space for me. I applied to seven different firms, but this is the only offer I got. How many did you apply to?"

Madison shrugged. "Only three, and all of them were in Dallas. I wanted to get on with MA Architects…they do a lot of skyscrapers and commercial building construction—that's what I really want to do—but they didn't even interview me. They wanted experienced architects, not new grads."

"Yeah, I heard the same thing. That's why I'm here. I figured I can get some experience and then move on. Doing upper-end homes isn't my thing. I like working with historic buildings; you know, renovations and additions that add to the style of the original design. That's what turns me on."

Madison felt a slight flush on her cheeks as his eyes continued to wander the curves of her figure. Turning away, she went back to her desk. "So did you meet with Mr. Parr during your interview?"

"Sure. What did you think of him?" He stuffed his hands in his trouser pockets. "I thought he didn't like me at first. With his squinty eyes I couldn't tell what he was thinking. I was about to write off the interview when he started asking me some questions. Grilled me, actually, about architectural theory and design. It made me feel like I was still in school."

Madison's cheeks flushed even redder. "I never met him. I met with Mr. Worthy. He didn't quiz me or anything. Just asked about school and why I wanted to be an architect."

Adam's gravelly snicker annoyed Madison. "You were lucky. I got the impression Parr's going to be a real taskmaster."

"Really? Sam, the receptionist, told me he was great to work for."

Adam went over to his desk and inspected the computer. "She's just a receptionist, Madison. Of course he's nice to her. She's not essential staff like we are."

He hit a key on the keyboard and the computer screen came to life. Madison observed his long, bony hands as they reached for the mouse, and decided that she didn't like them. For her, a man's hands had always been the starting point of an attraction, and if his hands did not meet her standards, she figured little else would.

"Looks like we have our schedule for the day." Adam nodded to his computer. "We're to head to human resources on the thirty-second floor, do our employee paperwork, and then attend a computer orientation meeting."

Madison had hoped to get right to work, not be bogged down in mindless meetings. "Sounds pretty boring."

Adam turned to her, grinning. "Not completely. Looks like we get to have lunch in the conference room with Mr. Parr. At least we're getting a free meal."

Madison's stomach did a nervous flip. "That doesn't make me feel any better. Maybe he's going to grill us while we eat."

Adam smiled for her, trying to appear reassuring. "Maybe he just wants to get to know his new employees. What better way to do that than over a friendly lunch."

***

After two hours of filling out IRS forms, deciding on IRA packages, and getting a brief rundown on the computer system, Adam and Madison were escorted to a luxurious conference room. A long, oval mahogany table with deep red leather chairs filled the room, while a sideboard of matching mahogany was pushed against the wall closest to the door. Wide windows overlooked scenic downtown Dallas, and along the walls were various contemporary metal sculptures done in gold, silver, bronze, and iron, depicting different city skylines.

"Mr. Parr will be along shortly, and we're waiting for the caterers to arrive with lunch," a pretty blonde secretary named Emma told them as she ushered them into the conference room.

Madison noticed how Adam's eyes traced the outline of Emma's sky blue dress, lingering over the swell of her ample breasts.

"I hope you two like Italian. Mr. Parr insisted I order from his favorite Italian restaurant for lunch," Emma went on.

Adam glanced up and smiled. "I love Italian. Will you be joining us, Emma?"

"I have letters to type for Mr. Parr." The curvy secretary gave Adam a dubious grin. "You two have a nice lunch." She quickly closed the door, leaving Madison and Adam alone.

"I think she likes me," Adam proposed with a touch of bravado.

Madison glared at him. "She was being polite, Adam."

He bobbed his eyebrows playfully. "There was a connection between us. Didn't you feel it?"

Madison studied him as he sauntered over to the picture windows. "Are you always this way with women?"

"What way?"

"Confident."

"Sure, I guess. I found with women it isn't so much a matter of confidence, but just getting up to bat. So many guys I know are afraid to talk to a woman they find attractive, and miss out on an opportunity." He pointed his thumb to his chest. "I make it a point to never miss out on an opportunity." His eyes once again glided over her figure. "Normally, with an attractive woman like you, I would ask you out, but since we're going to be working together, that would be a bad idea. Don't want to make work more stressful for either one of us by adding sex to the situation." His irksome snicker filled the room.

Madison felt her patience for her new co-worker quickly waning. "I'm amazed you haven't found Ms. Right with that attitude."

"Who says I want to find Ms. Right? I'm not interested in settling down any time soon. I want to get my career going first, get some money, and maybe when I'm in my thirties I'll start looking for a wife." He shrugged. "Men don't have to settle as young as you girls do. I mean, our biological clocks have no expiration date."

Madison's jaw dropped slightly. *I'm going to have to share an office with this butt wipe!*

"What about you?" Adam moved away from the window. "You got a boyfriend?"

"No," she answered flatly.

"Why not? You're not a lesbian, are you?"

Right when she was about to reply, the sound of the conference room door opening distracted her. Adjusting her attitude, Madison plastered a stellar smile on her face, expecting to meet her new boss, but when she turned, her stomach dropped to the floor. Standing inside the doorway, with an irresistible smile that melted into her soul, was the man from the elevator earlier that morning. His smoky eyes were glued to her, and as she felt the air in the room grow thin.

He had removed his suit jacket, and his white dress shirt allowed a tantalizing glimpse of his muscular chest beneath. His head tilted slightly to the side as he watched her, and Madison became undone as his assertive confidence overpowered the room like the heady bouquet of red wine rising from a glass. His thin, red lips dropped their smile when his gaze drifted to Adam, standing beside her.

"So how do you two like Parr and Associates?" he asked, walking into the room.

"Ah, Mr. Parr," Adam all but drooled as he rushed up to the man, "thank you so much for having us for lunch today."

Adam's sucking up did nothing to change Madison's quickly diminishing opinion of her co-worker. She stayed back as he eagerly pumped Mr. Parr's hand.

Adam stepped aside, and Madison swallowed back her nerves when she saw the handsome man once again turn to her. "We haven't met." He came toward her. "I'm Hayden Parr." He took her hand. "I was out of town the day Don Worthy interviewed you for the position. I wish I could have been here." He slowly squeezed her hand as his eyes searched hers. "You don't know how long I've been waiting to meet you, Ms. Barnett."

For a moment, Madison was perplexed by an odd sensation that she had met this man before. Quickly reminding herself of their previous encounter in the elevator, she chalked up her strange feelings to nerves.

"So, Mr. Parr," Adam interrupted, "I was wondering how long it would be before Madison and I got our first assignment."

"That's mighty ambitious of you, Adam. Considering this is your first day, don't you think we should see how you do before I throw clients your way?"

His amused chuckle reverberated about the small room, and Madison was instantly floored by the sound. That laugh was so familiar. Convinced she had met this man before, her mind struggled to recall any prior meeting with the seductive Hayden Parr.

"I know we're supposed to do a lot of secondary drawings and basic copying of plans until we get some experience under our belt," Adam went on. "And I understand why we have to do all of that, I really do." Adam clapped his hands together. "I was just hoping you would maybe...you might give us something," he shrugged, "exciting to do. Something to prove our worth, you know?"

"Prove your worth?" Hayden Parr slowly nodded his head. "Intriguing idea, and perhaps there is something I could send to you and Ms. Barnett." He turned cordially to Madison and his eyes twinkled. "Something that you both could do to show me what you've got."

Madison felt her knees growing weak as his eyes remained fixed on her.

A knock at the open door made all heads turn. Entering the room was a skinny, pale, balding man who wore gold-rimmed wire glasses over businesslike blue eyes. His black suit hung from his frame, and his tie had already collected a coffee stain or two.

"The caterers are downstairs. I was going to meet them at the back service elevators and escort them up. Ah, Ms. Barnett," the gentleman nodded to Madison, "welcome aboard."

Madison smiled. "Thank you, Mr. Worthy."

"Don?" Hayden Parr motioned to Adam. "You remember Adam Turnbull."

Don Worthy careened his long neck around to Adam. "Yes, of course. How are you, Adam?"

"Fine, Mr. Worthy," Adam chirped.

Don Worthy waved to Adam and Madison. "Why don't you two come with me and meet the caterers at the back entrance. I can show you the lay of the building."

"I think Ms. Barnett and I could use a few minutes to get to know each other while you and Adam meet the caterers," Hayden Parr asserted.

Her eyes flew to Adam. Terrified that this was her moment for a grilling from her new boss, she silently pleaded for Adam not to leave her.

"I'm with you, Mr. Worthy," Adam confirmed, avoiding her desperate gaze.

Her stomach tightened as Adam scurried across the conference room to the open door. Don Worthy patted the young man's shoulder before shifting his eyes to Hayden Parr.

"You need anything else?"

Hayden shook his head. "We're fine, Don. Just get the food. I think we're all pretty hungry."

Don Worthy smiled and pushed Adam out the door. He was about to follow the young man when Hayden Parr called to him.

"Shut the door, will you, Don?"

Don Worthy glanced back over his shoulder, and added, "Sure thing, Harry."

The words sent a lightning bolt of horror running through Madison's every atom. *Harry?* The name resonated through her mind as images of the night she had spent with the handsome stranger clouded her vision. *Could it be him?*

Her jaw was clenched so tight that her teeth were screaming in pain. She wanted to run out of the building never to return, but reason told her not to panic. Maybe it was just a coincidence and she was overreacting. Taking in a deep breath, she tried to quell the sickening feeling swirling in her gut.

"We should talk. Get to know each other since I missed the opportunity to interview you." He went around to the side of the conference table and pulled out a chair. "Sit."

Madison stared warily at him. "Are you going to quiz me about design theory?"

His small eyes crinkled upward as he gave her a confused smile. "Excuse me?"

"Adam mentioned your interview with him was more like a grilling session. I just want to know if that's what you intend to do with me."

He motioned to the chair. "I promise, no grilling. I simply want to know more about you."

"I thought all you needed to know was filed away in human resources, Mr. Parr."

"That's the business side of you. I wish to know the real Madison Barnett."

"The real me?" She shook her head and moved forward. "I'm afraid you'll be pretty disappointed." After taking her seat, she waited as he took the chair next to her.

His sleek hand caressed the smooth wood of the table, sending an unexpected tingle up her spine. His hands were expressive, strong, and for an instant she could picture those hands traveling over the curves of her—

"So where are you from, Madison?" he began, interrupting her fantasy. "I can call you Madison, can't I?"

"Sure." She fidgeted in the big chair. "I'm from Arlington. I grew up there and went to UT."

"Good architecture program." He rested his hands together on the table. "Go on."

"Um," Madison stumbled. "I really liked my classes in skyscraper design. There was a real challenge in combining form and function with a high rise building."

"Then why are you here with my firm designing lowly houses?"

Words failed her. *Oh crap!*

"I get it. You settled for this job, but you really want to build skyscrapers, is that it?" The sudden drop in the temperature of his voice made her flinch. It was cold and menacing; she feared ever making him angry.

"Ah, no," she quickly jumped in. "I didn't mean that. I look forward to working here, but you said you wanted to get to know me, and that was what I liked in school."

"You're right, I did ask to get to know you, and I appreciate your candor." He moved closer to the table, leaning over to her. "What else can you tell me?"

"Ah, I have a roommate named Charlie who is getting married soon." *Why did I say that?*

He chuckled, and her insides tingled again. "What about family. Parents? Siblings?"

"I just have my mom and an older brother who's in the Navy. My dad left when I was eight. He lives in California with his second wife."

"What does your mother do?"

"My mom's a school principle in the Arlington Public School System." She paused, mustering her courage. "Can I ask you a question?"

He sat back in his chair. "Yes."

"Why did Mr. Worthy call you Harry?"

It was then she saw it; the slightest break in his features that gave her a glimpse into his mind. He appeared confused and almost ill at ease about the question, and then the lapse in his composure was gone, replaced again by his daunting smile.

"Family nickname. My father always called me Harry as a kid. It stuck, and those who have known me most of my life, like Don Worthy, call me Harry."

She paused for a moment, mulling over his words. "I like Harry."

He gently patted one hand on the table. "Then maybe you should call me Harry."

"No, I should call you Mr. Parr, since you're my boss."

He angled closer to her and the smell of his cologne surrounded her. "When we're alone, and away from the prying eyes of others, you can—"

The door to the conference room flew open, cutting him off. The jarring sound of carts rolling along the floor and indistinct voices swept into the room as the caterers, along with Adam and Don Worthy, hurried inside.

Hayden stood from his chair and Madison sagged with disappointment, wanting a few more minutes alone with the man. She wondered if this "Harry" was her "Harry." If Hayden Parr was actually her memorable first lover, then what? How would she be able to look her boss in the eye and go on as if nothing had happened? Suddenly, the quicksand of her past was swallowing up her well-planned future. This was not supposed to happen. Millions of people in Dallas and she just happened to land a job with the one stranger she had met in a bar and surrendered her virginity to. She could almost hear Charlie laughing it up. Maybe it was possible for lightning to strike twice.

Chapter 3

"You really think it's him?" Charlie pressed, her blue eyes round with excitement. "How cool is that?" she went on as she carried a bottle of water from the kitchen to the living room.

Still dressed in her running outfit, she was slurping back a few sips of water as Madison sat on their green sofa cradling a glass of wine in her hands. "It's not cool, Charlie. He's my boss."

Charlie plopped down on the cushion next to her. "Aw, come on, girl. You two have a history."

"If it's him." Dread coursed through Madison and she took another gulp of wine, almost draining her glass.

Charlie observed as Madison reached for the bottle of zinfandel on the coffee table and refilled her glass. "By the way you're chugging that wine, I'd say it's him. Why didn't you just ask him?"

Madison nearly dropped the wine bottle on the coffee table. "Ask him? Are you kidding me? I need this job, Charlie, especially with you moving out. Somehow asking the man that just hired me if he was the guy I met in a bar five years ago seems like a hell of a way to get fired."

Charlie took the wineglass from Madison's hand and put it on the table. "He's not going to fire you. From what you told me about how he was acting, I'd bet he would love to hear that you were that girl who snuck out on him in the middle of the night."

Madison flopped back on the sofa. "Or maybe he doesn't remember…if it is him. I could be wrong about the guy."

"I doubt it. The way he flirted with you on the elevator, wanted to be alone with you in the conference room, it kind of sounds like he's definitely interested."

"Interested?" Madison snorted and snapped up her glass from the table. "You're reading way too much into all of this."

"What about the other guy you told me about…Adam? He seemed interested in you, too."

"He's a creep," Madison roared. "The idea of sharing an office with his skinny ass is almost as disconcerting as asking Hayden Parr if he's the guy from that night."

"Sooner or later, Mads, you're going to have to ask him. You can't just go into work every day and wonder about it. I know how you are, and this will eat away at you." Charlie stood from the sofa. "Besides, if he does suspect you're that girl, how long do you think it is before he says something?"

Madison groaned and chugged a long sip of wine.

Chuckling, Charlie headed toward their bedrooms, but stopped when a light knock sounded on the apartment door. The two women looked to each other, panic written all over their faces.

"Did she see you come home?" Charlie whispered.

Madison mouthed, "I have no idea," then set her wineglass on the coffee table. Charlie went to the door while Madison stepped up behind her. Anxiously, Charlie opened the door.

Standing in the hallway was an elderly lady with snowy white hair piled into a bun, thick glasses that magnified her round brown eyes, sallow skin, and dainty features that added an air of frailty to her diminutive figure. Wearing a metallic blue muumuu and silver slippers, she glided in the door with all the grace of a ballerina entering the stage.

"Mrs. Leder," Charlie uttered with a strain of civility in her voice. "Nice to see you, as always."

Mrs. Leder held out a white casserole dish in her hands. "Did you hear the guy with the python on four was visited by animal control? Apparently you can't have a python without a permit in Texas. Did ya'll know that?" She handed the dish to Charlie. "It's a rice pilaf with tuna. You girls need to eat better."

Charlie took the dish from her. "Mrs. L, you don't have to keep cooking for us."

Mrs. Leder waved a pruny hand at the young woman. "Nonsense; and if you had any brains, young lady, you might start learning to cook. You're going to have a husband to feed soon. I know you're both modern women, but men like having home cooked meals on the table when they get back from a long day at the office." She shook her finger at Charlie. "Makes them feel special."

"I thought that was what sex was for," Charlie blurted out.

Mrs. Leder took the comment in stride, grinning. "Sex is only a small part of marriage, Charlie. You'll learn that soon enough." She eyed the boxes piled against the far wall. "Are you just about finished packing?"

Charlie set out toward the kitchen, carrying the casserole dish. "Almost. I want to get everything moved over to Nelson's apartment before the ceremony, so when we get back from our honeymoon, everything will already be set up."

Mrs. Leder turned her thick lenses to Madison. "How do you feel about being on your own, Madison?"

"Umm." Madison wrung her hands. "I'm fine with it. I'm happy Charlie and Nelson are finally tying the knot." She glanced at her roommate who was standing by the kitchen counter, and begged to be rescued with her eyes.

Mrs. Leder went to the kitchen breakfast bar. "I'm sure you'll be finding someone soon, Madison. Pretty girl like you won't be on the market for long."

"Madison already has someone, Mrs. L," Charlie declared, coming toward the counter. "Her new boss."

"Yes, you started that job today." Mrs. Leder's eyebrows went up. "Is your boss cute?"

Madison grimaced, wanting to kick Charlie for saying anything. "It's not like that. He's my boss. We can't date each other."

Mrs. Leder let out a deceptively fierce cackle. "Why not? When I started working at the oil company after I graduated from college, I used to spend hours watching Duncan Leder's fine ass walk by my desk until I got the man to sleep with me."

Charlie and Madison both started laughing. "Mrs. Leder?" Charlie chastised. "You shouldn't say such things to us. We're young and impressionable, remember?"

Mrs. Leder snorted. "Young maybe, but you two are about as impressionable as a Botox-stuffed Orange County housewife picking out her fifth Mercedes." Her eyes settled on Madison. "Well, maybe not you, Madison, but your cohort in crime definitely knows her way around a man."

Letting her mouth fall open, Charlie feigned indignation. "I do not. I'll have you know I'm wearing white at my wedding."

"Only because your future mother-in-law will be in attendance," Mrs. Leder commented. "She needs to believe her son is marrying a nice girl, but we know better." She waved off Charlie's stunned expression. "I was young and horny, too, Charlie. If my mother-in-law knew what her son and I had been up to the night before our wedding, she would have never let me marry into the Leder family…but I did. Thirty-two years of marriage, two sons, and now I own two apartment buildings and four business offices in Dallas." She winked at Madison. "Just play your cards right. Don't jump into bed with him too quickly, and you might just end up with that big rock on your finger like your roommate." She pointed to the oval-shaped diamond set in platinum glistening on Charlie's left hand.

"Might be a little late for that," Charlie giggled.

"Charlie," Madison yelled.

Mrs. Leder leveled her eyes on Charlie. "Did I miss something?"

"Mads has already slept with her boss."

"No, it's not like that, Mrs. L," Madison quickly clarified. "I think he may be this guy I knew a long time ago. We had this…thing."

"A one-night thing, if you know what I mean," Charlie teased with a wink.

"Oh, I get it." Mrs. Leder grinned. "No need to explain." She looked Madison up and down. "So, what did he say when he saw you today?"

Madison twisted her hands together, mimicking the feeling in her stomach. "He acted like he didn't know me. He, ah, never got my name before when we...." She shrugged. "I never met my boss until today, and I kept thinking he seemed so familiar. I don't think I should say anything to him."

"Of course you should say something!" Mrs. Leder waved her hand delicately in the air. "Make a casual reference like 'Have we met before? You seem awfully familiar,' or you could ask, 'Do you go to such and such restaurant? I swear I've seen you there before.' That might jog his memory and get him to talk about it."

"I can't do that," Madison admitted, shaking her head. "What if it is him and he does remember me?"

Mrs. Leder's devious smile took ten years off her face. "Then I'd say you have one up on your boss."

Madison frowned. "I don't get it."

"Madison, honey, if you two did as you kids say, 'hook up,' then he has to play nice with you. He might not want everyone in his office finding out about your past together. Could cause problems for him, but it could be a real advantage to you."

Charlie playfully slapped Mrs. Leder's arm. "Mrs. L, I never knew you had a bad streak."

"Child, I know how to play this game." She turned her eyes to Madison. "I may not look it now, but in my day I was quite the catch. Duncan's father hit on me way before his son did. So by the time Duncan asked me out, I had his father right where I wanted him, and knew there would be no objections voiced to my dating his son." She patted Madison's shoulder. "If it's the same guy, use what you had together to help you get ahead."

Charlie turned to Madison. "Mrs. L is right, Mads."

Madison felt the apprehension in her gust twist even tighter. "I can't do that! He was...is a nice guy."

"Nice guys don't have one-night stands, Madison. The nice guys get to know a girl first. Don't let him get away with it." Mrs. Leder turned toward the apartment door. "This is war, girl." She gave a passing wave of her hand. "Return the dish to me when you're done."

"Thank you, Mrs. L," Madison and Charlie called almost in unison as the door closed behind the older woman.

After she was gone, Charlie turned to Madison with one arched eyebrow. "Take it from the former femme fatale who also happens to be our landlady…go for it with the hottie boss."

Madison went back to the sofa and picked up her wineglass from the coffee table. "You want me to take advice from a seventy-year-old grandmother with a penchant for tuna casseroles? I don't think so."

"What could it hurt to ask the guy, like Mrs. L suggested? Just bring it up casually."

Madison guzzled more wine. "Casually? I don't even know if it's him, Charlie. I wish you wouldn't have said anything to Mrs. L."

Charlie turned back to the kitchen counter. "Come and eat some of this tuna casserole with me. And don't be so worried about what your boss will think. Better to find out now if it's him. What if you really like this job? You don't want to blow it, do you?"

Madison toyed with the notion of saying anything to Hayden about her suspicions. While imagining him standing close to her, she felt that funny tingle in her belly return. The only other man who had elicited such a reaction had been her onetime lover. Her mind may not have wanted to believe he was her Harry, but her body was beginning to have other ideas.

***

The next morning, Madison was sitting at her desk and peering out her window at the clouds hovering about the adjoining buildings. A light trickle of rain was tapping against the glass as her mind kept rolling over the advice from her landlady. She was supposed to be copying plans for a builder waiting to start construction on a new home designed by Parr and Associates. Instead, she entertained the multitude of ways she could walk into her boss's office and ask him if he was the Harry. Every time she felt the courage to rise from her chair, that nagging voice in her head barged in, warning her not to rock the boat with Hayden Parr.

"You're somewhere else," Adam's voice cut into her thoughts.

She turned to his desk. "I was thinking about something."

"Obviously, you're about as thrilled with copying plans as I am." He stood from his chair and came up to her. "What do you say we sneak out for an early lunch together? My treat?"

Madison glared at him and wondered why Adam was suddenly being so friendly. She had grown leery of his passing compliments, attributing his every action to some ulterior motive. "Maybe we should just check to see if they have something scheduled for us today for orientation."

He leaned his elbows on her desk. "I ran into Emma this morning. We had a little chat and she told me our boss and Mr. Worthy were going to be tied up all day in client meetings. So we're on our own."

Madison took in the curve of his freckled forearms beneath his rolled up white shirt sleeves. "I don't want to have lunch with you, Adam."

"Why not? I think if we're going to be spending so much time together, we should at least know a bit about each other."

Madison picked up a number two pencil on her desk. "I don't think we should be taking off for early lunches on our second day on the job." Turning her attention to the plans on her computer screen, she proposed, "What if Mr. Worthy or Mr. Parr comes looking for us?"

Adam's acerbic laughter bristled against her skin. "I hope you're not that naïve, Madison. You can't think that our bosses actually give a damn about us. The first day, they give you lunch, pretend to be interested in your future plans, but after that you're simply a workhorse expected to produce." He went over to the window and took in the misty clouds. "Don't kill yourself for an employer. You're always replaceable, and once they've chewed you up and spit you out they will move on."

She thought of the way Hayden Parr's haunting eyes had lingered on her face. "I don't know…Mr. Parr seemed nice yesterday."

Adam's green eyes intently studied her. "What did you two talk about while I was with Don Worthy? You seemed awfully preoccupied while we were eating lunch."

Madison put on a nonchalant smile. "He just asked me some questions since we never got a formal interview together. You know, about why I became an architect…the usual."

"You're sure?" His red brows rose up his forehead, accentuating the freckles on his cheeks. "You two seemed almost cozy."

How was she going to put this guy off? While scrambling to find the appropriate answer, she heard their office door open.

"Glad to find you two with your heads together," Hayden Parr announced as he breezed into the room.

Madison's stomach immediately clamped down when she saw the handsome man. The cut of his dark brown suit highlighted his wide shoulders and trim waist. When his eyes found hers, she could have sworn there was a glint of some decadent thought shimmering back at her. For a split second, she pictured pushing the jacket from his shoulders and letting her hands—

"Mr. Parr," Adam exuberantly extolled, as he walked toward the man. "We didn't expect to see you today."

"No, I'm sure you didn't." Hayden's eyes shifted to Adam, but the amusement in them vanished. "The reason I stopped by was to discuss something you brought up yesterday, Adam."

Adam's ass-kissing smirk made Madison's stomach turn. "And what was that, Mr. Parr?"

Hayden glanced toward the window overlooking downtown Dallas. "You wanted to know when you and Madison were going to get your first assignment. Well, I may have something for both of you."

Madison cautiously stood from her chair. "Both of us?"

He brushed his hand across his chin as he gazed up and down her figure. "I was just meeting with my new clients. They have two acres in Turtle Creek and want something out of the ordinary; something that blends with the landscape and does not detract from it. They want a natural-looking house that is also modern in design and allows expansive views of the land from every room. These clients have a great deal of money to spend, and certainly want the house to reflect that wealth...but in a tasteful way," he added sarcastically. He stiffly shifted his hands behind his back. "I would ordinarily give this to one of my more seasoned architects, but I think I need a fresh approach with these people, some new ideas. I thought perhaps I would let the two of you take a stab at it. See what you come up with."

The excitement in Adam's twitching feet was almost more than Madison could bear. *Could the guy be more obnoxious?*

"Wow, that's fantastic." Adam dashed to Hayden's side, waving his hands about in the air. "I have so many ideas, Mr. Parr. I know you'll love them. I can see a ranch exterior that perhaps opens up to a grand hallway with—"

"That's very ambitious of you," Hayden interrupted. "Don't you think you should consult with Madison first, since it will be both of your ideas?"

Adam appeared surprised. "But I thought we were competing against each other. You know, have the best design wins kind of thing."

Hayden snickered. "That was not my intention, Adam."

"Why not have us compete against each other?" Madison debated. "Might give you a better idea of our design styles, and you will then have two plans to choose from instead of just one."

Hayden's eyes darkened as he pondered the idea. "I usually don't like pitting one architect against the other. Are you are both all right with this?"

"Great. I'm in," Adam said with way too much exuberance in his voice.

"I'm game," Madison concurred.

Adam rubbed his hands together and turned toward his desk. "I can't wait to get started on a presentation for you."

"Aren't you forgetting something, Adam?" Hayden questioned.

"What else do I need? You already told me what the client wants."

Madison folded her arms over her chest, displaying a smart grin. "The property, Adam. We need to see the property. What good is designing a house to blend with nature, if we don't have any idea of the nature it is meant to blend in with?"

The smile that spread across Hayden's lips was absolutely stunning, awakening the sleeping butterflies in her stomach.

"Very good, Madison. And you're absolutely right. You need to see the property." He glanced over at Adam. "Both of you."

Adam clapped his hands together and the loud noise made the butterflies in her stomach take wing. "Great. We can take a look at it whenever you like."

Hayden's intense eyes crinkled up at the sides as his grin widened. "How about now?"

"Okay," Adam agreed with a shrug of his shoulders.

"I have a car waiting downstairs to take us to the property." Hayden moved closer to Madison's side. "What do you say, Ms. Barnett, are you up for a quick spin with me?"

She leveled her eyes on him. "You don't play around, do you, Mr. Parr?"

"I like to cut right to the chase, Ms. Barnett. Games are for cards, not people."

For an instant, her eyes held his and the room around them disappeared. She remembered Harry saying the exact same thing to her so many years ago. It was Harry's voice and Harry's words.

"Then let's get this show on the road," Adam proclaimed.

The sound of Adam's voice grated against her spine. Madison didn't know how she was going to be able to work side-by-side with her aggravating coworker without stabbing her number two pencil straight through his ambitious little heart.

***

The black Town Car Hayden had hired pulled up in front of a spacious wooded lot with thick oaks, a few crape myrtle trees, and trails that cut through the high grass and light brush. Named for the Turtle Creek that ran throughout the exclusive neighborhood, any address in the affluent area was often prized by the socially ambitious and highly affluent.

"Two acres in this neighborhood is quite a find," Hayden stated as he stepped from the rear of the car. "My clients inherited the property from a wealthy aunt, along with a sizable amount of money to build their dream home."

"Why don't they want to build further out where they can get more land?" Adam probed.

"You don't pass on a chance to build in Turtle Creek, Adam," Hayden explained. "There are very few lots left in this neighborhood."

Madison glimpsed the stone mansions that rose up close to the curb on either side of the property. They appeared old and grand, with wide steps that climbed to thick, carved doors and colonial windows covering the façade of the first and second stories. The homes were opulent, impressive, and demanded the attention of the onlooker, but Madison thought they lacked originality.

"Whatever we design it will have to be set back," she muttered, waving to the property. "We can't give any hint of being natural with these homes on either side. It will take away from the aesthetic."

Hayden faced her. "What else?"

"We need to keep the front grounds intact and allow the home to blend in," she affirmed as she moved from the street to the curb.

"That's what I was thinking," Adam agreed. "We need more trees in front, actually."

Madison turned to him. "It's a lot, not a grove, Adam. Add more trees and you'll kill the grass and brush beneath. Better to leave the nature already in place intact." She shifted her gaze to Hayden. "Does the property back up to the creek?"

"The lot covers three hundred feet along the shore of the creek, right past the ridge." He waved to a high ridge rising up in the center of the lot.

Madison climbed from the curb onto the grass. "Let's go and see it."

"Wait, what?" Adam's face fell. "You don't want to actually walk through that, do you?"

She spun around. "Why not?"

Adam's hand swept down his black pinstripe suit and black leather shoes. "We're not dressed for hiking through an uncleared lot, Madison."

She glimpsed her short yellow dress and black flats. "If I'm willing to walk in this, Adam, you can get a little dirt on your shoes."

Aghast, Adam's green eyes rounded. "They're two hundred dollar shoes, Madison."

Hayden's alluring chuckle broke the tension in the air. "Come on, Adam, it will be fun." He removed his suit jacket and flung it in the back of the car. Tugging his yellow tie from about his neck, he threw it on top of his jacket.

Madison could see Adam's reservations about the trek through the property stamped all over his face, but he did not dare voice his refusal. Shrugging his jacket from his shoulders, Adam reluctantly left it on the backseat of the car.

"Come on, boys," Madison taunted, kicking off her flats and leaving them next to the curb. "Last one to the creek is a rotten egg."

Madison took off down a dirt path to the side of the lot, running along as the brush and grass scraped against her bare legs. The late morning sun had finally come out and was filtering through the trees as a gentle fall breeze brought goose pimples to her skin. She could not remember the last time she had just run through the grass, feeling all the zest for life of a child.

"Madison, don't go so far," Hayden's voice called behind her.

She ignored him as she darted along the narrow path. She could feel the cool, damp earth beneath her toes with the occasional crunch of a twig or leaves coming up from the ground. As she jogged along, she took in the topography of the lot, noting how it dipped sharply after reaching a rise, and when she continued down an embankment, she could smell the creek just up ahead. The ground beneath her feet became mushier, and soon brambles and thorny bushes closed in around her, sticking her with their burs.

She was picking a thorn from her calf when Hayden came up to her.

"You shouldn't have taken off like that," he chided, seeming a little out of breath.

His concern perplexed her. "Why? I'm fine. The only thing that can hurt me here would be a snake, and it's too cool for them to be up."

Hayden quickly glanced down at the ground. "Oh crap, I hate snakes." He glowered at her. "If I chased you up here only to step on a snake, I will fire you."

Madison had never seen a man afraid of snakes, and the look on his face when she had mentioned the possibility of a slithering visitor was absolutely priceless. She broke out in a fit of laughter.

"What's so funny?"

"You." She waved her hand at him. "Afraid of snakes." She started laughing again. "I thought you were this famous architect, all sophisticated, and here you are afraid of a little ole snake."

"Well, no one likes snakes, Madison." His anger cooled as he ran his hand through his wavy brown hair. "I'm not the big, famous architect. That was my father."

Her laughter slowly abated. "No, I'm pretty sure it's you. Your designs are the talk of Dallas."

His head cocked to the side, and the morning light catching in his gray eyes made Madison's toes curl into the soft ground. "Is that why you wanted to come and work with my firm? Because my designs are the talk of Dallas?"

"Do you want to know the truth, Mr. Parr?"

"Mr. Parr was my father. I'd prefer it if you called me Hayden."

She stared into his eyes, mesmerized by the way the sunlight made them look so transparent. "The truth, Hayden, is I really, really needed a job."

Hayden smiled and then chuckled. "Well, I did ask for the truth, didn't I?"

"Yes, you did." She angled her face upward to catch a ray of sunshine.

"Why are you so different out here?"

She shrugged and looked over at him. "Maybe because we're not in your office; out here we're free of constraints."

He dipped his head closer to her. "But I like constraints. I like it when people do what is expected of them."

Emboldened by her surroundings, she flirtatiously smiled at him. "And why is that?"

"Because I like control. I like order. Without it there is simply…chaos."

"I thought that was a good thing," she argued. "Chaos reminds us that we're alive."

Hayden peered into her eyes. "I can think of other ways to feel alive, Madison."

"Hey, where are you guys?" Adam's desperate voice cried from a patch of brush behind them.

Madison could feel the heaviness of reality returning to her shoulders. For a few blissful moments, there had been no office, no boss, and no sense of propriety coming between them.

"Over here, Adam," Madison called.

"Where?" Adam's voice was laden with panic.

"Over here," Hayden shouted, his eyes never leaving her face. "By the river."

The crash of brush to their right soon gave way to the figure of Adam. With a leaf or two hanging from his red hair, the man's face was bright red and his green eyes wild with fear.

"This was a very bad idea, Madison," he complained, coming up to their side. "There isn't a thing we've accomplished by making our way across this jungle."

"I don't know, Adam," Madison offered. "I think our little adventure was very informational."

Hayden's eyes curiously searched her face. "What did you discover?"

She motioned to the ridge behind them. "The drop from the ridge is a lot steeper than I thought and not visible from the road. The topography is going to be a challenge, especially if we're talking about a big house. We're going to have to somehow make this home fit into the ridge."

"I don't see it," Adam rebuked. "Why not just clear the ridge? Get a few bulldozers in here and flatten the land for what we need."

"What about the natural beauty of the property?" she persisted. "You'll destroy it with bulldozers."

Adam swatted at a passing insect. "I don't see it that way. The land will look a lot nicer from the street that way. Blend in with the other homes."

"Blending in is not what is needed here," Madison countered with a raised voice.

"Obviously, you two have divergent opinions on this project," Hayden broke in. "That's good. Put them in a design and let's see which one our clients like."

"Oww!" Adam shouted, grabbing his ankle. "I think something just bit me."

Hayden grinned at Madison. "Probably a snake."

Adam began wildly jumping about. "A snake!"

Once they returned to the car, Madison and Hayden checked the bite on Adam's ankle. Sitting in the backseat of the Town Car with his ankle hanging out the open door, Madison looked over the lanky red-headed man's pale skin.

"It's nothing, Adam," Madison reassured him as she examined the small red dot on his ankle. "It's just an ant or something."

"It's the 'or something' that bothers me," Adam mumbled, scratching his ankle.

"We can stop by a pharmacy and pick up something on the way back to the office, if you need it." Hayden shrugged his jacket around his shoulders.

"No, no," Adam answered, sounding stoic. "I'll be fine."

Madison retrieved her flat black shoes from the curb while Hayden adjusted the yellow silk tie about his neck. When she saw him struggling, she leaned over to him.

"Allow me," she offered, and began to straighten out his tie.

As she fit the knot into place under his neck, her hands caressed his soft cotton dress shirt. She could feel the heat from his skin beneath the fabric, creating a ripple of desire in her belly. The smell of his slightly musky cologne filled her nose; the sensation of his eyes, taking in her every gesture, only seemed to compound the waves of white heat tensing her insides.

"So how long do we have to come up with our plans?" Adam's voice intruded.

Hayden took a step back from her, giving her a polite nod of thank you. "Two weeks."

"Two weeks?" Adam echoed. "That's not a great deal of time to come up with an original design like this one. We need particulars like one story, two story, how many bedrooms do they want, kitchen styles, is there going to be a family room or a movie theatre, and—"

"Perhaps I should give the two of you the opportunity to interrogate the clients," Hayden interrupted. "I have their living requirements," he motioned to Adam still sitting in the back of the car, "like the things you mentioned, but I think you need to meet the couple, get a feel for them, and what kind of home they want."

Adam stood from the backseat and slipped on his jacket. "I already think I have a feel for them. They want to fit into this neighborhood." He glanced around to the other mansions that dotted the street until he spotted a contemporary one-story home nestled on two lush acres. The stone house seemed out of place and better suited for a Texas ranch rather than an upscale neighborhood. He waved to the house. "Except for that one. What an eyesore," he commented.

Hayden arched an inquisitive brow. "Actually, that's an award-winning home. It belongs to Tyler Moore, the owner of Propel Oil and Gas."

Adam snickered. "He sure didn't get his money's worth with that one. Any idea who designed it?"

Hayden smiled. "I did."

Adam's long face fell and Madison covered her mouth, hiding her giggle.

"I'm sure it looks great on the inside," Adam quickly offered, his face turning a deep crimson.

Hayden ignored him. "What about you, Madison? Do you have all you need to make your design?"

She perused the adjoining homes, and then looked back to the lovely green lot nestled between them. "I have an idea, but I would like to hear the clients tell me of their vision. It will help me with the final design."

"Fine." Hayden nodded his head. "They're having a party at the Turtle Creek Mansion Restaurant this weekend. You should go and meet with them."

"Hey, maybe I should meet with them as well," Adam voiced, easing in between Hayden and Madison. "It could help me with my final design."

Hayden smirked, sensing Adam's jealousy. "All right. It's formal. You'll need a tuxedo."

Adam pulled at his tie. "I have one."

When Hayden turned to Madison, she cringed, knowing what he was going to ask. "Do you have a gown?"

She held her head up confidently and smiled. "Sure," she lied.

As they climbed into the back of the Town Car, Madison's excitement about the coming project faded beneath her troubled thoughts.

Where in the hell am I going to get a fancy gown?

Chapter 4

"But you don't own a gown," Charlie lamented later that evening. "You can't afford something like that, Mads. You could barely afford your bridesmaid dress. Why didn't you tell him the truth?"

Madison stood behind the counter in the kitchen, holding up a saucepan of macaroni and cheese while Michael Bublé crooned "Feelin' Good" in the background. "What else was I supposed to do, Charlie? That scrawny ass-kisser, Adam, was telling him he had a tuxedo, and then the man turned to me and I...I couldn't tell him I don't own a gown, let alone can't afford to buy one."

Charlie waved a frustrated hand in the air. "Is that why we are listening to this song? You always play this when you're upset." She marched over to the CD player by the television and turned off the music.

Madison shoved a wooden spoon filled with cheese-covered macaroni into her mouth. "Maybe I could wear your bridesmaid dress to the party," she mumbled with a mouthful of food.

"You can't wear that hideous teal and chocolate disaster to your fancy party. They won't let you in the door in that thing."

"I've got to find something. I need to go to this, Charlie."

Charlie pointed to the saucepan in Madison's hand. "So what are you doing, stress eating because you don't have a fancy dress for the ball, Cinderella?"

"Better than stress drinking," Madison replied, carrying the saucepan to the breakfast counter.

"Nothing is better than stress drinking," Charlie reasoned, pulling out one of the wooden barstools next to the bar.

"Well, I would be drinking, but we finished up the wine last night when I was stress drinking because I discovered my boss might be that guy from the bar."

"And how is that working for you? Did you ask him about it?"

Madison dropped the wooden spoon into the saucepan. "No. When he took us to check out that lot, and we were standing there by the creek, alone, I almost did say something about it, but then Adam appeared. Today, I could have sworn it was him. He even has the same laugh."

"You need to talk to him, Mads." She pointed to the saucepan full of mac and cheese. "If you don't, you'll end up weighing two hundred pounds and you'll never catch a husband."

"I don't want to catch a husband, Charlie. I want to fall in love."

Charlie reached for the saucepan. "You're already in love, Mads. With the guy you met that night in the bar. If you ask me, you've been crazy about him ever since." She lifted the wooden spoon, shoveling the macaroni into her mouth.

"And now he might be my boss." Madison slapped her hand down on the countertop. "Who'll probably fire me after he sees my design."

"Any idea what kind of house you're going to draw?" Charlie asked, digging into the saucepan for more mac and cheese.

"I'm not good with houses, Charlie. In school I was always better with big buildings that had lots of light and windows. I could never get the feel for houses."

Charlie tossed the wooden spoon into the macaroni. "Now you've got me eating this crap, and I've got a wedding dress to fit into." Glancing over at her friend, she smiled. "You'll come up with something great, Mads. You always do. Your designs are good, really good. You wouldn't have gotten the job with Parr and Associates if they weren't. And I think it's exciting that your hottie boss is giving you such a great assignment."

"You should have seen this piece of property, Charlie, it was beautiful. I just hope I can make something to complement it." She frowned and dropped her eyes to the white countertop. "But what am I going to do about a dress?"

"There is someone we can ask." Charlie's blue eyes twinkled with devilish delight. "She probably has tons of fancy dresses you could borrow."

Madison instantly knew what her roommate was thinking and started shaking her head. "No way. I'm not going to ask her."

Charlie jumped from her stool and went around the breakfast bar to take Madison's hand. "Yes, you are. Now come on."

Three minutes later, they were standing in front of an apartment door not far down the hall from their place.

"This is such a bad idea, Charlie," Madison griped.

"No, it's not." Charlie raised her hand and knocked on the door. "She owes us for eating all of her tuna casseroles."

"Well, if it isn't my two favorite tenants," Mrs. Leder commented after opening her front door. "What happened? Did you set off the fire alarm in your kitchen again?"

"No." Charlie smiled sheepishly. "We have a favor to ask you." She gestured to Madison. "Actually, Mads needs the favor."

Mrs. Leder leaned against her doorframe, the folds of her bright red muumuu clinging to her slim figure. "Go on. What is it?"

Madison twisted her hands together as she peered into the Coke-bottle glasses of her landlady. "Do you have a gown I could borrow?"

***

Standing in front of a long, antique mahogany-framed mirror, Madison gazed at her reflection. The gold ribbons woven throughout the white satin, off the shoulder gown danced in the lamplight of Mrs. Leder's oversized bedroom.

"It's a little big in the waist and needs a few darts sewn into the bust line, but I think the length is perfect," Mrs. Leder suggested as she stood beside Madison.

As Madison took in the flowing gown in the mirror, she caught a glimpse of Charlie's scowling expression behind her.

"You don't like it?"

"No, I love it." Charlie gestured to the dress "I was just trying to picture what your boss is going to do when he sees you in it."

Mrs. Leder's cackle permeated the air. "He'll want to get her away from the party and into bed if he has any sense." She went to a mahogany dresser and opened a small wooden box on top of it. When she returned to Madison's side, she was holding a red pin cushion. "When is this party?"

"Saturday," Madison told her.

"Well, I will have to work quickly to make some alterations for you." She removed a pin from the red cushion and reached for the dress.

"Thank you so much for doing this for me, Mrs. L."

"This old dress needs a night out." Mrs. Leder pinched a section of the dress about Madison's waist. "Where is the party?"

Madison watched the woman's deft hands expertly pin the dress. "At Turtle Creek Mansion."

"Turtle Creek?" The older woman smiled. "I haven't been there in years. When my Duncan was alive we used to go there quite a bit for dinner."

"We need to find you a man, Mrs. L," Charlie spoke out, sitting atop Mrs. Leder's massive oak king-sized bed. "You need to go out again."

Mrs. Leder pinned a small dart in the waistline of Madison's dress. "No, my dating days are over."

"You still miss Mr. Leder, don't you?" Madison gently inquired.

"Sure I miss him." Mrs. Leder removed another pin from the cushion. "Been almost ten years since he's been gone, but I have my boys and my grandchildren to keep me happy. Love comes into your life in many different ways, girls. First, you have the love of your parents, then the love of a mate or partner, and in your golden years, if you're lucky, you learn to appreciate the love of your children, friends, and family. When we're young, we think falling in love is the most important thing, but as you get older you realize, it's only a part of real love. The art to loving is realizing that it never stays constant, you must embrace every dimension of it. Otherwise, you will miss out on the essence of happiness."

"Yeah, but what about sex?" Charlie implored, standing from the bed. "Don't you miss that?"

Mrs. Leder grinned. "I never said I wasn't getting laid, Charlie, just not dating." She winked at Madison.

Madison giggled as Charlie let out a low whistle.

"Mrs. L," Charlie chuckled, walking across the bedroom, "you're a bad ass."

Mrs. Leder secured another pin in the dress. "I'm old, Charlie, not dead."

"Who's the lucky guy?" Charlie pestered as she perused a collection of pug figurines on Mrs. Leder's dresser.

"So you can tell the whole building?" Mrs. Leder replied. "I don't think so. You're a hopeless gossip, Charlie Tonti."

Charlie spun around. "I am not!"

Madison turned to her roommate. "Oh, please. Who is the one that told everyone about Mila Jacobs being pregnant in 210?"

"And about Mrs. Hubert hiding a monkey in 516?" Mrs. Leder chimed in.

Charlie folded her arms over her chest and shifted her hip against the mahogany dresser. "Some minor indiscretions," she conceded.

Madison looked down the folded skirt of the gown. "It wasn't minor to Mrs. Hubert. She still won't talk to me."

"Yes, well, at least Lester the monkey is happy with my granddaughter," Mrs. Leder reported. "I hated taking Mrs. Hubert's monkey away, but if I let one tenant have a monkey then every tenant will have a monkey, and soon I won't have a building, I'll have a zoo."

"What about a guinea pig?" Charlie questioned. "Are we allowed those?"

"You hate guinea pigs," Madison asserted.

"Not for me…for you. So you won't be lonely when I move out."

Mrs. Leder pulled at the waist of the dress. "If you do get a guinea pig, I don't want to know about it." Mrs. Leder looked down at Madison's bare feet poking out from beneath the dress. "What about shoes? Do you have something to go with this dress? Something gold and in a high heel I think would be best."

Madison gazed down at her feet, wiggling her toes. "All the shoes I own are black, blue, or brown, and are flats. I never wear heels."

"Too many years up on ballerina blocks, huh?" Charlie joked.

Mrs. Leder grinned into Madison's beautifully carved face. "You were a dancer, Madison?"

"Not just a dancer, a ballerina," Charlie responded.

Mrs. Leder motioned to Madison's figure. "Explains why you stay so slim." She handed her the pin cushion. "I have a pair of heels you can wear. Might be a little big, but you can stuff the toes with tissue paper to make them fit."

"I can't take your shoes, Mrs. L. The dress is more than generous."

"Nonsense." Mrs. Leder shooed off her comment. "You need to look like a princess for your boss. We have to make sure he can't take his eyes off you the entire evening."

"Ooohhh," Charlie squealed. "This is so exciting."

"Better put your hair up, too," Mrs. Leder suggested, going to her closet in the corner of her room. "Pile it atop your head with a few strategic wisps coming down; that'll float his boat."

"Mrs. L, you are good at this," Charlie piped in.

"Years of practice," Mrs. Leder shouted from inside her closet.

As Madison listened to the two women chatting, a cozy sense of contentment swept over her. Never before had she likened herself to a character in a fairy tale—she had been too practical to waste her time with such daydreams—but now, as she stood at the threshold to some mystical story of enchantment, Madison began to allow her mind to embrace the promise of what could be. Perhaps Hayden Parr would turn into her Prince Charming, and with Mrs. Leder and Charlie as her doting fairy godmothers, happily ever after might only be a few days away.

Chapter 5

Friday morning, Madison was in her office, attempting to lay out her design for the house in Turtle Creek. Unfortunately, as she stared at the blank computer screen, nothing came to mind. She had spent two days volleying her eyes from her blank computer screen to the wide window overlooking the skyline of downtown Dallas. With thoughts of the party enlivening her panic, Madison considered what she would say when she met the clients. How could she get her design across if she had nothing on paper to demonstrate her ideas? The scratch of a computer mouse roused her from her worries, and she glanced over at Adam.

Hunched over his computer, with his jacket strewn about his chair and his white shirt sleeves rolled up, he was entranced by what he had drawn on the computer. In fact, he had never stopped working since they had returned from the property.

"Still not getting anything?" Adam queried, never taking his eyes from the drawing on the screen.

She sighed and sat back in her chair. "I can't wrap my head around it."

"Perhaps you just have the wrong concept. Why not try for something else...something a bit more mainstream?"

Madison wanted to snicker with contempt at his suggestion. She knew she was on the right track, but visualizing what she wanted for the property, while encompassing all the beauty the land had to offer, was turning into quite a challenge.

"No, I have the right concept, Adam."

He looked up at her, donning his boyish grin. "We'll see tomorrow night if the clients agree with you."

"Yes, we will."

"What are you two still doing in here?" Don Worthy admonished as he entered the open office door. "There's a staff meeting in the conference room on thirty-two. Better get down there before the donuts are gone."

"Thanks, Mr. Worthy." Adam stood from his chair. "We must have been so preoccupied in our work that we forgot."

Don Worthy clapped his hands, urging them into action. "Get going, both of you."

Madison was following Adam out of the office when Don Worthy stopped her. "How is your design coming along, Madison?"

"Good," was all she offered before darting out the door.

They took the elevator with a few of the other seasoned architects to the thirty-second floor. Madison rolled her eyes as Adam happily bragged about his newest plans to everyone in the elevator.

When the silver doors opened, the group made their way across a darkly paneled reception area and through a pair of double doors that led to the conference room. After grabbing a donut and a glass of water, Madison got comfortable in a red leather chair at one end of the oval mahogany table and waited for the meeting to begin.

"I hate these things," confessed a hushed, masculine voice taking a chair beside her.

Turning to the side, she met the deep brown eyes of Garrett Hughes, chief architect for Parr and Associates. "Don makes us come to these stupid meetings and then spends an hour talking about himself," he grumbled.

Madison noted the man's aquiline profile, dark stubble on his chin, and the cut of his expensive suit jacket. "Then why don't you take over the meeting, Garrett? After all, you're the man in charge of the architects."

Garrett reached for his cup of coffee on the table. "Everyone knows who is really in charge at Parr and Associates, and it isn't me or Don Worthy."

"Then who is it?"

Garrett turned his liquid eyes to her. "The same man who has taken a fancy to your…talent." He took a sip of his coffee. "Harry has great plans for you."

"You call Mr. Parr 'Harry'?"

He nodded, replacing his cup of coffee on the conference table. "Ever since we belonged to the same fraternity in college and discovered we shared a common interest."

"What interest is that?"

Garrett just grinned at her. "How did you like UT at Arlington?"

"I liked it a lot. Good school."

"I know. Harry and I graduated from there."

Madison sat upright in her chair. "Hayden Parr went to UT in Arlington?"

Garrett's brow furrowed. "I thought you two knew each other from there. I assumed that was why you applied here."

Madison stared at the man in disbelief. "Are you saying Mr. Parr mentioned knowing me before…that he remembered me from UT Arlington?"

Garrett shrugged his wide shoulders. "He never said so. I just assumed you two were—"

Don Worthy's bellowing voice echoed about the room, interrupting Garrett. "Okay, let's get started everyone."

Garrett turned away and Madison settled back in her chair, her mind reeling from the disclosure. It was the first hard evidence she had to confirm her suspicions that Hayden Parr had been the man in the bar. Now what did she do? Confront him? Bring it up in passing conversation? Or should she ignore it all together? As Don Worthy's monotonous voice began to drone on about quality control issues, Madison debated the proper course of action to take. However, no matter what she planned, Madison feared it would likely have the same outcome: unemployment. And that, more than confronting Hayden Parr, terrified her.

***

After the meeting concluded, everyone was filing out of the conference room when Madison spotted Hayden at the entrance talking to Garrett Hughes. The two men were laughing when she came toward the door. Hoping for a clean getaway, she lowered her eyes and quickened her pace.

"Madison," Hayden called as she passed through the doorway, "do you have a moment?"

Shit.

She turned to him. "Sure, Mr. Parr."

His eyes wandered up and down her plain green cotton dress and black flats. "Good," he waved down the hall, "let's talk in my office."

She noted the smirk on Garrett's face as he walked away. Going up to Hayden's side she kept up her pleasing smile, hoping to hide the abject terror coursing through her veins.

A few doors down the hallway, they came to a modest pair of oak double doors, and Hayden reached for the handle. "There is something we need to discuss," he insisted, opening the doors.

His office was not as grand as she had envisioned. With a slew of crammed bookcases, his diplomas, and a few framed accolades on the faded steel blue walls, it appeared cluttered and almost plain. The dark blue carpet beneath her feet seemed to match the sinking feeling in her chest. As Madison approached his black desk situated before an expansive picture window, he came up behind her and gently pressed his hand into her back, guiding her to a black leather chair in front of his desk.

The touch of his hand sent a shudder down her spine. The pit of her gut exploded with heat that shot to the valley between her legs, making her feel a little lightheaded. Never before had a man's touch excited her so. Then, she remembered that night with him, the way he had held her while dancing and the white hot surges of desire he had awakened in her.

Don't lose it now, Madison.

"Am I in trouble?" she asked, taking her chair.

"No, not at all. Don Worthy came to me before the staff meeting." He casually rested his hip on the edge of his desk. "He was in your office and saw what you've been working on...or should I say what you haven't been working on." Hayden paused and waited for a moment before asking, "Is there a problem?"

She sat stiffly in the hard, black leather chair. "I'm just having trouble finding inspiration."

He leaned back, appearing surprised by her statement. "You seemed pretty inspired the other day when we were at the property."

"That was then. Now I'm desperately trying to find something that will do justice to the land. I know Adam is working away on some lavish design, but I want to—"

His hand cut through the air. "Never mind about Adam. This is about you and your idea."

He stood from the desk and had a seat on the chair next to her. Unexpectedly, he reached for the arms of her chair and pulled it closer to him. The show of strength surprised her, and Madison was convinced her boss would notice the flush on her cheeks as he angled closer to her.

"When we were walking about the property the other day, what did you feel about the land?"

She swallowed hard and tried like hell to concentrate on the question, and not the tantalizing nearness of his lips.

"I remember liking how green and woodsy it felt. Kind of like an escape in the big city. You know, sort of like a woodland hideaway." She licked her lips, suddenly feeling her mouth go dry.

His eyes focused on her lips, and he wiped his hand over his brow. "Anything else?"

She took in a deep breath, willing her heart to slow down. "It reminded me of when I spent summers at my grandfather's horse farm outside of Arlington. There was a creek a lot like the one the other day. I used to love playing there."

He crossed his ankle over his left knee, seeming a little nervous. "That explains why you were so comfortable in the brush...and with the snakes."

She shrugged. "I was a tomboy growing up. I learned a lot about nature during those summers."

"So use that. What did you like best about the property?"

She tilted her head to the side and a strand of brown hair fell across her cheek. "The high ridge and how it dipped to the creek." Without thinking, she twirled the loose hair about her finger. "But I think I liked the wooded atmosphere around the creek the best. I want to incorporate that view into the house somehow."

Hayden's eyes lingered on her finger, playing in her hair. "Sunroom, family room, or den perhaps?"

She let go of her hair and shook her head. "No, part of the atrium entrance. Where you walk in the front door and immediately see a twenty foot wall of windows that opens on to the creek. With rooms that flow off from there, but at the same time allow an unheeded view of the creek. Like a long corridor with rooms on either side. One side built up on the ridge, the other a flight down and facing the creek."

Hayden's eyes expanded from two small orbs of worried apprehension to wide gray marbles filled with wonder. His whole face appeared to change before her, making Madison smile.

"Wow," he exclaimed with a dip of his head. "Now there's something I would never have envisioned." He stared at her with admiration shining in his eyes. "That's truly a house worthy of the land. So what are you waiting for? Draw that."

Madison's body sank into her chair. "I've tried, but every time I begin, the dimensions seem too much for the foundation, and then there are the structural components. There will have to be a lot of steel beams used to hold the main rafters in place, especially since it will be built at quite an angle."

He took her hand. "Just draw it, Madison. Besides, the only part of a building that matters is its foundation. The rest is just for fun. Remember that when you are designing and worry about the logistics later when the engineers come on board. Right now we just need a vision."

Heat erupted between her legs and tingling exploded in her stomach. His hand felt like fire against her skin. She was overwhelmed by his touch, but at the same time terrified of it. Madison had never reacted like this with a man. Even during that night, she remembered feeling intensely attracted to him, but not like this. Was he her Harry? She had to find out.

"There's something I've been meaning to ask you."

"Ask me anything you like." He let go of her hand, sat back in his leather chair, and crossed his legs again.

She tried to remember the advice Mrs. Leder had given her. "Do you…have you ever…listened to Nina Simone?"

Hayden froze. For several seconds he did not move or even appear to be breathing. Madison was not sure if that was a good thing.

Great. I scared him to death.

Slowly, the inviting smile returned to his lips. "Nina Simone. I haven't listened to her in years. But yes, I used to love her music." He furrowed his brow. "Is she some kind of inspiration for your plans?"

Her hope sank to the dark blue carpet below. She had been a fool. If he was her Harry, he did not remember their night together. Hayden Parr had no idea who she was; Madison was convinced of that now. All of her worrying had been for nothing.

"Yeah," she finally answered, "her music helps me to draw."

He rose from his chair. "Then I suggest you get to it. The party is tomorrow night, and I think it would be wise to have some kind of rough draft to show the clients."

She stood up. "Yes, Mr. Parr."

"Hayden," he corrected.

The excitement she had felt before fizzled out of her. "Yes, sir," she mumbled, and quickly turned for the doors.

"Madison," he called to her as she placed her hand on the doorknob.

When she faced him, her smile had slipped a little and she fought to look as if nothing had changed between them.

"Tell Adam to come and see me when you get back to your office. I want to go over his design before tomorrow night."

Swallowing back her disappointment, she opened the door. "Of course, Mr. Parr."

Dashing from his office, she fought to hold her emotions in check until she reached the elevator. Only when the silver doors closed did she let out a long, loud breath between her gritted teeth.

"You're an idiot, Madison Barnett." She forcefully wiped her hand over her forehead. "How could a man like that ever want a stupid girl like you?"

***

Madison spent the rest of the afternoon at her computer, diligently developing her design. She refused Adam's invitation to join him for lunch, and continued working until five o'clock rolled around and the shuffle of the others on their floor drifted in through their open office door.

"I guess that's it for the day," Adam remarked as he shut down his computer. "You ready to head out?"

Madison stretched out her back and then shook her head. "No, you go on. I'm going to stay for a while and get a bit more done."

Adam went to the corner table with the large printer on it. The hum of the printer filled the air as it churned out a hard copy of Adam's design.

"It's just a rough sketch, Madison. You don't have to have it completed." After glancing over at her drawing, he pulled the large copy of his design from the printer and began rolling it up.

She nodded to his desk. "Is yours almost finished?"

"Not quite, but it is good enough for the Martins."

"Who are the Martins?"

He sheepishly grinned. "The clients. Mr. Parr told me about them. Old friends of his family…that's why he is giving us a shot at the plans. He couldn't afford to piss off a real paying client with two new grads for architects." Adam went back to his desk. "Anyway, I wouldn't kill yourself over this, Madison. Mr. Parr is probably going to ignore whatever we come up with and give the project to Garrett."

"Did he tell you that?"

"He didn't have to. When you came in after meeting with him, you looked down in the dumps about something. I figured he wasn't happy with your design."

"No, he actually seemed rather excited about my design."

"Could have fooled me." He slung his blue backpack over his right shoulder, gripping the rolled up paper in his hand. "Are you sure I can't talk you into leaving? We could go around the corner to Rory's and grab a beer."

"No thanks. I've got to finish this." She motioned to her computer screen.

"Suit yourself. If you ever feel the need for a drink, the invitation is always open." He hurried into the hall.

Relieved to finally be alone, Madison took her chair and shifted her attention to the design on the computer screen. The house was beginning to take shape. As she began to lengthen out the rear porch that she had inserted overlooking the creek, Adam's words came back to her.

Why was she bothering if all of her efforts were for naught? Sighing as she shaded in a section of the extended porch with her mouse, Madison considered if she should finish the design she had started. Maybe someday, someone would like it.

"Yeah, maybe someday."

It seemed her life had been an endless string of "maybe somedays." She had placed so much hope on someday, that the reality of today had been pushed aside. Madison had waited for someone special to someday come and change her life, but that someone had never appeared. Instead of losing her virginity to a man she loved, she had given it to a stranger, and when that stranger turned out to be like every other man she had met, the reality of her life came crashing down around her. There was no someday…only today.

Even the special attention Madison thought she had been receiving from Hayden Parr had been her imagination. Like her silly infatuation with Harry, she had built her relationship with her boss into something it obviously wasn't. Maybe she had built up Harry to be something he wasn't as well. As her mind wandered back to that night, Madison tried to find subtle hints or words that would allay her apprehensions, but there was nothing. No sweet endearments whispered in her ear, no gentle caresses or prolonged embrace. It had just been sex…really good sex, but sex all the same.

"It's time to grow up, Madison," she voiced, hardening her resolve to put away the past. "It never mattered. It was nothing more than a one-night stand, and no one's ever found happiness in the arms of a stranger."

Chapter 6

The poufy gold and white skirt of her long dress was bunched around her hips as she struggled to reach for the release on her seat belt. Sitting in the front seat of Charlie's blue Honda Accord, Madison waited as a valet came toward the car door outside of the entrance to Turtle Creek Mansion Restaurant.

"Don't forget your plans," Charlie said, handing her the cardboard tube containing her computer generated drawing. "Text me when you're ready to go. I'll probably still be over at Nelson's unpacking." Her eyes swerved back to the pile of boxes she had stacked in her backseat.

"You're sure you don't mind picking me up?" Madison finally hit the button on the seat belt release. "I can grab a cab home."

"No. I'm happy to come back and get you. That way I can leave Nelson to do the unpacking."

The car door opened and a sharply dressed young man in black pants and a red vest held out his hand to Madison.

"You look great," Charlie declared. "Go get that hottie boss."

Madison smiled warmly for her friend, ashamed that she had not told Charlie the truth about Hayden and how he had forgotten all about their one night together.

"Thanks, Charlie," she uttered, before stepping from the car.

Clutching her small gold purse and the round cardboard tube with her design, Madison stopped before the grand entrance to the restaurant and glanced up at the impressive Rosewood Mansion on Turtle Creek.

Built over a century earlier by a cotton baron, the stately home was designed as a High Renaissance Italian villa, complete with heavy decorative white moldings above the grand domed entrance and long arched windows. Short, protruding balconies on the second and third floors were wrapped in heavy white iron railings. The patio leading to the doorway was covered with red brick inlaid in an arched pattern, resembling waves on the water. A white canopy covered the walkway to the main entrance, while all about the greenery had been strewn with white tea lights. As she neared the doorway, with its white triangular pediment rising majestically above, Madison sucked in a nervous breath and smoothed out the front of her gold and white gown.

"Here we go."

At the oversized wooden doors, an attendant dressed in a black tuxedo politely smiled and waved her inside. The stately mansion had long ago been converted into a fashionable hotel, and as Madison entered the warmly decorated lobby with its modern custom artwork, she reveled in the estate's original magnificence of hand-carved fireplaces, marble floors, and stained-glass windows. To the right of the lobby was a narrow hallway with a stand announcing that the Mansion Restaurant was closed for a private party. Following a line of well-dressed guests down the hallway, Madison made her way toward the elegant leaded glass doors that opened into the restaurant.

Passing through the doors, she was enticed by the murmur of voices and greeted by a warmly lit bar. With deep honey-colored paneled walls and burnt sienna leather furniture surrounding black tables, the cozy room oozed elegance. A wall of niched alcoves behind the dark-stained bar offered a glimpse of the alcoholic brands offered. At the far end of the room, a selection of dark beige and amber plush sofas stood on a black, white, and gold-tiled floor across from a stately hearth encased in a high taupe marble mantle. About the room, the formally attired guests sipped on tall martini glasses filled with a red concoction. Before Madison could even begin to wonder what the drink was made of, a waiter decked in all black approached her side.

"Cranberry martini, miss? It's the signature drink for the party." He held out a silver tray filled with the specialty drinks before her.

Rearranging the awkward cardboard tube and purse under her left arm, Madison reached for a glass. "Thank you."

The waiter disappeared behind her and Madison raised the edge of the wide-rimmed glass to her lips. First the tartness of the cranberry tickled her taste buds, and next the pungent rush of alcohol hit her.

"They'll have to carry me out of here if I drink this."

Casually stepping to the side, she put the strong drink on an empty table in the corner of the room, pretended to adjust her gold clutch purse under her arm, repositioned her tube, and then she slinked away.

Leaving the bar, she made her way to the main dining room. Dark, carved panels of rich wood decorated the walls, but the centerpiece of the room was not the impressive walnut and white marble inlaid mantle with its depiction of the old cotton baron's family crest, it was the wall of stained glass windows boasting the crests of the relatives of the influential family that had built the massive mansion. Along one side of the room a white linen buffet service waited, while chefs wearing high white hats stood at the ready to serve the guests. The dining room tables were covered in white linen, set with glistening white china and shiny silver stemware, and in the center sat an arrangement of bright red carnations. More vases of red carnations were scattered about the room, and decorated the buffet tables. An open pair of leaded glass doors allowed the cool night breeze into the room from an adjoining patio.

Eager to check out the contents in the selection of silver chaffing dishes, Madison slowly sauntered past the buffet tables and her stomach rumbled in protest. Nervous about the entire evening, she had skipped lunch, fearing that food would have only added to the distress pervading her already queasy stomach.

At the entrance to the patio, she savored the feel of the nippy fall breeze on her hot skin. Then, a familiar laugh made her breath catch in her throat.

Standing by an outdoor fireplace of orange stucco and dressed in a fitted black tuxedo was Hayden Parr. In the pale light of the dozens of cast iron lanterns that were strewn about, his gray eyes appeared magically aglow. His rugged features were accentuated by the dancing shadows of light, making his strongly carved chin and sharp cheekbones even more luscious. In his hand was an old-fashioned glass of dark yellow liquid that matched the dark yellow furniture spread about the patio. He was talking to a beautiful brunette with stunning cheekbones, catlike brown eyes, and a lean figure, not unlike his. Draped in a black and white satin gown that gathered at the waist and collected on her right shoulder, she looked every inch the woman Madison knew she could never be: sophisticated, stunning, and irresistible to men. As she chatted with Hayden, she affectionately placed her smooth white hand on the sleeve of his black tuxedo jacket.

The well of jealousy that overtook Madison was unexpected; she wanted to scratch the woman's eyes out. Feeling the desire drain from her body, Madison was about to turn away when Hayden's eyes found her. Suddenly, she felt naked beneath his gaze. He seemed to drink in every inch of her, and without hesitation she knew what he was thinking. Any woman worth her weight knew that look when she saw it in a man. It was primal; it was instinctual, and utterly carnal.

Putting his drink down on a nearby table, Hayden abandoned the woman at his side and came up to Madison. "You look absolutely wonderful," he purred in a voice akin to black velvet.

The rush of heat to her cheeks only compounded the tingling in her belly. "Thank you, Mr. Parr."

He grinned, looking sexy as hell. "None of that Mr. Parr stuff tonight. We're out of the office and this is a party. Call me Hayden." He took her arm. "Come, there's someone I want you to meet."

He escorted her across the patio to the woman waiting in front of the large fireplace. As she came closer, Madison noticed the way she watched her, smiling with appreciation rather than malice.

"Mike, this is the young architect I was telling you about, Madison Barnett," Hayden proclaimed as he came to a stop next to the beautiful brunette. He turned to Madison. "I would like you to meet my sister, Michaela Chaplin. Everyone calls her Mike."

Mike held out a sleek hand clad in a wide diamond tennis bracelet and an assortment of diamond rings. "Madison, great to meet you. Harry has been singing your praises to everyone who will listen."

Hayden frowned. "My sister exaggerates, as usual."

Mike laughed and slapped her brother teasingly on the arm. "He never praises his architects, but you he has simply gone on and on about." She smiled, a mischievous smile that hinted at the playful demeanor beneath the exquisite alabaster face. "You see, Harry is one of those bosses that believes praise needs to be earned." Her brown eyes swept over Madison's face. "And you have definitely earned it."

Hayden reached for the tube beneath her arm. "Is this your design?"

"Yes, I finished it this morning."

As he unscrewed the red plastic top from the tube, he said, "Working after hours. I like that."

Mike shook her head. "Must you talk shop so soon? The poor girl doesn't even have a drink, Harry."

Hayden glanced over to Madison's hands. "We can remedy that." He waved to a passing waiter. "Bring us three cranberry martinis."

Madison was about to protest, but then thought better of it. She would just have to pretend to drink.

Hayden went to a black iron table next to them and began to spread out the long sheet of paper with her computer drawing. His eyes studied the paper for several moments, making Madison itch with nervousness.

Stay calm. Just stay calm, Mads.

"This is very good, Madison," he finally admitted in a hushed tone. "Very good."

When he looked up at her, the fire in his eyes was so intense Madison thought she would be utterly consumed.

He tore his eyes away from her and glanced about the small crowd braving the chilly night air on the patio. "Let's go and find Stevie and Pat. Show them what you've got."

"Stevie and Pat?" Madison inquired.

"The Martins. They are the clients and hosts of this party."

"It's their fifth wedding anniversary," Mike explained. "The third marriage for each," she reported with a wistful roll of her eyes, "but at least they haven't killed each other yet."

"Mike, play nice," Hayden scolded. "They're my clients."

"They're your neighbors, Harry." She leaned in closer and lowered her voice, adding, "And I know why you're so hot to build this house for them. You just want to buy their house across the street and tear it down."

"That's because it's an eyesore, Mike. I want their property, not their house."

"Why do you want their property?" Madison questioned.

"Because they own five acres on Exall Lake that I want to build my dream home on." He sighed. "My current house is…a problem."

Mike let go a deep, hoarse chuckle that surprised Madison. "He means his current house is being sought after by the bloodsucker he was married to. The pretentious bitch wants everything he owns and then some. I swear, Harry, I don't know why you married that social climbing gossip whore. I told you it would never last."

His face reddened and his lips blanched as he mashed them together. "Enough, Mike," Hayden snapped. "You don't have to remind me of your reservations about Ellen. I get plenty from Mom and Dad, I don't need it from you, too."

"Fine, fine." Mike pouted. "I still don't know why you want to give her your house. Two years of marriage hardly seems worth it."

"I'm not giving it to her. She is fighting me for it, and…. This is not the place to discuss it." He glanced over at Madison apologetically. "Why don't you stay here and I will go and get Stevie and Pat?"

"Sure thing, Mr. Parr."

When he exited the patio, Madison noted the way his hands were curled into fists. He walked away, and she admired the cut of his tuxedo from behind and the way his butt—

"You'll have to forgive my brother, Madison." Mike's voice pulled her back from her lurid observations. "Talking about his ex always puts him in a foul mood. But I think you can help with that."

"Me?" Madison knitted her brows. "What can I do?"

Mike's elegant hand waved down Madison's dress. "My brother always had a thing for tiny, slender brunettes with green eyes ever since he graduated from UT Arlington. Before that he was a real player. Harry never met a woman he didn't like in his college days. I think he dated half the women on the Arlington campus." She winked. "You remind me of Ellen in a way. She has your face, but not your smile." She paused, and slowly a knowing grin eked across her red-painted lips. "I think you might be just what he needs."

"Another reminder of his ex-wife?" Madison curtailed her desire to snicker. "I don't think so, Mrs. Chaplin."

"You misunderstand me, Madison." Mike stroked the front of her gown, fondling the satin. "My brother needs someone to listen to him. He has no one these days, and I worry that he spends too much time alone."

"I'm just his employee, Mrs. Chaplin. I don't plan on being anything else."

Mike's deep chortle reminded Madison of Hayden's soulful laugh. "I wasn't suggesting that. I was merely saying he could use someone in his life that isn't going to judge him based on his success or bank account. He's had enough women doing that."

Madison had no idea what the strange woman was alluding to, but she decided to venture a guess. "Are you saying you want me to be his friend?"

"Why not? Don't you need a friend, Madison?"

Madison nervously gripped her gold purse and shifted it under her arm. "I guess we could all—"

"Here are your martinis, ladies," a short waiter broke in.

Madison took one of the red drinks from his tray, while Mike picked up the two others being served.

"Thank God." Mike took a large gulp from the glass in her right hand, downing the contents in one swallow.

Madison watched in amazement as the woman finished the drink. Just as the waiter was about to turn away, she stopped him.

"Here." She placed the empty glass on his silver tray. "Bring me two more like that one," she held up the drink in her left hand, "while I finish this one."

The young man just grinned. "Yes ma'am."

Mike surveyed the guests in the main dining room beyond. "You've got to have at least three stiff drinks in you to be able to put up with this pretentious group."

Madison held her drink, but refrained from taking a sip. "You don't like these people?"

"Honey, snake charmers have more merit than half the people in that room." Mike nodded to the leaded glass doors to the dining room. "The only reason I'm here is because Harry asked me to come."

A very handsome man wearing a black Armani tuxedo eased up behind Mike and wrapped his arm about her slender waist. "Still drinking like a fish I see, Mike."

He was tall, over six foot, and his toned body oozed sophistication and sex appeal. Black, wavy hair tinged at the sides with gray outlined his determined, square jaw and high forehead. As his deep-set, dark eyes lingered over Madison's dress, his thin lips curled into a seductive smile.

"Tyler, it's good to see a friendly face amid this den of thieves," Mike commented, giving his chiseled cheekbone a peck. "I didn't know you were coming."

Tyler grinned at her and then tipped his head to the side. "Moe and I decided to come at the last minute."

Mike waved to Madison. "Tyler Moore, meet Madison Barnett, Hayden's newest architect at the firm."

Tyler held a tapered hand out to Madison. "Ms. Barnett. It's a pleasure."

Madison felt the man's eyes linger over her face and figure, causing her pulse to quicken.

"Tyler is a client and owns Propel Oil and Gas." Mike patted his tuxedo sleeve. "His house has even won Hayden an award for architectural design."

"I remember. The stone contemporary home in Turtle Creek," Madison stated. "Yes, Mr. Parr showed it to me and another architect last week. Lovely place, Mr. Moore."

"Thank you, Ms. Barnett." Tyler turned to Mike. "Have you seen my wife?"

"Probably signing autographs." Mike shifted her gaze to Madison. "Tyler's wife is Monique Delome, the writer."

The name rang a bell with Madison. "Really? I love her books."

"I'll be sure to let her know. Thank you." Tyler glanced around the patio. "If you see her, Mike, tell her I'm looking for her." He checked the gold Rolex on his wrist. "We need to get home before my mother has Eva clothed in Chanel and picking out her first Mercedes."

"How is Barbara doing these days?"

He offered a sad smile. "Still coming to terms with Gary's death, but she's been spending more time with Eva, which is a good thing."

"I was sorry to hear about your stepfather, Tyler."

"Thank you, Mike. Give your parents my best." He kissed the elegant woman's cheek, and nodded to Madison. "Ms. Barnett. I hope we meet again."

"Thank you, Mr. Moore."

Madison went to Mike's side as Tyler Moore gracefully strolled away.

"Damn, that man has still got it," Mike muttered, lifting her drink to her lips.

"I can't believe he's married to one of my favorite authors," Madison remarked.

"Apparently, they met in college and dated for a while, but nothing ever came of it. At least, not until they met up again a little over two years ago…then the romance turned serious." Mike gulped back another mouthful of the red martini. "Seems the second time around everything worked out for them." Mike turned her dark eyes to Madison. "What about you? Do you have a man in your life?"

Madison shook her head. "No, ah, I—"

"There she is...Madison," Hayden called from the patio entrance.

When she whipped her head around, she saw Hayden walking in beside a middle-aged couple. The man was almost as tall as Hayden, but with thinning black hair speckled with gray. Wearing a black tuxedo with a red cummerbund about his thick waist, his arm was linked with an attractive blonde. She glided along in a silk gown of azure with a cream beaded bodice and flowing skirt. With a beautiful creamy complexion and scintillating blue eyes, the woman was draped in glistening gold jewelry about her neck, wrists, and ears. Her smile was warm and inviting as she eyed Madison across the patio.

"Madison Barnett, this is Pat and Stevie Martin, old family friends, and your new clients," Hayden announced with a flourish of his hand.

Madison put her drink down on the table next to her design before stepping forward. Taking Pat Martin's hand, she uttered, "It is a pleasure to meet you both."

"Has Mike been keeping you entertained?" Pat Martin nodded to Hayden's sister.

Mike raised her empty martini glass, giving the man a dubious smirk. The contempt in her brown eyes was palpable. "I've been giving her the lowdown on your sordid past, Pat."

"Hayden has just been telling us about your design," Stevie Martin began, ignoring Mike, "and I must say we are both very excited to see what you have drawn for us."

"He told us you went to UT Arlington." Pat Martin gestured to Hayden. "Same as Hayden. Did you two know each other from school?"

Madison's eyes shot to her boss.

"No, I never knew Madison before she applied to our firm," Hayden divulged.

Madison was shattered. She had still hoped that perhaps he did remember her, but as time went on, it was becoming evident that he didn't have the slightest clue as to who she was.

"So is that it?" Pat Martin waved his hand over the long paper Hayden had left on the patio table.

"They're wonderful, Pat, you'll love them," Mike blurted out, and then pointed to Madison's untouched martini on the table. "Are you going to drink that?"

Madison gaped at Hayden's sister, not sure of what to say.

"How many has she had?" Hayden softly demanded in her ear.

"Two," Madison mumbled.

"Don't worry, big brother," Mike snickered. "We're among friends."

Hayden picked up the drink from the table and handed it to Madison. "Keep this away from her."

"These are quite impressive, young lady," Pat Martin commented, lifting the large sheet of paper from the table with his chubby hands. "I see you're trying to build the house into the ridge." He turned to his wife, holding out the plans. "I told you that's what I wanted."

"I didn't think it could be done," Stevie Martin confided in a soft voice.

"It can be," Hayden assured the couple. "It's just going to cost you and require a bit more planning as far as the engineering specs go."

"I like that the creek is so close to the back." Stevie Martin gestured to the rear of the home on the drawing. "And these are windows?"

Madison motioned to the plans. "All along the rear of the atrium, tying in the entrance and the back of the house, is one sweeping room. I have all the rooms running off that main room in both directions, with the second story coming off the atrium via a set of climbing stairs. That portion of the house will be built into the ridge, but overlooks both the front portion of the property and the rear, while the first floor rooms will only have views of the creek. It will give you more of a secluded feel from the street." She glanced over at Hayden, and he gave her an encouraging smile.

"I like it," Stevie Martin affirmed with a curt nod. "It blends in with the property."

Pat Martin returned the plans to the patio table, frowning. "Ambitious, yes, but isn't there another architect coming to show us his ideas?"

Madison's hopes were instantly dashed.

"Yes, Adam Turnbull." Hayden glanced back at the dining room doors. "Who should have been here by now."

As if on cue, Adam—decked out in a tuxedo with shiny lapels and a lopsided black bow tie— appeared in the dining room entrance. His red hair was sleeked back, accentuating his long face and skinny neck. In his hand was a cardboard tube, and when he spotted Hayden and Madison by the fireplace on the patio, his smile broadened, reminding Madison of a salesman in a used car lot. He took off in a determined stride as he approached their party. When his smile morphed into his usual pompous grin, all of Madison's contempt for her haughty office mate reignited.

"Madison, what a lovely dress," Adam commented, with all the sincerity of a well-seasoned politician running for re-election.

"Hello, Adam. You look very elegant." She then took a quick sip of the drink in her hand, yearning for the bolster of alcohol in her system.

"Adam," Hayden waved toward the Martins, "these are your clients, Pat and Stevie Martin."

Adam enthusiastically gripped Pat Martin's hand, pumping it up and down. After complimenting Stevie Martin on everything except her shoes, Adam's overzealous eyes returned to Hayden.

"I'm not sure how much Mr. Parr has told you about my design."

"I haven't said a thing, Adam," Hayden insisted, holding up his hands.

Adam beamed at the Martins, tugging at the cardboard tube under his arm. "Well, when I viewed your property and the surrounding homes, I knew I could give you exactly what you wanted. I got such a wonderful vibe from the land and the neighborhood, and what I drew reflected the essence of everything I absorbed there."

"Absorbed?" a confused Stevie Martin asked.

Madison took another badly needed sip of her cocktail.

"Absolutely," Adam went on. "The Turtle Creek area is so esteemed, so prestigious, and the homes there are some of the most brilliant representations of classical architecture. Like this mansion we are in now." He dramatically waved his hand about the patio, looking more like a bad actor in a B movie than an architect. "I wanted to capture the essence of that in my design for you." He then pointed to the perplexed looking Martin couple.

Hayden took a step toward Adam, rubbing his hand across his chin. "Why don't we dispense with the explanations and just show Pat and Stevie the drawing, eh, Adam?"

"Ah, sure," Adam agreed, appearing a bit befuddled. Opening the top of the cardboard tube under his arm, Adam approached the black iron table behind Madison.

She moved to the side, and waited as he spread his plans out over hers. When her eyes craned over his shoulders to get a peek at his finished design, she recoiled. The massive, three-story home had wide colonial windows, Doric columns, and a triangular pediment over the front entrance. Resembling an ancient Greek temple with its Greek Revival design, Madison thought the home appeared nothing at all like what the Martins had wanted. She shifted her eyes to the middle-aged couple as they eagerly scanned the plans, the disappointment etched on both of their faces.

Mike came forward, interested in the plans on the table. "Jesus," she gasped.

"Yes, it's certainly big," Stevie Martin commented.

Adam took it as a compliment and smiled voraciously. "Yes, I have six bedrooms with bathrooms upstairs, and a grand-sized kitchen, family, living, and dining rooms on the first floor." He gestured to the rooms drawn on the first floor. "Plus, there is plenty of space for a media room."

Pat Martin studied the plans. "What about blending in with the property? We want it to be natural, like the land."

"Oh, it will." Adam touched the drawing, pleading his case. "I have included wide windows on the rear of the home in the family room, den, dining area, and even the kitchen. A large deck will come off the back and go down to the creek."

"I don't understand," Stevie Martin voiced, eyeing the plans. "What about the ridge? Is this going to be built in front of it or on top of it?"

Adam placed his hands behind his back and rocked cockily on his black, shiny patent leather shoes. "I think to make the house blend in with the surrounding homes, we will need to eliminate the ridge, or at least flatten it a bit, so you can get a great view of the creek."

Hayden's eyes turned to Madison, and for a split second she detected the frustration in them.

"We want to try and preserve the beauty of the land, Adam," Pat Martin pointed out. "By taking out the ridge we will be compromising the integrity of the property."

"I believe you also have to be true to the architecture surrounding your home," Adam debated. "You will stand out like a sore thumb if you venture too far from the established designs in Turtle Creek."

An uncomfortable silence filled the air, making Madison hide her sly grin by taking a sip from her drink. It seemed the arrogance Adam had shown her from day one had spilled over into his approach to architecture. With him more was better, and the biggest house on the block was obviously the best.

"Well," Pat Martin finally spoke up, glancing to his wife, "we have a lot to consider, don't we, Stevie?"

She smiled encouragingly at Adam. "It certainly would be the biggest on the block."

"You could see it from space," Mike ribbed.

"Okay." Hayden patted Adam on the shoulder. "Why don't you get something to eat while I talk to Pat and Stevie, all right?"

"Sure thing, Mr. Parr."

Hayden dipped his head to Madison and nodded toward the dining room doorway, insisting that she join Adam. She gave him a weak smile, placed her drink on the edge of the table, and adjusted her purse under her arm.

Adam waited off to the side for her, and as the two stepped toward the dining room doors, he placed his hand in the small of her back.

"I think that went rather well."

The alcohol Madison had hurriedly downed was now urging her to speak her mind. She wanted to tell Adam what a mistake he had made with the Martins, but decided there was no point in deflating his overblown ego so early on in the evening; she would leave it to Hayden to handle Adam. After all, he was Hayden's problem and not hers.

Chapter 7

As they entered the dining room, Madison glanced back at Hayden and the Martins. They were huddled together, engrossed in their discussion. With her sole objective for the party accomplished, she wanted to quietly slip out the door and hurry home. The nervousness of dealing with the Martins forgotten, she began to feel the annoying little pokes and twinges of her fitted dress and tissue-stuffed, high-heeled gold shoes. While she was picturing curling up with a good book in her warm ups and fuzzy slippers, Adam took her hand.

"Now we have all night to get to know each other…outside of the office that is," he said with a leering gaze. "You really do look beautiful in that dress, Madison."

Uncomfortable with the clamminess of his hand, she tried to shake it off. "Thank you, Adam."

He tightened his grip on her. "I know we didn't get off to the best start, but I really would like to be friends, good friends."

"We work together, Adam. We don't need to be friends."

He moved closer to her. "I think we do."

"Madison," a sultry voice called over her right shoulder.

When she turned, Hayden was standing behind her. Her body tensed when his eyes peered down at Adam's hand in hers. "I need to speak with you."

Instantly, she let go of Adam's hand. "Of course."

"Is this about the designs?" Adam butted in. "Because I have a few more things I would like to—"

"No," Hayden barked, cutting the young man off, "this is about something else entirely."

Seeming relieved, Adam gave a slight shrug and then nodded. Letting Hayden take her elbow, Madison allowed him to pull her away. When they went to a corner of the dining room, Hayden let go of her arm, and his eyes surveyed the room before he finally spoke.

"I'm sure you already know the Martins are very interested in your design." He lowered his head. "They were very impressed with you. I have to say, so was I."

"Thank you." Her voice was barely above a whisper.

"However, they have some changes they want to make, quite a few changes actually. I want to find out if you're all right with that."

Madison nodded. "It's their house. I'll do whatever they suggest…as long as it's structurally possible."

"Good answer." He slowly grinned, appearing pleased. "We need to speak more about this tonight, but not here." He glanced over at Adam standing by the buffet tables, taking in their every word. "How did you get here? Did you drive?"

"A friend brought me. She's going to pick me up later."

He hesitated, his lips smashing together in an unflattering scowl. "I'll take you home. We can talk in my car."

Her stomach tangled into a huge knot. "You really don't have—"

"I said I would take you home."

The hint of anger in his voice disturbed her. Great, the last thing she needed to do was piss off her boss. "All right. Thank you," she added, hoping to appease him.

He peered over her shoulder to Adam. "Anyway, you looked like you needed rescuing."

She followed his eyes to see Adam hovering over the buffet tables, inspecting the food and trying to strike up a conversation with an older couple next to him. The way his tuxedo hung on his lanky frame reminded Madison of a something she would see at a prom and not a fancy party. "Adam is harmless," she declared, as she swung her eyes back to him.

The first thing that struck her was how the cut of Hayden's tuxedo was nothing like Adam's; he looked dark and tempting in the precisely pressed fabric. Adam's high school attempt at formal men's fashion only amplified Hayden's magnetism.

"Don't say anything to him. I'll give him the bad news on Monday. I don't need him causing a scene or bothering the Martins."

"Yes, Mr. Parr."

Hayden inched closer to her, and the smell of his musky cologne overtook her senses. "What did I tell you about that?"

Madison gazed boldly into his eyes. "This is business…Mr. Parr."

The scowl on his face twisted into an intrigued grin. "I can see you're going to be very difficult to handle, aren't you?"

Feeling that tingle of electricity at the nearness of him gave Madison a rush of courage. "I was being assertive and not difficult. If I were being difficult, I would have refused your offer to take me home."

His grin became a full-on smile. "And which one are you most often, assertive or difficult?"

She returned his smile. "That would depend."

"On your mood?"

Madison kept him waiting before finally answering, "No, on the man."

The laughter of a group of men by the patio doors distracted him. "Let me see to the Martins, grab your design, and I will meet you out front. Give me about ten minutes."

"Ten minutes?" Her eyes took in the half-full dining room. "What about the party?"

"I didn't come here for the party." He abruptly headed toward the patio doors. His lean figure cutting across the room reminded Madison of a hero in a Greek play. Strong, smart, and with a dash of hubris in his step, he looked irresistible. As Madison watched his sleek body maneuver through the light scattering of guests, she felt that white heat rise up from her gut, obliterating all other thoughts.

Oh, I'm in trouble.

"What did he say?" Adam excitedly asked, coming up to her.

Madison pushed the smoldering desire that Hayden had awakened back down into her gut. "Nothing. He just had a question or two about something related to my design."

Adam peeked out the patio door. "Does he have any questions for me? Maybe I should go and ask him."

He had taken a step forward when she held his arm, stopping him. "No, Adam. Mr. Parr only had questions for me because…I didn't do as thorough a presentation as you. That's all," she elaborated, amazed by her quick thinking.

"I guess you're right." Adam's attention shifted to Madison and his eyes dropped to her hand on his sleeve. "Hey, why don't we get some food, grab a table, and we can talk?" He placed his hand over hers. "I want to know all about you…every interesting detail."

She slipped her hand out from under his. "Actually, Adam, I'm feeling rather tired. I was up late last night finishing my plans." She swiped her hand along her brow. "I guess the excitement and the cranberry martini has gotten to me. If you don't mind, I think I'll go home."

"You can't go," he objected, his voice cracking with distress. "We have so much to discuss."

She gave him an apologetic pout. "I'm sorry, but I really should go."

"I'll show you to your car."

She rested her hand on the lapel of his tuxedo jacket, smiling flirtatiously. "There's no need, Adam. You enjoy the party; get something to eat." She waved to the buffet. "I'll see you Monday."

Leaving Adam behind, Madison made a hasty retreat from the dining room, anxious to meet Hayden. Dodging guests, she pulled the gold purse from under her arm and retrieved her cell phone. When she reached the lobby, she stopped, taking a moment to send a quick text to Charlie.

No need to pick me up. Got ride home.

Very quickly Charlie texted back. *With who?*

Hottie boss.

Hottie boss sex?

Not like that, Madison typed into her phone.
I'll sleep at Nelson's. Jump his bones.
It's business, Charlie.
Yeah, right. Details in morning.

Madison shook her head at her roommate's suggestion, not wanting to admit that she had secretly hoped for such an ending to the night. She was pretty much convinced that Hayden was her Harry, but was also painfully aware that their one night together had meant nothing to him. After her conversation with Hayden's sister, Mike, she had a good idea of the kind of man Hayden had been when they had met up in that bar: a campus playboy. She couldn't help but wonder if he was still the same Lothario he used to be, or if his failed marriage had scared him further away from commitment. Common sense told her that another night with her boss would be a huge mistake, but despite all the dire warnings from her head, her heart was slowly caving to him. Her head spinning with questions while her stomach twitched with nerves, Madison rested her hand against her forehead as a slight pounding—the after effects of the strong drink, no doubt—began to add to her discomfort.

Leaving the warmth of the lobby behind, she exited the thick wooden doors at the entrance and stood beneath the white canopy that stretched over a row of steps to the bricked drive. A brisk breeze blew past, making her rub her hands up and down her bare arms, regretting not bringing some sort of wrap. Slowly descending the cascade of cement steps to the valet podium, Madison's mind leapt ahead to the events to come with Hayden. Those persistent butterflies zoomed to life at the thought of being alone with him. Again her practical mind jumped in, tempering her excitement.

Straighten up, Madison. You have to work with the man, she silently berated.

Suddenly, something wrapped around her, and when Madison looked down, she saw a man's black tuxedo jacket enveloping her.

"You're cold," Hayden's voice purred in her ear.

When he came around in front of her, adjusting the jacket about her shoulders, she spied his muscular torso through his sheer white dress shirt. His eyes searched hers as he held up her cardboard tube.

"Adam cornered me as I was leaving." He pulled a valet ticket from his trouser pocket. "I had to almost threaten him with bodily harm not to harass the Martins after I left."

The valet came up to Hayden and took his ticket.

"Do you think that will work?" Madison tucked the tube under her arm. "He seems pretty relentless."

"He'll listen. I set Mike on him before I left. I told her to keep an eye on him and trust me, she will."

"I liked your sister."

Hayden raised his dark brows, making his eyes appear slightly sinister. "Really? I find that surprising. Mike usually offends everyone."

"She's honest, not offensive," Madison reflected. "Only people who are hiding from the truth will be offended by it."

He snickered while placing his hands in his trouser pockets. "Yeah, well, my sister is a master at pissing everyone off. My parents, her ex, even my ex."

"I got the impression she didn't like your ex-wife."

"No one liked Ellen." His handsome face sobered. "My mother begged me not to marry her. She said I was going to regret it, and she was right."

"So why did you marry her?"

He took in a deep breath of the cool night air. "When we met I was…looking for something, and I thought I'd found it in her."

The lights from outside the mansion cast a tempting glow, drawing Madison's attention to every fleck of gray in his eyes. "What were you looking for?"

The left side of his mouth curved into a half-grin. "How do you do that?"

"Do what?"

"Get me to talk, open up, and…I can't seem to keep my thoughts to myself when I'm with you."

"Surely there are some thoughts you're holding back, Hayden."

Then she saw it; that irrefutable flash of desire in his eyes.

The bright beam of headlights made her turn away. A black Range Rover with tinted windows pulled up to the podium, and the young valet attendant jumped from the front driver's side of the car. He came around and opened the passenger door for Madison.

Hayden rested his hand against her back and gently ushered her toward the car. The sensation made Madison close her eyes for a second, relishing the feel of his hand.

After slipping into the front seat, she watched as Hayden tipped the valet and then went around to the driver's side of the car.

"Where do you live?" he inquired, pulling the seatbelt over his shoulder.

"Behind the SMU campus on Rosedale. It's a big blue apartment building." She set the cardboard tube in the backseat.

"How long have you lived there?"

She watched his smooth hands glide over the wood and leather steering wheel as they pulled out of the fancy bricked driveway. "A little over a year. I moved in with my roommate, Charlie, after I finished my degree at UT. It was close to where I was doing my internship."

"And where was that?"

"It was on my resume."

"Madison, do you know how many resumes I saw? I had thirty people apply for the jobs you and Adam got. Forgive me if I can't remember every detail on your application."

"I interned at Pellerin, Everly, and Walters."

"I know Curtis Pellerin," he told her. "We've shared some clients. How did you like working for him?"

"He was very nice to me. He even wanted me to stay on, but it wasn't what I was looking for."

"And Parr and Associates was?" he snickered. "I find that hard to believe."

She took in a deep breath, debating if she should lie her butt off or tell him the truth about her high-rise aspirations. "Actually, no. I wanted to get on with MA Architects. My dream is to build skyscrapers...buildings that touch the sky."

"I understand. I was just like that when I was in school. I didn't want to take over my father's firm, but by the time I graduated with a master's degree in architecture I was warming up to the idea.

However, if given the chance, I would love to build skyscrapers, too."

"Then why don't you?"

"Because Parr and Associates has a great reputation with home design. It's taken a long time to build up that reputation, and after being in this business for a while, I discovered I like the simplicity of designing homes. I know some big building architects, like over at MA, and the headaches associated with designing and building those steel and glass beasts are enormous." He paused as he turned to her. "Besides, pleasing homeowners has its rewards. When you see the finished product and know people are going to be living inside of something you created, building a life and raising a family, it makes it all worthwhile. You'll see when Pat and Stevie build your design. It gives you a sense of accomplishment."

"You told me that they wanted to make some changes to my plans. What kinds of changes?"

Arching back slightly, he appeared uncomfortable with the question. "They love it as is, but that could change as we get down the road. Homes are an ever-evolving process during construction."

Confused by his comment, Madison cautiously studied his profile. "I thought we needed to talk about the changes to my design. That's why you offered to take me home, isn't it?"

His gaze locked on hers. "I lied."

"Why did you do that?"

He diverted his eyes to the road ahead. "You know why."

A zap of dread mixed with excitement tore through her. The statement could have meant a number of things, but instead of pursuing questions about his intentions, she kept quiet and eased back in her seat. She had the answer she had been hoping for. Hayden Parr was interested in her…very interested.

***

When his black Range Rover parked in front of her blue five-story apartment building, the recessed entrance of glass doors and dim lights loomed ahead. As she debated between inviting him up or dashing for the entrance, Hayden spoke out.

"I'll see you to your apartment." He turned off the engine and climbed out before she could protest.

As he came around and opened her door, a flutter of panic seized her. The sensation reminded her of their first night together. He had brought her back to his apartment, and had opened the car door of his Porsche for her. When he had reached for her hand, his touch had instantly calmed her, giving her the courage to forge ahead.

"Give me your hand," he urged, snapping her back from the past.

Hesitantly, Madison took his outstretched hand, and when their fingers met, a burst of electricity passed through her. She considered if he had felt it too, but his frosty eyes were impossible to decipher.

Pulling her to him, Hayden shut her door, and still holding her hand, led her toward the building entrance.

"Oh, my plans," she glanced back at the car, "I left them in the backseat."

"Leave them. I'll bring them to the office on Monday."

Neither of them spoke as they walked the rest of the way to the glass doors, and when he opened one of them for her, she let go of his hand, disappointed to lose the warmth of his touch.

Inside, they slowly made their way to the pair of silver elevator doors in the lobby as Madison's mind clamored for something to say.

"You really don't need to see me up. I'll be fine." She eased his jacket from around her shoulders and held it out to him. "Thank you for this."

Ignoring the jacket, he pushed the elevator call button. "There is something we need to settle between us."

"There is?"

He took the jacket and slung it over his arm. "Yes, we have unfinished business."

The silver doors slowly cranked open, and he held them as she stepped inside. Once he had followed her in, he motioned to the console.

"What floor?"

"Five."

He punched the button, and while the doors were slowly closing he moved next to her.

"What 'unfinished business'?" she asked, clutching her purse to her chest.

With an amused grin, he noted the apprehension in her green eyes. "You're keeping secrets from me."

She swallowed hard. *I'm keeping a hell of a lot more than that from you,* she thought, but insisted, "I'm not keeping anything from you, Hayden."

"Are you sure about that?"

She stood beside him as the car climbed upward, hunting for things to say to him; witty comments or alluring statements to offset the torment he was creating in her.

"I don't keep secrets," she finally offered, figuring it was close to the truth.

Once they arrived on the fifth floor, she moved toward her apartment as she searched her purse for her keys. Hayden followed her, and she was acutely aware of his presence.

"I think you keep a great deal to yourself, Madison. You don't say much, but your eyes give you away."

She found her keys and spotted her apartment just ahead. Quickening her step, she moved to work the lock on her door. "I think most people are like that."

"Perhaps, but none of them are like you."

Her hands shaking, she unlocked the deadbolt and glanced back at him. "I'll take that as a compliment. Good night."

She was about to open the door when he placed his arm in front of her, barring her way. "Aren't you going to invite me in?"

Staring into his eyes, she knew she couldn't resist him...and if he entered her apartment, she'd be his for the taking. "Why?" she defiantly questioned.

His face inched closer to hers. "Invite me in, Madison."

"I don't think that would be a good idea. You're my boss."

He leaned back slightly, as if the challenge of her answer had been unexpected. "Is this your assertive side or difficult side?"

"This is my needing to keep my job side, Mr. Parr."

He lowered his arm and took a step closer to her, placing his face right in front of hers. The nearness of his lips caused every molecule in her being to scream with protest.

"I would never use my authority as your employer to make you do my bidding. I don't want that kind of control over you. I would prefer a very different arrangement."

She was at a crossroads; if she let him in, their relationship would invariably change, and she would be vulnerable. Yet feeling his eyes on her at that moment, she wanted to be vulnerable to him, wanted to be so much more than his employee. Despite the loud remonstrations in her head, she pushed her door all the way open and stepped inside.

Flipping on the overhead lights, she set her purse on a table by the door, dropping her keys next to it. Madison listened as he came in behind her and quietly closed the door.

"Where's your roommate?"

"Out," she curtly replied.

The sound of her deadbolt being secured behind her made her tremble. Determined not to show him any fear, she turned and faced him. Jarred by a memory, she was transported back to their night together. She had stood before him, in almost the same way, filled with all the trepidation, excitement, and lust that was now coursing through her veins. Only then she had not known what to expect. Tonight, she hungered for it.

He inched closer, his eyes riveted on her. "Will she be out for the entire evening?"

She backed away, bumping into a pile of Charlie's boxes, and one tumbled over. After retrieving the box, he came to her side and took it from her hands.

"Are you moving?"

She avoided his eyes. "No, my roommate is. She's getting married in two weeks."

Lifting the container, he replaced it on the pile by the door. Then, after tossing his tuxedo jacket to the sofa, he made his way deeper into her living room. Glancing about, he spotted the CD player.

Madison followed his movements as he perused her music selection in the storage towers on either side of the CD player. He stopped when he saw a CD cover still out next to the player. Switching on the CD player, he waited as the sound of a man's soft voice filled the living room.

"Michael Bublé. You like the classics?"

She nervously rubbed her hands together. Why did the room suddenly feel so small? "Not usually, but there is this one particular song."

Hayden pointed in the air as the bluesy rendition of "Feelin' Good" began. "This song?"

She nodded as he slowly approached. "It reminds me…of someone."

He stopped before her. "Who does it remind you of?"

"It doesn't matter."

He held out his hand to her. "Dance with me?"

The way he said the words, the tone of his voice, was just as it had been when he had taken her home from the bar that night. Madison wondered if this was his move; the way he seduced women into bed. Perhaps what she had thought was special, was merely his tried and true method of seduction. Shaking her head, she went to walk past him.

He held her arm, and whispered, "Dance with me." The need in his voice was hypnotic, and more desperate than she had ever heard him sound.

"All right, one dance." She ran her hand up and rested it on his shoulder.

When his arm came around her waist, pulling her to him, she let out a little gasp of surprise. He held her close, and slowly swayed side to side as the music swirled about them.

"There is something I've wanted to ask you since the moment we met."

His hot breath teased the nape of her neck. "What is that, Hayden?"

He gazed into her eyes. "Why did you leave me that night, Mary?"

All the emotion she had been holding back since first realizing who he was came crashing down around her. "You're Harry!"

Jerking away from him, she slapped her hand over her mouth. Madison went to the breakfast bar by the kitchen and punched her fists into the bar, taking in several deep gulps of air.

"You had to know it was me," he commented, coming up behind her. "Or did you forget about me...forget about what we shared?"

"I thought you were the one who had forgotten, the way you acted. When I asked you about Nina Simone...I figured I had just been a one-night stand that had meant nothing."

"I wasn't sure if you would run out on me again if I told you who I was, so I decided not to say anything." He put his hands on her shoulders. "When I woke in the morning and found you gone...Christ, you should have told me you were a virgin."

She spun around. "How did you know that?"

"I saw the sheets, Madison. You need to give a guy some warning that he's going to be the first, especially a stranger. I wanted to find you and see if you were all right, but I didn't know where to begin. You could have at least told me your real name."

Her back smacked into the bar behind her. "What difference does it make if I gave you a fake name? You told me your name was Harry."

"It is Harry." He leaned closer, resting his hands on the countertop behind her and pinning her between his arms.

"That's not your real name, Hayden, so don't jump all over me for not telling you my name, all right?" She paused, catching her breath. "How long have you known it was me?"

His lips hovered above hers. "From the moment I saw you in the elevator."

She angrily broke free of his arms. "Did you know it was me when I applied to your firm?"

"Of course not. I didn't hire you, Don did. I saw your application, but I never knew your name, Madison. How could I've known it was you?"

"You should have said something that first day in the conference room."

He grabbed her arms. "If I had, would we be standing here now? Would you have opened up to me, talked to me like you have?"

His body was inches from hers. The heat coming through his shirt felt like summer and his hands were strong, forceful, and utterly compelling. She wanted to push him away, but the longer she stared into his eyes, the more Madison felt her resistance floundering.

"Please tell me you haven't made a habit of picking up strangers in bars since me." He let her go and stood back. "I could never pick up another girl in a bar after you, do you know that?" He turned away and went to the CD player.

"Why not?"

He turned off the music. "Because you left a hell of an impression on me, that's why."

"No less of an impression than you left with me," she shouted.

"What is that supposed to mean?"

She waved her hand in the air, getting ahold of her anger. "So what do we do about this situation?"

"Do?" He went to the sofa and picked up his jacket. "Nothing. This changes nothing between us."

She waited as he eased the tuxedo jacket around his shoulders. "I think it changes everything." She looked down at her hands. "Do you want me to quit?"

He came up to her. "No, you have talent, Madison. I want you to stay with Parr and Associates."

"Even knowing what happened between us, you think we can still work together?"

"Why not? I need a good architect...not a girlfriend." He paused, and for a moment she thought he was going to kiss her, but then he simply nodded his head. "I'll see you Monday morning."

When he quietly closed the front door behind him, Madison shuddered. They had cleared the air, discussed the past, and he had made his intentions known for their future. It was going to be all about business from now on.

Securing the deadbolt on the door, she thought ahead to the coming days and weeks they would be working together. How would she be able to look him in the eye without thinking of that night? Wondering if every time he looked at her, if he was thinking about that night, too.

Making her way through her living room to her bedroom, she envisioned her life with Hayden Parr, and the constant burn of desire the man elicited from her every time he drew near.

"How am I going to survive this?"

Chapter 8

Monday morning, Madison arrived at the entrance to the Renaissance Tower buzzing with a blend of excitement for her coming design for the Martins, and trepidation over seeing Hayden again. The entire weekend she had gone over and over his disclosure, wondering how to proceed. Madison knew she should put the incident behind her and move on with her new job and her life just like he had suggested, but there was something about the man that ate at her.

"There is no way you two are going to be able to work together," Charlie had advised that Sunday morning when Madison had stood in the kitchen and told her the news. "Admit it, Mads, you're attracted to him and he's attracted to you."

"I thought he was attracted to me, but maybe I was wrong," Madison had proposed. "He said he wanted me as an architect and not a girlfriend."

"You don't actually buy that crap, do you?" Charlie had laughed and then rolled her big blue eyes. "Lord, if this is just your first week at this job, I can only imagine what next week will bring."

Now riding in the elevator to her office on the thirty-third floor, Madison had already decided that she could not afford to get involved with her boss. After all, he was the kind of man she had always steered clear of; the sexy, successful kind that would dump her in the end for someone far more sophisticated and prettier.

By the time she reached her office door, she was convinced that she could work for Hayden. Sure it would be difficult, but she knew with time the awkward feelings would fade, and then their relationship would be "strictly business."

Opening the door to her office, she was relieved to see that Adam had not arrived yet. She knew the obstinate man would be asking a thousand questions about the party, questions she still was not sure how to answer.

Having just put her purse down on her desk, Madison was removing her blue pantsuit jacket when she heard a knock on her door.

"Madison," Emma called as she came into the office, "Mr. Parr wants to see you first thing."

Madison quickly slipped her jacket back on. "Is there a problem?"

Emma shrugged. "He just told me to come and get you."

Shoving her purse in the bottom drawer of her desk, she hurriedly followed Emma out of the office. Just as the two women were turning down the hallway that led to the elevators, Adam came tearing around the corner, carrying his blue backpack.

"Hey, where are you two headed?"

"Mr. Parr asked to speak to Madison," Emma informed him without stopping.

Adam turned and began to follow them down the hall. "Is this about the designs for the Martins? Does he want to see me, too?"

"Just Madison," Emma clarified.

"He'll probably want to speak to you next." Madison tried to sound hopeful.

"Right," he mumbled as he stopped walking. "I'll be in my office, Emma."

When they reached the elevators, Emma turned to Madison. "How are you getting along with him? Has he hit on you yet?" She snorted. "I've heard he's hit on every unmarried woman in the office."

"He's not that bad, Emma. Just a bit overzealous."

"Mr. Parr was never keen on hiring him."

The elevator doors opened and when Emma stepped inside, Madison quickly came alongside her.

"What are you talking about?"

Emma hit the console button for the thirty-second floor. "I overheard him telling Garrett Hughes and Don Worthy to keep an eye on him. Said he didn't trust the little weasel." Emma waited until the doors closed and then grinned at Madison. "I think he only hired him because he's a friend of the family or something like that."

Madison stood gaping at the petite woman. "How do you know all of this?"

Emma tipped her head to the side. "I'm his secretary. I overhear everything that goes on in his office."

The short ride ended and the doors opened on the reception area of the administrative offices. Emma walked from the car on her sturdy black heels, headed past the double doors, and moved quickly down a hallway until they came to Hayden's office. Smiling at Madison, Emma knocked once and waited until Hayden's voice called, "Yes, come in."

Madison scooted in the doors and her stomach sank when she saw Hayden sitting behind his wide black desk in front of the massive picture window. His unnerving eyes were all over her, and her thoughts immediately went back to the last time they had seen each other. Heat rose to her cheeks, and she lowered her eyes to the dark blue carpet.

The doors behind her closed and a soft whoosh of air tickled against her back.

"Madison, come in."

Glancing up, the first thing she noticed was the way his tailored black pinstripe suit accentuated his firm body, and how his dark brown wavy hair was still damp from his morning shower. Thinking of artic winters to cool the inferno in her belly, she approached his desk.

"I want to discuss your design for the Martin house." He came up to her while waving to a computer table shoved against a bookcase in the corner of the room. "We have a lot of work to do to get these plans ready before I can send them on to the engineers." He placed his hand behind her back and guided her to the corner of his modest office.

"Yes, Mr. Parr."

"I know the Martins loved your design, but I spent the day yesterday going over some changes I think we need to make." Pulling out the chair before the table, he waited as she took a seat.

On the computer screen her design was already up, with twenty yellow Post-It notes attached to the border of the screen. She was reading the scrawled handwriting on the notes when Hayden came up behind her and rubbed against her shoulder as he leaned over the table.

The swell of molten lava that shot up from between her legs was devastating. Her hands gripped the edge of the desk as she closed her eyes.

"Here," he said, his mouth inches from her right ear. "I think you need to expand that center beam in the atrium."

She opened her eyes to see his finger pointing at the large atrium she had designed as the focal point of the home.

"You're also going to have to thicken up those walls to take the weight of that wide ceiling you have drawn," he added, teasing her ear with his breath.

"Yes, Mr. Parr." The smell of his cologne was making her dizzy.

"Then there is the whole issue with the second story. We're going to have to fix it."

Her mind woke up, and she glared over her shoulder at him. "What's wrong with it?"

His face was inches from hers. She could smell the hint of coffee on his breath and see the slight ridge of his thick brow shadowing his eyes. Up close, he appeared less overwhelming and for an instant he was almost…tender.

"The second story needs to be balanced with the lower floor of the home." Hayden veered his gaze to the computer screen. "You drew it shorter and we're going to have to figure out the dimensions of these second-story rooms so they don't end up being tiny bedrooms." He stood back from her, and the rush of cold air that took his place made her shiver. He paused, observing her. "You all right?"

She glanced over her plans. "Just chilly."

He patted her shoulder. "I'll get you some coffee. I'm in need of another cup myself." He strolled to the office doors. "How do you take it?"

A memory of standing in his kitchen as he made her coffee during their first night together came back to her. "Black," she answered, blotting out the pictures from the past. "I always take it black."

At the office doors, he stuck his head outside. "Emma, can you get us two coffees? Black, please."

When he came back to the table, he stood to the side and pinched one of the yellow notes from the computer screen. "This is something we have to address...this wall of windows." He motioned to the long row of high windows she had covering the back of the home. "You're going to have a real structural problem with the support of the second story here. Those beams running across the top of the windows are going to have to be at least eight inches to take the weight."

She sat back slightly in her chair. "My calculations are six."

After he crumpled up the yellow note in his hand, he threw it into the black wastepaper basket beside the table. "Your calculations are wrong."

"You do realize I put several additional cross sections in the joists to offset the additional weight, right?"

He stared at her design on the computer screen. It was several seconds before he spoke again. "So you did. Do you think it's enough?"

She could sense that he was testing her. The first lesson she had learned in design class was always stand behind your design, no matter what. "Yes," she confidently expressed. "It'll support the weight."

The smile he gave her was absolutely enchanting. "Glad to hear you remember rule 101 of design."

"I remember a lot of things."

His smile fell a little and she waited to see what his response would be, but he said nothing. Frustrated, she focused her attention on another note stuck to the corner of the computer screen. After reading his almost illegible handwriting, she pulled the yellow paper from the computer.

"You should have been a doctor; you write like one."

That made him laugh. "How would you know what a doctor's handwriting is like?"

"My father is an orthopedic surgeon. His writing is almost as bad as yours. At least that's the way it looked on the birthday cards he sent me."

"Are you two close?"

Madison's heart hardened at the thought of her father. "No. He has a new family in California. He forgot about me and my brother almost as soon as he left. I haven't seen him since I was thirteen."

"You're lucky that you didn't have a father to live up to. Try following in your old man's footsteps and see what it's like being compared to him at every turn."

Madison took in his profile and noted the quivering muscles of his clenched jaw. "I would rather have too much of a parent in my life than never have them at all. We can always forget what we don't wish to remember, but we can never forget what we never had."

He eased closer to her chair. "I'm sorry. You're right, I should be thankful I had a father who played an important role in my life. Forgive me for being so...callous."

A gentle knock on the door made him leave her side and head across the plush carpet. Behind the door Emma was waiting, holding two white mugs of coffee in her hands. Taking the coffee from her, he returned to the desk and handed Madison a mug.

"That should warm you up."

She watched as he avidly took a sip of his coffee; his Adam's apple bobbed up and down as he swallowed. For a second, she wished she could glide her lips along his neck, and tease that Adam's apple with her tongue.

Desperate for a distraction, she took a gulp of the coffee and winced, having burned her tongue. Plopping the mug on the table, she raised her hand to her mouth.

"What is it?"

Fanning her face, she stood from her chair. "That was…really hot coffee."

He rested his hand against her cheek. The cool touch of his fingers only made her feel even hotter than the coffee.

"I'll be back," she muttered, and then dashed for the office door.

Swerving to the left as she bolted out his office door, she found the ladies room at the end of the short hallway and ducked inside. Hoping to cool her torrid desire, she went to the sink and flipped on the cold water. Patting the back of her neck and cheeks, she slowly reined in her emotions.

"You snuck past me," Emma stated as she entered the restroom. Her dark blue eyes drew together. "You okay?"

Madison turned off the water. "I just got a little dizzy."

"Are you getting that flu going around?" Emma came up to the sink, swaying her ample hips. "Everyone is getting it in the office."

Madison reached for some paper towels. "I just haven't been sleeping very well. Must have caught up with me."

Emma leaned against the sink next to Madison and flicked her shoulder-length blonde hair with her hand. "I'm sure it's all the excitement about having your design chosen for the Martins' house. Mr. Parr was very excited, too. He said you wowed the Martins."

"Really? He said that?"

"Yeah, he was telling me about the party until his bitch of an ex-wife called him." Emma checked over her pink-painted fingernails. "She usually calls about once a week to complain about something. I hear yelling from his office, and that's how I know it's her. She drives him nuts."

"His sister told me a little about her. Apparently, no one likes her."

"Can you blame them?" Emma checked her reflection in the mirror. "I've heard Mr. Parr say time and time again that he will never remarry. That woman turned him off completely. He always says he'll never trust another woman. He's been too badly burned."

Emma's words resonated with Madison. The difficult distance between them suddenly made sense. It was not her, it was his past. Funny how the cruelty of someone she had never met could impact her life. Kindness from strangers had to be experienced directly, but suffering could impact her no matter the degree of separation. It made Madison wonder if the human heart was not the resilient rock reported throughout legend, but a fragile crystal more easily shattered than sustained.

Wiping her hands on the paper towels, Madison gave Emma a half-smile. "I should get back."

"Sure, thing." Emma fluffed her blonde locks as she stared in the mirror. "Can't keep the boss waiting."

***

Back in her office, Madison sat at her desk and dutifully incorporated the boatload of changes Hayden had suggested into her design. But as she worked on her computer, her thoughts kept returning to what Emma had told her in the bathroom. Maybe it was time to give up on her fantasies about her boss. Some men, no matter how enticing, were never meant to be.

"Hey, I'm glad the Martins liked your design," Adam remarked from his desk.

Madison had forgotten about his disappointment after meeting with Hayden earlier that day about the Martins' decision.

"Thanks, Adam. What you came up with was really beautiful, it just wasn't what they were looking for. But you'll find a client that wants it. I'm sure of that."

"I know that. I'm not worried," he cockily asserted. "There will be no shortage of clients looking for that design at this firm. I'm sure before the year is out I'll be working on construction plans like you."

Madison sat back in her chair and let out a long sigh. "Yeah, well, you may not be too happy about it. Mr. Parr made a ton of changes. It's gonna take me another week to work all of this out, and then I still have to get started on the construction plans, engineering prints, and all the other designs required for the permits." She rubbed her hands along her temples. "It's giving me a headache just thinking about it."

"You need a break." He stood from his desk and came over to her side. "Leave that stuff for tomorrow and go home. You look beat."

Despite his arrogance, there were times when she felt Adam could be genuinely kind. Right now, Madison didn't want to go home to an apartment full of boxes. What she needed was a few hours to forget everything.

"Adam, how about that drink you promised me? Are you up for that, or do you need to get home?"

"No, ah...." His eyebrows went up in surprise. "We could go to Rory's and grab some beers if you'd like." He studied her eyes, appearing slightly concerned. "You all right, Madison? If you need a friend, you know I'm here for you. No strings or anything, just friendship."

Madison turned his words over in her head, and she was reminded of something Mike had said to her the night of the party. "Don't you need a friend, Madison?" Perhaps she had been right. If there was no hope of having the man she wanted, then what difference would it make if she ended up with someone else? Even someone like Adam was better than being alone.

"I'm fine, Adam," she heard her voice say. "Rory's sounds great."

Chapter 9

Rory's Bar was a restaurant and sports bar that many of the employees in the surrounding buildings went to for a quick lunch or much-needed after work drinks. The dimly lit décor was a mixture of posters of famous Dallas sports teams and sports paraphernalia. Framed team jerseys, trophies, autographed photographs, and a collection of baseballs, footballs, and basketballs cluttered the paneled walls.

As Adam and Madison meandered across the dark wood floor to the U-shaped bar with its Tiffany-style pendant lights and decorative glass racks hanging from above, the sound of a prerecorded football game blared from a television set up across the room.

Taking a burgundy leather upholstered bar stool, Madison soaked in the ambience of the crowded bar. All around men in suits with loosened ties or women wearing business attire sipped on drinks, munched on peanuts, and filled the air with the hum of conversation.

"Busy place," Madison commented as she removed her purse from her shoulder and placed it over her lap.

"It's always busy in here." Adam dropped his backpack on the floor by the bar and took a barstool next to her. "I used to come here a good bit before I joined up with Parr and Associates. It always stays packed until after ten at night."

"When was this?"

He reached for a bowl of peanuts on the dark wood bar. "Whenever I came to Dallas to see family. I would always stop by here for the food."

"I thought your family was in New Orleans."

"My parents are there, but I have aunts and uncles, as well as a few cousins, here."

She wrestled her blue pantsuit jacket from around her shoulders. "So is that why you came to Dallas?"

"That and the job."

A very attractive bartender with dark hair and liquid blue eyes came up to them. Wearing a blue T-shirt that accentuated his toned arms, he sported a deep five o'clock shadow. "What'll it be?" he asked in a husky voice.

"Ah, beer is good for me. Draft," she returned.

Adam held up two fingers. "Two drafts."

The bartender pulled two tall Weizen glasses from a rack above Madison's head and went to the other side of the bar to the draft tap.

"I never thought you would take me up on my offer for drinks," Adam began.

She tore her attention away from the bartender's well-formed ass. "I guess after everything that happened last weekend with the Martins, I realized we really don't know much about each other, and if we're going to work together we should be friends."

Adam leered playfully. "See, you're warming up to me. I do that to everyone. Yeah, at first nobody likes me, but after a while, once they get to know me, I grow on people."

Madison was not sure how to respond to that. "Oh, well, then I guess I'm warming up to you."

Their bartender returned with their beers, and after giving the man a friendly smile, Madison eagerly reached for her drink. She quickly downed a deep sip while Adam pulled his wallet from inside his suit jacket.

"I'll get this." He flung a twenty dollar bill on the bar.

Their sexy bartender picked up the bill and scurried away.

Adam gripped his beer and raised his glass to Madison. "To working together."

She tipped her glass against his. "To working together."

After Adam had taken a hearty drink from his beer, he plopped the glass on the bar. "You know, I still don't understand why the Martins didn't go for my design. It would have looked great in that neighborhood. Been the biggest house on the block."

Inwardly sighing, Madison placed her beer on the bar. "I don't think they were going for the biggest, Adam. They wanted something more—"

"Artsy?" he injected.

She refrained from commenting, and instead nodded in agreement.

"When I was in college, my designs won awards and my professors said I was one of the best students they had ever taught. Which makes it inconceivable to me why the Martins didn't go for my house. I know everyone has an opinion, and I'm not knocking your design," he patted her arm, "but you have to admit, mine would have totally rocked that property."

Beginning to doubt her decision to join Adam for a drink, Madison reached for her beer.

"My father always believed I was going to make it big in this business," Adam went on. "When I got on with Parr and Associates, he wasn't surprised. He was, however, upset that I got turned down by several local New Orleans firms." Adam winked at her. "My old man tried to pull some strings so I could stay there, but the firms weren't hiring. So I came to Dallas. I don't regret it. I can really make a name for myself here, and one day I'm going to open my own firm."

"I can definitely see that," Madison declared with a faint smirk.

"I've got a cousin here who wants to help set me up in my own place later on down the road. She helped me get this job. She was the one who encouraged me to come to Dallas to find work."

Madison rested her elbow on the bar, bracing herself for the onslaught of "me talk" she feared she was about to get from Adam. Just as he was about to open his mouth to continue, a hand slapped Adam's shoulder, making the slender man flinch on his stool. But when the perpetrator of the act emerged from behind Adam, Madison gasped.

"Mr. Parr," Adam croaked, sounding as surprised as Madison felt.

Madison was undone by the flicker of anger she saw in Hayden's small gray eyes.

"Well, I didn't expect to find you two here…together," he grumbled as his eyes stayed on her.

Adam stood from his stool. "Yes, we were having an after work drink to celebrate Madison's first professional design."

"Really?" Hayden grinned at Madison. "And you didn't invite me?"

She knew in that instant he was toying with her. "We didn't think our boss would be interested," she coyly fired back.

"Of course I would be interested, Madison. Why would I want Adam to have all the fun?" He slapped Adam's back hard, making him wince slightly.

Madison swiveled around on her stool and picked up her beer while Adam offered Hayden his barstool. Hayden greedily took the seat next to her, leaving Adam to head further down the crowded bar in search of another stool.

Hayden leaned over to her. "Really, Madison? Him?"

"It's just a drink."

He scowled at her. "I'll make sure of that."

She didn't like the edgy tone in his voice. "What are you going to do?"

Before he could answer, Adam returned carrying another stool. Placing the barstool next to Hayden, Madison watched anxiously as Adam reached across for his beer.

"Beer?" Hayden commented, pointing to his glass. "No, we have to really celebrate." He motioned to the good-looking bartender standing close by. "Steve, get us a round of shots. Tequila. Patron, if you've got it."

"Sure thing, Mr. Parr," Steve with the dreamy eyes called back.

"You know him?" Madison murmured to Hayden.

"Why? Do you want a date?"

"Would you be jealous if I did?"

He gazed into her eyes, making that desire he always stirred within her come shooting to the surface. "Yes, I would."

His words hit her like a tidal surge crashing into a rocky shore. She had thought he didn't want her as a girlfriend, and that there was no possibility of anything between them. Yet, in an instant, everything changed.

"Well, Mr. Parr," Adam broke in, "what brings you here?"

Hayden spun around to Adam. "I was going to head home and saw you two strolling over here. So I thought I would join you. You don't mind, do you, Adam?"

"No, hell no." Adam grinned happily. "This is great. It gives me and Madison a chance to get to know our boss. Find out what kind of guy you are."

Madison cringed and reached for her beer, quickly downing half the glass in one gulp. When Steve returned, carrying three shot glasses in his hand, she considered Hayden's intentions. Was he out to get all of them drunk, or just her? She didn't think him the kind of man to take advantage of an inebriated woman, but at this point she would take him any way she could get him.

Steve retrieved a bottle of Patron tequila from beneath the bar and slowly poured the clear liquid into each of the shot glasses.

"Ah, I'm not a big tequila drinker," Adam confessed.

The comment made Hayden smile. "After tonight you will be, Adam. I guarantee it."

Steve placed each shot glass before them, and stood waiting for them to drink as he held the bottle of Patron in his hand.

Hayden reached for his glass first, and motioned for Adam to join him. When his eyes shifted to Madison, she reluctantly picked up her drink and quickly slurped down the bitter-tasting alcohol. Adam and Hayden drank together, grimacing when they slapped their glasses on the bar.

"Another," Hayden ordered, waving to Steve to refill Adam's glass.

"Oh, I don't know," Adam whined.

"Nonsense, we have to do two," Hayden insisted. However, when Steve went to refill Madison's glass, Hayden placed his hand over it. "None for her. Just me and Adam."

She angled closer to him. "What are you doing?"

He ignored her and smiled encouragingly for Adam. "This is just between the boys, Madison."

Steve topped off their shot glasses, and both men tossed back the contents in one swallow. After slamming their glasses on the bar, Adam wretched and wavered on his stool. When Hayden pointed to Adam's glass, urging Steve to fill it yet again, Madison scowled.

"Last one," Hayden affirmed.

"You're not drinking," Adam stated, pointing to Hayden's empty shot glass.

"I'm done," he admitted. "This one's all about you, Adam."

"Oh, no. Not another one," Adam protested.

Hayden pushed the full shot glass closer to him. "You can't wimp out on me now, Adam."

Rising to the challenge, Adam took the glass in his hand.

Madison watched in disgust as Adam drained the glass and banged it on the bar in a show of triumph. Hayden applauded, making Adam blush with pride.

It did not take long after finishing the tequila shots for Adam to sway on his stool. The one shot Madison had downed had made her feel tipsy, so she was sure Adam was in much worse shape.

"I think it's time we get you home," Hayden suggested to him.

"We just got here." Adam waved an unsteady hand about the bar. "The night is still young."

Hayden stood from his stool. "Come with me."

Adam picked up his backpack from the floor, and with great difficulty slung it over his right shoulder. The two men then headed toward the entrance. Figuring their evening had come to an end, Madison put on her jacket while Steve cleared the shot glasses from the bar.

"What do we owe you, Steve?"

The handsome man smiled. "Not a thing. Mr. Parr has an account with us. I'll put it on his tab."

As the bartender went to another group of customers waiting across from her, she picked up her purse.

"Where are you going?" Hayden questioned, coming up to her.

She looked behind him. "Where's Adam?"

"In a cab on his way home," he told her.

"How did you get a cab so quickly?"

"I called one the moment I saw you two walk in here."

Her mouth fell open. "You planned this! You got him drunk intentionally to what...humiliate him?"

Hayden took her arm. "I did it to get him away from you."

"What are you doing?" She tried to jerk away, but Hayden kept a firm grip on her arm as he pulled her toward the door.

"It's time to go," he growled.

When they were finally outside on the street, he released her arm. There were still some people milling about, but the bustling activity she had always seen on the downtown streets during the day was gone. The sun was setting and red streaks colored the evening sky. Glancing over at Hayden as he adjusted his suit jacket, she wasn't sure if she should hit him or thank him for rescuing her from Adam.

"You didn't need to get me away from Adam. I told you before, he's harmless."

"Harmless? Did you see the way he looked at you?" Hayden's eyes bore into her. "I'm a man. I know that look."

"What look?"

"He has plans for you, and I'm not about to stand by and let that little weasel...." He wiped his hand over his face. "Forget it. Just don't spend any more time with him." He motioned ahead to their office building. "I'll take you home."

Pissed off, she started down the sidewalk, determined to ignore him. "I'll drive home."

He came up behind her and grasped her arm. "You've been drinking and I cannot let you drive."

She yanked her arm away. "You've had more than me."

"I know. That's why I texted my driver after I saw your boyfriend into a cab."

"Adam is not my boyfriend."

"I'm glad we've established that fact." He moved closer and let his lips hover right in front of hers. "Now I'm going to take you home, so I suggest you cooperate with me, otherwise I will throw you over my shoulder and carry you to the car."

The image of him manhandling her made her mouth go dry. She slowly nodded her head.

He grinned and took her hand. "Besides, you don't have a good track record with men in bars."

***

In the back of a black Town Car, Madison settled against her leather seat as their driver maneuvered the crowded expressway north toward her home. Watching Hayden's profile as he frowned at the thick jam of cars ahead, she considered all she knew about the man.

What he'd done with Adam at the bar was out of character for the Hayden Parr she had come to know over the past few days. She had not considered him the jealous type, especially after what she had learned from his secretary, Emma. Madison also realized that his possessive actions meant he was just as bothered by her as she had been by him. Or at least she hoped as much.

"Why did you pull that stunt back there with Adam?" she posed after a long silence.

"I told you. I didn't like what he was thinking. You need to keep away from him."

"I share an office with him, Hayden. It's going to be rather hard to keep my distance."

His scowl made the lines on his brow appear deeper. "I'll arrange for you to get an office of your own tomorrow."

"And what do you think everyone will say? They will think you're giving me special treatment."

"You wouldn't be the only one." He slowly released a long breath between his gritted teeth. "There is something you need to know about Adam. He's my ex-wife's cousin. Ellen asked me to help him out last year when he was finishing up in college. I agreed to grant him an interview, and then his father, Ellen's uncle, got involved, calling me and pushing me to hire his son. He's some big attorney from New Orleans. Ellen is from there, and when our marriage went south, her family rallied around her. Then, her uncle threatened to cause problems for Parr and Associates. So I had no choice but to hire the little shit." His hands clasped tightly together. "I had hoped Adam would prove himself, so that when it was revealed he was Ellen's cousin, it wouldn't have mattered. Unfortunately, with his behavior lately...I don't know how much longer I can keep him."

"His behavior? Are you talking about at the party?"

"You really don't know, do you?" He shook his head. "Adam has been going around to the men in the office bragging about getting you into bed. First, it started with Emma, but when she confronted him, he turned his attention to you. That's why I followed you two to the bar. I knew what he had in mind."

"That doesn't mean I was going to sleep with him, Hayden." She folded her arms and sunk deeper into her seat. "I can take care of myself. I don't need you coming to my rescue."

"That's exactly what you do need, Madison." The car pulled behind an eighteen-wheeler that had slowed to exit the expressway. "You're still that innocent little virgin I picked up in that bar. You have no idea what men are like."

"I'm not that girl anymore." She raised her voice. "I stopped being that girl after that night with you."

"Let's talk about that night, shall we?" His voice rose to match hers. "Why were you out picking up a stranger in the bar in the first place?"

"Why do you think I was there? To get laid, Hayden."

"And you chose a stranger in a bar to lose your virginity to."

"Apparently not a stranger anymore," she quipped.

"Do you know what could have happened to you? For the entire night I sat at the end of the bar and watched those men coming on to you. I swore if you got up to leave with any of them, I was going to stop you."

"For a man who was so worried about me, you were sure anxious to get me into bed."

"I was not," he fumed. "I was...." His voice trailed off as he glimpsed their driver in the front seat. Leaning in closer, he demanded, "Just tell me, why did you go to bed with me that night?"

She sighed, releasing the tension their conversation had created. "I was nineteen and every girl in my dorm had done it. They kept asking me what I liked, how I did it, about my first time and...I guess I wanted to find out what all the fuss was about."

"Peer pressure. You lost your virginity to a man you had no feelings for because of peer pressure?"

She turned away from him and stared out the passenger window, feeling lower than dirt. "Yeah, I know what that makes me, Hayden."

The silence that surrounded her was more painful than his words. Madison's eyes began to fill with tears, but she willed them back, not wanting him to see how much he had hurt her.

"I'm sorry, Madison. I shouldn't be judging you. Why you did it is your business and not mine. Far be it from me to understand a woman's reasoning."

She sniffled and glanced back at him. "Why did you take me home that night?"

The question seemed to send a ripple of discomfort through him. His arms stiffened, his back became straight as a board, and his face shadowed with aggravation. Madison instantly regretted her question, but something inside of her needed to know the answer.

"You seemed like a nice girl, and I didn't want anything bad to happen to you."

There was something in the way he spoke that made her doubt his answer. She sensed there was more to it than he was willing to admit.

"If you thought I was such a nice girl, then why did you sleep with me?"

His body relaxed as the car came to a halt at a red light. "Because a part of me also hoped you weren't such a nice girl."

"I'm sorry I disappointed you."

He chuckled lightly, making Madison sigh. His laugh was getting to her. "You didn't disappoint me, Madison." The light changed to green and the car moved forward on to Lovers Lane. "I hope I was the one who didn't disappoint you. Your first time should be special, and I just wish I would have known, that's all."

The driver turned off, heading toward her street. "I appreciate that, Hayden, but I have no regrets."

His eyes pivoted to his passenger window. "Well, I certainly do have regrets…quite a few, actually."

When the Town Car parked in front of her blue apartment building, Madison suddenly didn't want their conversation to end. She had never been very good at seducing men, but now she struggled to find some way to get him to come up to her place.

"Would you like to come up and have some coffee?" She tried not to wince, thinking the invitation too obvious.

He gave her one of his delicious smiles. "I would love that."

After Madison had exited the car, Hayden leaned over and said something that she could not hear to his driver. As Hayden came up to her side, the black Town Car pulled away from the curb.

"Why is he leaving?" she questioned, pointing to the car.

Hayden escorted her to the glass doors of her building. "He's going to get a cup of coffee and will come back for me later."

Heading up in the elevator to the fifth floor, Madison was a complete wreck. Was it a good sign he sent the driver away, or a bad sign that he was expecting the driver to return? Or did he send the driver home and tell him not to come back until morning? Her head was fuzzy with questions. She was even thinking ahead to the kind of coffee she had in her pantry and if he would like it.

"Will your roommate be joining us?" he inquired as they stepped out of the elevator.

"Ah, I doubt it." She pulled her door keys from her purse. "Charlie has almost moved out, except for her bed and some clothes. She still comes here to pick up mail and stuff, but with the wedding so close she spends all of her time at her fiancé's place."

"What does Charlie do?"

"She's a law student and a paralegal at the law firm where her fiancé works. He's a civil rights attorney." They stopped before her door. "Nelson's a great guy."

"Obviously why your roommate is marrying him." Hayden took the keys from her hand and placed them in the lock on her door.

"I don't know, she could have married an asshole, but then I wouldn't have agreed to be a bridesmaid. But I guess I would have to be her bridesmaid even if he was a jerk. I'm just glad she—"

"Madison," he interrupted. "Why are you so nervous?" He turned the lock and pushed her door open.

"I'm not nervous," she argued, walking in her doorway.

"Of course you are. You talk a lot when you're nervous."

He was placing her keys on the table by the door when she turned to him. "And how would you know that?"

He shut the door and folded his arms over his chest. "You did the same thing that night. I couldn't get you to shut up until I kissed you."

Madison set her purse on the table by the door. "I don't remember it that way."

He walked up to her, causing her to inch toward the kitchen. "How do you remember it?"

"I don't remember…talking."

"Well, we did. You told me you were studying architecture." He followed her to the kitchen. "You were having trouble with one of your classes. Intro to Architectural Design, I think it was."

She hurried behind the breakfast counter. "Coffee?"

"We had coffee that night, yes."

She went to the coffeemaker on the countertop. "No, do you want coffee?"

"If you're having some." His voice was right behind her.

She spun around to see him standing in the small kitchen. He was so close, making her momentarily forget what she was going to do.

"I take it black," he stated, snapping her out of her stupor.

Turning back to the coffeemaker, she muttered, "I remember."

"What else do you remember?"

Opening the cabinet above her head, she reached inside. "What difference does it make? What I remember or what happened." She slammed a bag of coffee on the counter. "It's behind us, Hayden."

"I'm not so sure about that," he whispered in her ear.

This time she did not turn around to face him. His hips pressed into her butt, and when his hand skidded over her right shoulder, gripping her jacket, she trembled. Madison stood perfectly still as he peeled the jacket off her.

"What's changed your mind?" she softly pleaded. "Today at the office you were so indifferent to me."

He threw the jacket on the counter in front of her. "I wasn't indifferent. I was trying to keep you from getting to me, but it didn't work." His hands went around both of her shoulders, slowly turning her to face him. "When I saw you go off with Adam, I couldn't take it anymore. I can't stand to see you with other men."

When her eyes met his, any reservations she had about being with him vanished. Her back smashed into the countertop as he slowly advanced. Her heart was beating faster than a hummingbird's wings as his face moved inch by inch closer to hers.

His hands reached around her waist. "Tell me you've been thinking of me."

She arched away from him, not sure if she was ready for this. "Thinking of you...I don't understand."

He eased into her, pulling her body against him. "Say you want me, Madison."

Her eyes darted about his face, trying to register the moment. "Why?"

Hayden lowered his mouth closer to hers. "I need to hear that you want me."

She hesitated—her mind telling her to not give in—but she caved. "Yes," she breathed, "I want you."

His mouth crashed into hers, sending shivers down her spine. His kiss was enticing, provocative, and utterly powerful. When his arms engulfed her, almost squeezing the air from her lungs, Madison did not care. She wanted to stay like this with him. Sliding her arms about his neck, she opened her mouth; letting his tongue trace the tip of hers, encouraging her to give in to him, promising more to come. Her inhibitions began to disintegrate and her hands started roaming the contours of his back, gingerly running over the curve of his muscular butt.

When her hands squeezed his hard ass, he laughed and lifted her onto the kitchen counter. His kisses traveled over the slopes of her neck, nipping her flesh along the way.

"You taste even better than the first time," he murmured into her shoulder.

Tossing her head back, she searched his eyes. "How can you possibly remember how—?"

"I remember everything about you."

She didn't want to believe him, but somehow his words rang true…because she had never forgotten him, either. Running her fingertips along the curve of his square jaw, she smiled.

"And here I thought I was the only one having a hard time forgetting that night."

She kissed his neck, and then nipped at his Adam's apple, causing Hayden to suck in a desperate breath. Her hands eased inside his suit jacket, and she was about to push the material over his shoulders when the jingle of keys working the lock to the front door made them both look away.

As the front door pushed open, Hayden moved back from the counter, allowing Madison to jump down. When Charlie strolled into the apartment, Madison rolled her eyes. *Great. Perfect timing!*

"Who is that?" Hayden asked, his arm still about her.

"My roommate."

"Hey there," Charlie called when she saw Madison in the kitchen. But then her smile faltered when she spotted Hayden next to her. "Oh, wow, did I interrupt something?"

Madison moved away from him. "Charlie, what are you doing here?"

"I still technically live here, Mads." She motioned to Hayden. "Who's this?"

"Hayden Parr," he replied, adjusting his jacket.

"You're Madison's boss?" Charlie's eyebrows rose up her forehead.

Madison wanted to groan out loud as she watched Charlie's zealous blue eyes running up and down Hayden's lean, tight body.

Hayden went up to Charlie and extended his hand. "I hear congratulations are in order for your upcoming nuptials."

Shaking his hand, Charlie grinned at Madison. "Yeah, less than two weeks away. Madison is going to be one of my bridesmaids."

Hayden glanced back at her over his shoulder. "Yes, she was just telling me all about it."

Charlie snickered. "I'll bet." Her eyes twinkled with mischief. "You know, Madison still doesn't have a date for my wedding. You interested, Mr. Parr?"

"Charlie!" Madison shouted.

Hayden chuckled as he shook his head. "I should be going."

"Don't leave, Mr. Parr," Charlie pleaded. "Stay and have a drink with us."

"No, thank you, Charlie." His eyes lingered on Madison, causing a warm rush of heat to shoot up from between her legs. "It's been a long day."

He made a move toward the front door, and Madison rushed to his side. "I'll walk you downstairs."

Pulling the door open, he turned to her. "No, stay here. I can send my car tomorrow to bring you to the office."

"No, I'll find a ride to work, but thank you."

"Are you always so determined?" He held up his hand. "Forget I said that." For a split second he stood in front of her, as if wanting to kiss her, but then his eyes swerved to Charlie standing in the living room, watching their every move. "Good night," he added, then slowly closed the door.

"You and the hottie boss?" Charlie shouted almost as soon as the door had closed.

Madison wheeled around. "Jesus, Charlie. Of all the nights for you to come home."

Charlie grinned while sauntering up to her. "Are you going to tell me what happened? This morning he was untouchable, and then I come in the door and he's all over you."

"I'm not sure what happened," Madison admitted, brushing her hands over her hot cheeks. "All I know is we spent the morning working on my design for the Martins' house, and it damn near drove me insane. I had to run to the bathroom to splash cold water on my face."

Charlie's belly laugh echoed about the bare living room. "I guess he felt the same way."

"I went out with Adam, that dipshit from my office, after work for drinks." Madison retreated to the kitchen. "I thought Hayden didn't want me, so…."

"You went for a guy you had no interest in," Charlie answered, filling in her words. "I get it. That's your MO with men. Go after the ones you don't want because you don't think you're good enough for the ones you do want." Charlie followed her to the kitchen and took a stool by the breakfast bar. "So what happened with Adam the sleaze?"

Madison returned the bag of coffee to the kitchen cabinet. "Hayden came into the bar and challenged Adam to a drinking contest. Adam got buzzed after three shots of tequila, then Hayden shoved him in a cab and insisted on taking me home." She folded her arms and leaned back against the countertop. "Believe it or not, he says he never forgot about me after that first night together."

Charlie clapped and yelled, "Hot damn!" She came around the bar and hugged Madison. "See? He wants you. This is so great." She let Madison go. "You have got to bring him to the wedding."

"He's my boss. I need a job more than I need a boyfriend."

"Who cares if he's your boss? Nelson was my boss, but I'm going to be Mrs. Nelson Peevy in two weeks. You can have the same with your Mr. Parr."

Madison shook her head. "I don't think he wants another wife. The last one he had burned him on women."

"So unburn him. Teach him what a good woman can do for him."

"How do I do that?"

"There is no science to this, Mads. Every man wants someone who will listen to him, and be there for him. Just do that for your Mr. Parr and I know he will come around in time. Loving someone is easy; trusting them is hard."

"What if it doesn't work out and he wants to get rid of me? I need this job, Charlie."

Charlie patted her arm. "But you want this man more, Mads. You've always wanted him, and if you don't go for it, give him all of you, you will never be able to give yourself completely to anyone again. People are like chapters of a book. You have to close one in order to open another, and your chapter on Mr. Hayden Parr has remained open ever since that night." She softened her voice and proposed, "Just trust what you're feeling, Mads. Never listen to your head where men are concerned. The heart is the true gauge of our emotions, because it is the only place inside of us that always remains connected to our souls."

Chapter 10

Entering the offices of Parr and Associates, Madison felt like a call girl heading to the home of a customer. Paranoid about the way the low-cut, red silk dress clung to her slim figure, she had tossed a casual black jacket over her shoulders before leaving the apartment, much to the ire of her roommate.

"You're ruining the effect," Charlie had griped.

"I can't go to work like this," Madison had balked, waving her hand down the tight dress.

"Honey, how many times did I look like a hotel-bound hooker when I left to go to work with Nelson? Part of the art of snagging a man is letting him know that if he doesn't grab you, someone else will."

"I'm not you, Charlie."

"Mads, do you want this guy?"

Madison had hated to admit Charlie was right, but she also hated stooping to such tactics to keep Hayden interested. "If I bend over, you can see right down my dress."

"That's the idea," Charlie had gleefully agreed.

Safely inside her office, she shut the door and went to her desk. While putting her black purse away in the bottom drawer, the jarring ringing of her office phone made her grab at her chest.

"Ah, this is Madison Barnett," she answered, not sure who would be calling her.

"Good, you're in." His voice was low and intense. "I'm coming up to see you, so don't wander off."

"Yes, Mr. Parr."

Tossing aside the jacket, she was instantly glad she had taken her roommate's advice and donned the sexy dress. Hurrying back to her desk, she pulled up her design plans. Better to make it look like she was into her work when he walked in her office.

Minutes ticked by as she stared at the computer screen, anticipating his arrival. Flustered by the whirlwind of her emotions, Madison covered her face with her hands, but raised her head when she remembered the makeup she had taken extra time that morning to apply.

"Shit!" She reached for her purse, wanting to check her makeup.

The strap of her purse caught on the handle of the drawer. Just as she was tugging to set her purse free, the office door opened, scaring her and sending her purse flying across the room to land at Hayden's feet.

Mortified that the contents of her purse, including her tampons, had spilled over the floor, Madison rushed toward the door. Hayden was already leaning over and picking up the contents as she knelt beside him.

"I'm so sorry, Mr. Parr."

He handed her a pink and white wrapped tampon package along with her lipstick. "There's no need to apologize, Madison…not to me."

Beet red, Madison hastily stuffed her lipstick, tampons, and her wallet back into her small black purse.

Taking her elbow, Hayden helped her from the floor. "I came by to give you some more suggestions for your plans," he explained while glancing back at the open office door.

"Ah, sure." Madison went across the room to her desk.

When she heard her office door close, she turned back to him. The leering grin on his handsome face was cataclysmic. Her breath caught in her throat. *Oh God help me!*

"Why did you wear that dress?" His voice was dripping with irritation.

Dropping her purse on her desk, Madison waited as he came across the room to her side, his eyes burning into her. "I, ah," she stumbled as she patted her hand down the front of her dress, "my roommate suggested it."

"Don't wear such provocative clothing. I don't want men ogling you in the office. You need to dress more...." His eyes lingered over the red dress. "Conservatively."

"Yes, Mr. Parr," slipped out of her mouth before she could stop it.

He chuckled, filling her body with desire. It took everything Madison had not to rip the fitted dark blue suit from his body. Christ, she had never wanted a man like this before.

His lips were inches away, taunting her. "I have to go to a luncheon this morning and then I have meetings all afternoon, but I'll be back here after five." He waited a moment before adding, "Wait for me, after everyone else goes home, and then we can go to my place."

"Your place?"

"Yes, so we won't have any interruptions while we work on those plans of yours." Hayden smiled, killing her. "I'll cook us dinner."

She cocked one dark eyebrow at him. "You can cook?"

His eyes slowly went over every inch of her body. "Among other things." As he turned away, he added, "At least you will have peace to work alone in your office today. Adam called in sick this morning."

"Is he all right?"

"Just a dented ego, I suspect. I'm sure he'll be back tomorrow to drive us all mad." When Hayden reached the door, he looked back over his shoulder at her. "And don't go out anywhere today. Stay in your office. I don't want anyone seeing you in that dress."

Alone in her office, Madison leaned against her desk, taking in a deep, calming breaths. "Damn, I need to listen to Charlie more often."

***

Madison spent the rest of the day at her desk, attempting to work on her plans. As she reconfigured roof angles and wall depths, her mind was constantly thinking about the night ahead. She knew what would happen when she went to his home, and she wanted to be with him just as much as he seemed to want it. The only question she had was, then what? After they had slept together, what would happen to their professional relationship? It was hard enough to call him Mr. Parr now, knowing of their past, but how would she feel being both his lover and his employee?

Staring at the house drawing on her computer screen, she tried to fathom when her life had taken a turn toward the difficult. Men had never been a big complication for Madison—having put as little energy into her love life as she had put into her exercise program—but what was budding with Hayden was different…and a lot more intense than anything she had ever known.

"Hey, Madison," Emma said, knocking on her open door. "Mr. Parr wanted me to drop off these engineering scales to you." She came in the door and approached Madison's desk, carrying a manila folder in her hand.

Madison waited as the attractive blonde placed the folder on the edge of her desk. "Thanks, Emma."

She motioned to Adam's desk. "Enjoy your day off from the asshole."

"Yeah," Madison replied as she opened the folder. "Mr. Parr mentioned he was out sick today."

"Sick my ass. I heard Mr. Parr telling Mr. Hughes about Adam's confrontation with him yesterday evening outside of the building."

Madison looked up from her folder. "What confrontation?"

"I thought you knew." Emma's face lit up, happy to spread more gossip. "Mr. Parr caught Adam drunk at Rory's Bar down the street. Apparently, after they had words, Mr. Parr put him in a cab and sent him home." Emma rolled her eyes. "I don't think that boy will be around much longer. When Mr. Parr sets his sights on you, you don't last long in the firm."

"Mr. Parr doesn't strike me as the type to set his sights on employees," Madison related. "He seems pretty fair with people."

"Oh, Mr. Parr's fair all right, until he's ready to get rid of you. Then he can be real relentless."

Madison sat back in her chair, digesting what Emma had just told her. "Have you seen him do that? Be relentless with an employee?"

Emma glanced back toward the open office door, and then slowly came toward Madison's desk. "There was another architect that worked here right before you came. Her name was Doreen. She and Mr. Parr were very close. He really looked out for her. There were rumors that she and Mr. Parr were seeing each other after hours, and then one day I came in and she was gone. No notice, nothin'. Everyone suspected he got rid of her."

A heavy knot formed in Madison's chest. "You think he got rid of this Doreen because they were seeing each other?"

"No one knows for sure. All I can say is that Mr. Parr's not a skirt chaser, like your cohort." She nodded to Adam's empty desk. "He has always been really professional with the staff here. I've heard him say he never gets involved with his employees." Emma shrugged. "Maybe he only gets rid of the ones he gets involved with."

With a shaking hand, Madison put the folder to the side of her desk. "Ah, thanks for these."

"Sure thing," Emma pronounced, heading toward the door.

After she had left, Madison began to reconsider her dinner with Hayden. Was he out to get rid of her? She shook her head, shooing away the negative thoughts. That was not the Hayden Parr she knew. After all, they had a history together. Or was that history the reason he had set his sights on her to begin with?

***

It was after five, and the activity inside the offices of Parr and Associates had grown faint as employees hurried home for the evening. With each sound of a door shutting, footsteps in the hallway, and mumblings of "good night," Madison's apprehension grew.

Emma's words had haunted her all afternoon, and like a damning bit of evidence that sticks in the craw of a hung jury, Madison was teetering back and forth between what to do and what not to do with Hayden Parr. The plans on her computer screen had suffered for her preoccupation; having accomplished little after Emma's visit, she was sure Hayden would be furious. Rubbing her hand behind her sore neck while visions of unemployment paraded across her mind, she wondered how in the hell it had come down to this.

Listening to the stillness around her, she debated if it might be better for her to go home and pass on Hayden's invitation. She had switched off her computer and was reaching for her purse when she heard the faint sound of rustling outside her open office door.

Turning around, she saw him. There was a faint hint of a five o'clock shadow covering his chin and square jaw. He looked tired, his dark blue suit slightly rumpled, but to Madison he was like water to a parched soul.

"Are you ready?"

She stood from her chair. "I was about to go home; my home."

"No, you're coming home with me," he argued, closing the door.

She twisted her hands together. "Maybe we should reconsider. It might be a—"

"Reconsider? I don't think so." His lips angrily mashed together as he came up to her. "Don't tell me you're having second thoughts about me already."

"I can't afford…I mean, if I lose…I don't want to be another Doreen," she finally got out.

His dark eyebrows went up. "Doreen? Do you mean Doreen Irwin?"

She glared into his eyes, attempting to be assertive. "You fired her because she had an affair with you. Is that what you plan on doing with me?"

His burst of laughter was exuberant and completely unexpected. He clasped her wrist and pulled her to him. "Baby, where on earth did you get the idea I had an affair with Doreen?"

She did not know what took her off guard more: his question, or the fact that he had called her baby.

"I, ah, heard about her. Everyone thinks you fired her because she slept with you. I don't want to end up like that, Hayden."

He ran his thumb along her lower lip. "Madison, Doreen left because her husband, who was serving in Afghanistan, got injured. She went to Virginia to be with him in the hospital."

Madison pulled away. "Why does everyone think you two were seeing each other?"

"Doreen and I were friends, nothing more, and if some people in this office thought we were more than that, then they didn't know her. I respected the hell out of her. She was holding it together every day, waiting to hear if her husband was alive or dead. No one knew what she was going through except me and Garrett. She didn't want anyone else to know and we respected her wishes."

Relief washed through her. "So you didn't fire her?"

"Or sleep with her." His eyes swept down her red dress. "You, on the other hand...I have every intention of taking you to bed and keeping you there. So if you have any reservations about what is going to happen between us, tell me now."

"What if we don't work? Are you still going to keep me as an architect in your firm?"

He stood before her, seeming to gather his thoughts. "Madison, you're a talented architect, and I'm always striving to keep talented people here. However, you also happen to be a woman I desperately want, and I never compromise when it comes to my desires. We'll find a way to make this work."

Did he say desperately want? Flustered, she reached for the back of her chair. "How...?" Her voice cracked and she cleared her throat. "How do you plan to do that?"

"We'll have to balance our work life and private life."

Her brow crinkled with uncertainty. "Balance? That sounds complicated."

"No, not complicated, just cautious." He ran his hand through his hair. "Look, Madison, I've got one bad marriage under my belt to prove that I'm not very good at relationships. What I want is for you to agree to be my lover. I could go through the banalities of dating, but I can't waste time with romantic nights out, weekend getaways, or emotional ties. What I said before is true; I don't need a girlfriend. What I want is someone to share my bed." He stepped closer to her. "I promise if you agree to this arrangement, you will enjoy it."

With her hand still tightly gripping the back of the chair, Madison stood for several seconds, unsure of what to say.

He sighed, looking over her features. "Do we have a deal?"

His statement sank to the inner reaches of her heart, wiping away her fairy tale hopes. So this was just about sex, nothing else. Madison knew she should walk away, but her feet never moved from her spot on the floor. Could she live with this? For the first time in her life, here was a man she wanted, and if all she could be was his lover and little else, wasn't that worth a chance?

Staring into his handsome face, she lingered over his thick brow, intense eyes, and carved cheekbones. Could she be that kind of woman where it was just sex? Summoning her courage, she swallowed back the thousand reservations cluttering her mind and nodded her head. "All right, Mr. Parr. We have a deal."

Taking her hand, he quickly pulled her to the door. "Good. Let's get out of here."

Letting him lead her away, Madison became acutely aware that this was one of those turning points in life that were often praised by poets and railed against in Sunday morning sermons; that instance where you handed yourself over to passion, and let the cards fall where they may.

***

As the red sun was setting over the rooftops of the premier neighborhood of Highland Park, Madison followed Hayden's black Range Rover down a wide street with elegant estate-like homes on either side. When they came to a black gravel driveway, she peered through her windshield in amazement at the contemporary two-story home in front of her.

It felt nothing like Hayden, with sharp, oblong angles, pale cream-bricked walls, a slanted slate roof, and long glassed in corners along the first floor. To the side, a cream-bricked chimney rose up the exterior of the home, while long dark cement steps were carved into the tiered landscape leading to a recessed front door surrounded by glass. There was no grass or green gardens surrounding the home, just circular beds of dark gravel with a trimmed landscape of creeping periwinkle and Irish moss.

Turning off the engine of her Nissan Rogue, Madison decided that the house gave off a very strange vibe. It was as if the structure was trying to be something it was not; an architectural achievement that missed its emotional mark. An instructor from her freshman days had once told her that "a house needs heart to be a home. If you don't put your heart into it, no one else will either." For Madison, that was exactly what the house lacked, heart.

"I know it doesn't seem like much," Hayden conceded, coming up to her car, "but the house has got a lot more to offer on the inside."

Madison gazed about the surrounding homes. "Which one is the Martins' place?"

He pointed to a two-story home directly across the street that looked to be an awkward blend of traditional and modern styling. Built of natural stone, the drab, square home had four narrow arches along the façade that encased windows, and a wider arch that surrounded the modest front door, with dark windows and a jutting balcony on the second floor. The property was heavily wooded with thick oaks, crape myrtle trees, and weeping willows.

"Why would you want to tear down the house?" She sized up the home with a skeptical eye. "You could always renovate it."

"No." He directed his scowl to the homes along the street. "Better to tear it down and start fresh."

"Could be expensive," she remarked, turning to him.

"But worth it." He came up to her. "That way I could build something huge to piss off my ex, while she lives in this house."

"Are you sure you want to live across the street from your ex?"

"No, but I want to keep an eye on the house I designed. If a judge makes me give it to Ellen, I plan on at least being close by to make sure she doesn't burn it to the ground."

"You think she would do that?"

He gazed upward to the second story of his home. "Yes. She would do anything to spite me."

They made their way up the wide cement steps to his recessed glass front door. He punched several numbers into a keypad to the right and the house lit up. Then, the front glass door popped open.

"The house is electronic, with an advanced security system, and sensory lighting to follow you from room to room." He pushed the glass door open and waved her inside.

"Is the security something you added before or after the divorce?"

His dark eyebrows went up in amusement. "You're funny."

The quarter sawn oak floors shined beneath the recessed lights, while a straight white iron railing and oak staircase was the centerpiece of the foyer. A row of white pillars encased the staircase, and looking up Madison could see an open second story with skylights framed in white beams that looked out into the night sky, covering the central atrium. The aesthetic of the design was clean, modern, and simple. A sunken living room off to the side of the entrance was decorated with classic modern furniture in black and beige, with a wheat Berber rug and prints of painted leaves done in black frames hanging in a row along the wall. An unadorned fireplace was set into the plain wall without a mantle or screen.

Hayden shut the front door and punched in some more numbers on the keypad to the left.

"Does that mean I'm trapped here for the night?" Her voice echoed in the open entrance.

Hayden came up to her and removed her black purse from her shoulder. "It's the only way I can guarantee you won't run out on me again."

"I didn't think you would want to wake up and see me last time. Isn't that what one-night stands are supposed to do?" Crossing in front of the stairs, she spotted an arched entranceway to the left.

"I hope I didn't give you the impression that you were meant to be a one-night stand."

She went to the arched doorway and peered into a circular den with high white walls, the same oak floors, and an adjoining kitchen divided by a stainless steel-covered breakfast bar. Glancing back at him, she shrugged. "Imagine if I had stayed; the awkward morning after conversation and such." She ambled through the doorway and into the den.

"I've imagined that morning after with you for a long time," he disclosed, coming through the archway behind her. "And I don't think it would have been awkward."

"Maybe not awkward for you, but for me it would have been unbearable."

"Is that why you left? You were embarrassed?" he questioned, moving to the kitchen counter and placing her purse on the stainless countertop.

She noted the plush white sofa and big screen television mounted on the wall in front of it. "I didn't want to get a million questions from you about who I was, and why I had picked you up in that bar. You figured out in the morning that I was.... I'm just glad I wasn't around to see your reaction."

After removing his suit jacket and tossing it over a white metal chair by a glass breakfast table, he went to the built-in stainless Sub Zero refrigerator. "Perhaps, but I would have still liked an explanation." Reaching inside, Hayden pulled out an already open bottle of zinfandel. "I hope wine is okay with you. It's all I have."

"Wine is perfect," she assured him, walking toward the kitchen.

Done in white with stainless Miele appliances, the kitchen reflected the clean lines and modern feel of the rest of the home.

"Why would you have wanted an explanation?" Madison leaned her backside against the chilly countertop. "If you had known ahead of time that I was...what I was, would it have really changed the outcome that night?"

After retrieving two wide-rimmed wineglasses from a white cabinet, he placed them next to her on the countertop. "Yes, it would have."

She lightly laughed, fingering the stem on one of the crystal glasses. "Do you really believe that, Hayden?"

He popped the cork out of the wine bottle and filled the glass she was fondling. "There are certain things you do with a virgin, Madison. If I had known, I would have been…gentler." He set the bottle down on the shiny stainless counter and lifted a glass to her. "Drink this."

She opened her mouth to protest, but the darkness in his eyes made her reconsider. Dutifully she took the glass, and under his watchful gaze, sipped from the wine. When she went to lower the glass from her lips, Hayden's hand went to the base, tipping it back to her mouth.

"More," he commanded.

She gulped more of the dry wine as he closely observed. After half of the wine was gone, he took the glass away. Madison pouted, wondering what he was up to, when he placed the glass on the countertop. Resting his hip along the edge of the counter, he folded his arms and stared at her dress.

The seconds ticked by, making Madison rub her hands together. Then, he picked up the bottle of wine and filled the other empty glass.

"There is something I want to know before we proceed."

She swallowed hard and nodded her head.

"How many lovers have there been since me?" he inquired, lifting his wineglass to his lips.

"What?" She had not expected that question.

He sipped his wine, amused by her reaction. "I want to know how many men you have been with since your first time with me."

"I haven't been with anyone else since you." She picked up her wineglass, eager for more alcohol, and hastily gulped down the pale yellow wine.

He put his wineglass down, raising his eyebrows with interest. "It's been five years. Why have there been no others?"

Madison sagged against the counter, dreading him hearing her confession, and slapped her glass down on the stainless countertop. "I was never interested in being with any other men. No one was ever…right."

"Was that my fault?" He moved her glass out of her reach.

She rolled her head back, afraid to look him in the eye. "Yes. I've constantly compared the men I dated to you, and they always came up short."

His deep laugh reverberated about the austere room. "I'm glad to hear I made such a lasting impression."

She went around him to get her wineglass, but he moved it further away. "No, I want you sober." After it was safely out of reach, he returned his intense gaze to her. "Do you have any questions for me?"

Did she have any questions? Madison almost laughed out loud. "Yeah, about a million of them, but I can't think of any right at this precise moment."

"If that's the case, the time has come to take off that dress," he said in a matter-of-fact voice.

Overwhelmed by the request, Madison's eyes darted about the kitchen. *Is he serious?*

"Take it off. Take everything off. I want to see your body," he firmly insisted.

She touched her fingers to her forehead, feeling a little lightheaded. "Shouldn't we go upstairs first?"

"Would you feel more comfortable if I took off my clothes?" Hayden took another sip of wine.

"God, no. I think one naked person in your kitchen is enough."

He chuckled and drank again from his wineglass. She opened her mouth to say something, but he beat her to it. "That's enough talk." He hiked his index finger from the side of the wineglass and pointed to her dress. "Take off your clothes, Madison."

Deciding it was better to go along, Madison reached for the zipper on the side of her dress. After dropping her eyes to the floor, her shaking hand lowered the zipper, and she kicked off her black flats. Gently placing the red dress on the countertop next to her, she hesitated as she reached for the clasp on her light beige bra.

"All of it." He put the glass down on the stainless counter.

Hayden's eyes stayed on her as she finished undressing, but when she lowered her beige bikini underwear to her ankles, he turned away. He snapped up her glass from the countertop and handed it to her.

"Drink this. You look petrified." The insistence in his voice warned her not to refuse.

She quickly emptied the glass, and as soon as she lowered it from her lips, Hayden once again took it from her and placed it on the counter.

He came up to her, his gaze sweeping over the curve of her hips and the swell of her breasts. Madison instinctively covered her naked body with her hands, but he stopped her. Moving her hands to her sides, he told her, "Don't be embarrassed." His fingers brushed along her jaw. "I want you to be confident in who you are and how you look. Self-assurance is very sexy in a woman. Consider this a lesson in confidence."

"It's kind of hard to be confident with you staring at my naked body."

He lowered his hand and nodded to the countertop behind her. "Face the counter," he ordered, his menacing voice a tad softer. "Place your hands palms down on the countertop and spread your legs apart."

She knew at some point in the evening they would end up in bed together, but she didn't understand why he was behaving this way. Slowly turning to the counter, she placed her palms on the cool stainless countertop. The chill in the air and the cold touch of the counter made goose pimples rise on her skin. Shifting her weight, she spread her feet apart, gulping back her nerves.

"Relax." His voice was right behind her. "I want to see what you feel like in my hands."

Madison closed her eyes, picturing his seductive hands on her. The images stoked her desire as she waited at the counter, listening for any movement behind her.

When his hand cupped her right butt cheek, she jumped. "You're just like you were that first night. You jumped when I touched you then, too." His hand crossed over her hip and came around to the patch of dark hair between her legs. Roughly he reached into her folds, driving his thumb into her. Madison gasped as it pumped in and out, rubbing hard against her flesh.

She dropped her head, overcome by the sensation as a cascade of tingling rose up from her inner reaches.

"Do you like this?"

"Yes," she moaned, rocking her hips against his hand.

He jammed his thumb in deeper, making her jump. His thumb became more insistent, probing deeper and driving her mad. He was causing the heat to build in her lower gut, and she whimpered against her growing need for release. Then his hand stopped, and when he removed his thumb, she almost collapsed against the counter. The weight of his body moved out from behind her. Breathing hard, she spun around to face him.

"Why did you stop?"

His eyes measured her reaction, but his face was coolly placid. "Because I want you to finish."

"What?"

He leaned back against the opposite counter. "I want to watch you while you please yourself, then it will be my turn."

Hayden put his thumb—still wet from her—in his mouth and sucked on it. The gesture at first repelled her, but as blood pounded in her ears and her body begged for relief from the tight grip of tension, she became entranced by how he moved his thumb in and out of his mouth. She inched across the kitchen to him, not knowing if she could do what he asked, but she also realizing she wasn't ready to walk out the door...not yet.

He removed his thumb from his mouth and angled closer to her. "Do it."

A twinge of apprehension clutched her stomach, but she forced the unwanted feeling away. If this was what he wanted, then so be it.

Her hand skirted over her stomach, and before she slid her fingers into her very wet folds, she looked up at him. Keeping her eyes on him, she moved her fingers back and forth over her sensitive nub. Madison slammed her lips together when that delicious tingle returned. Tilting her head back, she delighted in the way his eyes grew round with lust.

Hayden grabbed her shoulders, surprising her, and spun her around. Spooning against her back, he placed his hand over hers and guided her fingers.

"Come for me," he murmured.

His fingers were squeezing into her, causing an explosion in her belly. She didn't care that Hayden was her boss, or about her job, all she wanted was for him to go on forcing her hand, making her weak with desire. When that powerful wave of electricity devoured her, Madison bent over, cried out, and barely registered Hayden's arm about her stomach keeping her from collapsing to the floor.

His kisses on her back made her straighten up. "There, that wasn't so hard, was it?"

She rested her head against his shoulder. Letting her hand fall to the side, Madison closed her eyes and relaxed against his chest, feeling the soft fabric of his white shirt caress her back. Then, Hayden lightly traced the outline of her folds and she tensed.

His fingers dipped into her and she arched her back against him. "Now let me show you how to do it better."

He pinched her nub, hard, and Madison cried out. "Easy," he cooed in her ear. "Give in to me."

As he rubbed her tender nub between his thumb and forefinger, a rocket of white heat soared up from her groin. The intense sensation made her lurch forward.

"Oh God, Hayden, please...I can't," she begged, pushing his hand away.

But Hayden ignored her. "Yes, you can. You've got to play hard to come hard, baby."

The overwhelming waves of lust were rolling through her like a thunderstorm over a vast desert. Her body ached with such blistering desire that Madison was sure her legs were going to give out, but as Hayden held her to him, she gave in to the ecstasy taking over her body. Almost instantly, the powerful climax barreled up out of nowhere. It was not the gentle tingle that she was used to, the one she had reached in the darkness of her bedroom late at night.

No, this was something much more powerful. When it grabbed hold, her legs lost all of their strength as her inner reaches clamped down. She wanted to scream, but her body was so racked by a myriad of sensations that when she opened her mouth, nothing came out.

"That's it," Hayden breathed as she bucked in his arms. Slipping his fingers into her, he gently stroked her insides as her wet flesh pulsated around him.

Madison didn't know how long they stood like that, him holding her up as she lingered over the relaxation coursing through her muscles.

"That was better."

"Jesus." She stood upright and turned around in his arms. "It's never been like that before."

He searched her face and then swept a stray brown hair away from her forehead. "Not even when you were alone?"

Her eyes dropped to his red tie and a blush stained her cheeks, but Hayden put his hand below her chin and forced her eyes to return to him. "Don't be embarrassed with me. Ever. How am I to please you if you don't tell me what you like?" He rested his hands on her shoulders and slowly turned her around. "Now walk out of the kitchen and head toward the stairs to the second floor."

Confused, she glanced back over her shoulder at him. "Where are you going?"

"Nowhere." He patted her behind. "I'll be right behind you watching that incredible ass of yours."

Her stomach danced at the compliment and she headed out of the kitchen, conscious of the swing of her hips. Reaching the steps in the foyer, she glimpsed him coming toward the stairs. He had undone his red tie, leaving it hanging about his neck, and was unbuttoning his shirt. Unnerved by the lust she saw swimming in his eyes, Madison trotted up the stairs.

At the landing, he caught up to her and pulled her into his arms. Hayden tugged her to the right and down a short hall to the master bedroom. He was nipping at her neck and pushing her across the wheat-colored Berber carpet toward a Japanese-inspired, platform king-sized bed in the center of the room. When her calves hit the pale walnut bedframe, she was not sure if she should flop back on the low bed or try to sit down on it. Hayden alleviated her conundrum when he picked her up in his arms and settled her on top of the burgundy bedspread.

She sat up on her elbows and waited as he tossed his tie to the floor, struggling to free his white dress shirt from around his shoulders. Glancing up, Madison noticed the oak paneling that went all the way up the cathedral ceiling. A matching pale walnut dresser stood alone against the far wall, while a half-open oak door offered a glimpse of the master bathroom beyond. Then, she spotted the fireplace set into the wall, which matched the one on the first floor in austere design.

"What were you thinking when you designed this place?"

Hayden stared at her, dumbfounded. "Is that want you really want to ask me right now?"

"I've been trying to figure out what bothers me about this house, and I think I just realized…you weren't happy when you drew it." She sat up slightly, spying his ripped abdominal muscles beneath his shirt.

He came toward the bed. "No, I wasn't happy when I designed it. Ellen and I were fighting at the time." He threw the shirt to the floor. "We were always fighting."

Madison's eyes never wavered from his strong arms, wide shoulders, and muscular chest.

He arched an eyebrow at her. "Is there anything else you would like to know?"

She shook her head.

"Are you sure?" he persisted, grinning.

She shook her head again.

Reaching for her hand, he lifted her from the bed. Instead of kissing her, he turned her around and swept her brown hair away from her shoulders. Hayden stood behind her, kissing her right shoulder as his fingers glided between her legs.

"Like silk," he whispered, caressing her folds. "Get on the bed."

Bashfully avoiding his eyes, she went back to the bed and stretched out on the burgundy bedspread.

Tilting his head to the side, he let his eyes travel over every inch of her. "You are exquisite." He gracefully moved to the nightstand next to the bed and opened a small drawer. Reaching inside, he pulled out a red foil packet and flung it on the bed next to her. Standing at the end of the bed, he unzipped his dark blue trousers. "On your back. Spread your legs apart and close your eyes."

She was a little surprised that she liked how he took control and found his instructions comforting. There was no second-guessing as to what he wanted, and also little chance of her becoming flustered due to her inexperience. Closing her eyes, Madison lay back on the bed and spread her legs wide apart, waiting for him.

Seconds ticked by and her heightened senses searched the room for the slightest hint of what was to come. She thought she heard the rustling of clothing, and then felt his weight on the end of the bed. Madison anxiously waited for his arms, but when his hands ran up her inner thighs, an excited breath escaped her lips. What she felt next was not his body enveloping her, but his fingers spreading her folds apart. When his mouth closed over her, she gasped. His tongue zeroed in on her tender nub, teasing it with circles, making her body tremble. When his teeth nipped at her, she covered her hand over her mouth, silencing her scream.

Madison writhed on the bed, but he held her firmly to him and bit down even harder. She moaned as he tortured her with his teeth, and just when she was about to push him away, a thunderous wave of rapture overpowered her. She rose up from the bedspread, screaming out just at the moment her orgasm swept over her. Her nerve endings were exploding, and every muscle in her body quivered. The rhythmic pulsations in her loins seemed to go on and on, longer than anything she had ever known.

Collapsing onto the sheets, a trickle of sweat ran down her brow. As she wiped it away and opened her eyes, she spotted Hayden rolling the condom over his erection. Madison inspected every inch of his naked body, from his wide shoulders to his ripped abdomen and narrow hips. When her eyes settled on his large member, she stared at it. Madison couldn't remember him being that big before; but then again, she had been too afraid to look at him the last time.

As he settled on top of her, an odd sense of relief washed over her. No longer nervous, her hands caressed his skin, and she marveled at the taut muscles in his firm, round ass, back, and shoulders.

Hayden kissed her lips, but this was not a tender kiss like they had shared before; this one was saturated with need. As his hands explored her body, her nervousness returned. He immediately registered the change in her and pulled away.

"What is it? Are you afraid?"

She shook her head. "I'm just nervous."

He combed her long brown hair away from her face. "I have an idea." He patted the bed. "Roll over on your stomach."

Madison looked to the bed. "Why?"

His lips came closer to her ear. "Do as you're told, baby."

Before rolling over, her green eyes gave him a wary sideglance. He waited patiently as she got comfortable on her stomach, and then he raised her hips. Pulling Madison to her knees, he stroked the white skin on her butt before prying her legs apart. When his fingers found her moist flesh, he began stroking her.

"Now you're ready," he murmured.

His fingers dipped deep into her wetness, and when he pulled out, he spread her folds apart.

Madison closed her eyes as his tip nudged against her sex. She tensed, knowing what was coming. Instead of him pushing into her, his fingers once again teased her nub.

"You need to relax," he softly said.

This time he was gentle as he fondled her, and Madison enjoyed the way he rhythmically moved his fingers back and forth. Tossing her head to the side, her hips gyrated against his hand. She could feel the delicious tingle building in the shallows of her gut, but then Hayden thrust unexpectedly into her. The fullness that he created caused Madison to wince slightly. Hayden held her shoulders as he sank deeper into her flesh. Slowly, he entered her again. Wrapping his arms about her waist, he eased out, but then he dove in hard and deep. He rammed into her again, but instead of feeling uncomfortable, Madison discovered she liked it better when he was rough.

"Do it like that again."

He complied with her wishes, and it did not take long for him to push her over the edge. Clasping the bedspread in her hands, she fought to suppress her scream, and just as Madison caught her breath, Hayden flipped her over and pulled her onto his lap.

"I want to see your face."

Her flesh spread apart as he lowered her hips over his erection, but unlike the first time, there was no discomfort, only intense pleasure.

"Rise up and down. Put your hands on my shoulders for balance."

Keeping her eyes on him, she did as he instructed, slowly riding him. It felt better this way; she liked being in control. Madison began to move faster, hungry for more. His hands encouraged her to ride him harder. She was panting against him, clutching his shoulders as she felt her muscles tighten. Hayden was biting her neck, and his fingers kneaded into her hips, urging her to move faster. Then, just when she thought she could take no more, her climax erupted. She buried her head in his shoulder, desperate to suppress her scream.

"Madison," Hayden cried out as his body shook with his release.

Keeping his arms about her, he gingerly lowered her to the bed.

"I liked being on top," she divulged, while snuggled against his chest.

"I could tell." He sat up and removed the condom. "I hope I wasn't too rough."

"No, I liked it."

He dropped the condom to the floor and rolled with her over to the nightstand. "We'll try another position this time."

Madison watched as he plucked another red foil packet from the drawer. "Can we do it the rough way again?"

He came back to her side. "Are you sure? You're going to be sore in the morning."

"I don't care." She lay back on the bed, eying the muscles in his arms as he ripped open the red foil packet with his hands. "That's the last thing on my mind right now."

***

Hunger eventually drove them downstairs to the kitchen. Removing a package of uncooked chicken from the refrigerator, Hayden opened it and plopped a chicken breast on a cutting board while Madison searched the refrigerator for the wine.

"Your fridge is empty," she chided, pulling out the bottle of zinfandel.

"I've been meaning to get to the grocery store. Be thankful I have this for us." He waved to the bagged salad and chicken on the stainless countertop.

Madison tugged at the white long-sleeved shirt she had put on to come downstairs. She could still smell his cologne on his collar, awakening the memory of how he had made love to her again and again. Blushing, she picked up the bottle of wine and refreshed her glass, hoping for some cool relief.

"You don't have to cook. We could order a pizza or something." She took a sip of her wine.

"I don't mind cooking for us."

She took another sip from her wineglass and observed his lean, muscular torso as he stood by the countertop, wearing only his dark blue suit pants. "Do you usually cook dinner?"

"Rarely. I'll either grab something on the way home, or have dinner meetings with clients." He motioned to his wineglass. "Can you refill mine, too, please?"

She added the chilled wine to his empty glass on the countertop. "It doesn't sound like you have much of a life."

As he began slicing the chicken breast on the chopping block, he nodded in agreement. "My business demands a lot from me. It was the same with my old man."

Madison rested her hip against the metal countertop, taking in the stark white and steel kitchen. "You ever get the desire to throw a splash of color on the walls?"

"Frequently," he chuckled. "Ellen was the designer. I just built the place. I wanted to go with warm, earthy colors, but she felt it would detract from the simplicity of the home."

"It's cold," Madison stated without thinking. "I mean, it's pretty and all, but it needs more. You have an earthy exterior, one that blends with the land, but it feels like it's...." She tried to find the right word.

"Cold?" Hayden filled in the blank.

"No," she asserted. "Lifeless. There's no life here. It's almost like a show house. Perfect furniture, appliances, wood floors, but there are no stains, no muddied footprints, no happy voices."

He put down his knife and stared at her. "Are you asking why we didn't have kids?"

"No, I'm asking why your home doesn't appear lived in. Homes are meant to be lived in, Hayden."

"Maybe because this wasn't a home, it was just a house. By the time we finished building this place, and Ellen had completed the decorating, neither of us felt at home. I think we began to drift apart long before we got married."

Madison took a sip of her wine. "Is that what happened? You two drifted apart?"

"Actually, I don't know what happened. One day I thought we were happy, and the next she wasn't happy anymore. We met in college. Ellen was a few years younger than me and studying interior design. When I got out of graduate school with my masters, she still had another year to go with her undergraduate degree. So I waited until she finished school before I gave her an engagement ring. After that everything changed."

"Changed how?"

He went to the cooktop and removed a skillet from the cabinet below. "I was working at Parr and Associates by then, and my father was retiring and leaving me the business. She started wanting things. A car, jewelry, clothes, and then one day she suggested we needed a house…something unique, and she wanted me to build it. So I did." He paused and looked around the kitchen. "The only problem was, the more I gave her, the more she wanted. It seemed like nothing was ever good enough."

Madison's insides rolled with disgust. "Probably one of those ultra-chic, size zero women who only wear high heels, max out your credit cards, and could…never mind."

"No, Ellen wasn't that bad. I would never have married her if she had been like that."

"Then why did you marry her?"

"I thought we shared some common interests, and Ellen seemed like the kind of woman who would be there for me, but something was always missing."

"Like what?"

"We never talked." He flipped on the gas burner and placed the skillet over the flame. "I guess I never realized until I was married how important it was to be able to talk to the person you share your life with. In the beginning, you think marriage is about the sex, then about the house or kids, but at the end of the day it's about being able to roll over in bed and have someone listen to all of your bullshit, and sometimes laugh at your jokes."

"That sounds nice. The talking part."

He went back to her side and collected the chicken on the countertop. "What about you? What's your heartache?"

"My heartache?"

"Who broke your heart? That's why you're not married or engaged like your roommate, right? So, let's hear it? Who was stupid enough to let you get away?"

She gripped her wineglass, grimacing. "I didn't have any heartache. Dating for me has always been akin to having a tooth pulled. It's painful, awkward, and leaves me doubting myself for days if not weeks later. My roommate would argue that I dated the wrong men; the kind I could never care about."

He sat back against the counter. "Why did you do that?"

"I don't know. I never felt I deserved a great guy. I always thought they wouldn't want me."

"And now, what do you feel?"

She put her glass down on the metal countertop. "You're the only one I could ever.... The thought of having sex with other guys I dated...." She ran her hands over her arms. "I couldn't do it."

He carried the sliced up chicken breast to the waiting skillet. "Is that why you ended up with me that night, because you figured it would be better to have sex with a stranger than a man you knew?" He obtained a bottle of olive oil, stuffed with sprigs of rosemary, from the side of the cooktop and drizzled a bit into the skillet.

"Silly, huh?" She dipped her head to the side, blushing.

The sizzle of sautéing chicken filled the kitchen while Madison nervously grasped her glass. She waited as he went to the sink and washed his hands.

"Why didn't you say anything that night about being a virgin?" he finally demanded, wiping his hands on a nearby towel.

"I wanted to appear sophisticated for you." She motioned to him. "You seemed so worldly, and I was like a...country bumpkin."

He came up to her and took the wineglass from her. After placing it on the counter, he dipped his head in front of her. "Hardly a country bumpkin. You have a sophistication all your own, Madison. Why can't you see that?"

"I don't have any sophistication. I'm not one of those uber hot women men like you drool over."

"How do you know what kind of woman I drool over?" Shaking his head, he went back to the chicken. "Maybe I want someone fresh, naïve, and uncomplicated, like you."

"If you say so...Mr. Parr," she said with a sly grin.

"I see I'm going to have my work cut out for me with you," he mused.

As she watched his long hands stir the chicken, an idea came to mind. "You know my roommate is getting married next week," she began softly, "big church wedding and all. I'm going to be a bridesmaid."

"So I've heard."

"Well, I was wondering...do you want to be my date?"

"That's not a good idea, Madison," he stated in a cold voice. "I thought I explained that to you. We need to separate our work life and private life, and that includes being seen together after hours. People will get suspicious. I can't afford that right now."

She had forgotten about this being just about sex, but the way they had talked in his kitchen like a regular couple had given her hope that maybe he had not meant it.

Madison picked up her wine, more confused than ever. A week ago she was only concerned with her career; today she had entered into a relationship with a man who was beginning to make her feel like an underpaid sex worker. Would it always be like this with him? Or with time would his feelings for her grow into something more? Perhaps they just needed time to get to know each other. Anything was possible when two people cared about each other. After all, fairy tales were based on fact, weren't they?

Chapter 11

Madison awoke to the bright sunlight streaming in through the wide corner window and casting shadows across the rumpled bedspread. As she stretched out her arms, the soft cotton sheets caressed her naked body, but when she turned to the side, she found that the bed was empty. Touching the pillow Hayden had used, she smiled, and then the sound of running water came from the bathroom.

Swinging her legs over the side of the low bed, she stood and made her way to the half-open bathroom door. The bathroom was done in white with pale beige marble countertops and sleek, silver modern faucets. In the corner, a man's round butt and long legs could barely be seen behind the fog-covered door to the shower stall. Inching closer, she let her eyes roam up his back as the water cascaded over the ropelike muscles. A surge of warmth erupted between her legs, making her want him all over again. Reaching for the silver handle on the shower door, Madison ached to touch him.

When she entered the shower, he grabbed her and pulled her beneath the spray of hot water. Before she could even get a "good morning" out, his lips were on her. Pressing her backside into the tiled wall, his hands went to work, roaming over her breasts, hips, and stomach. When his fingers slipped between her legs, caressing her delicate folds, she stiffened.

"Are you sore?"

"A little," she shyly confessed.

"I know just the thing for that." He turned away and opened the shower door, reaching to the towel shelf to the right.

Madison admired his wide shoulders, and on a whim raked her nails down his back all the way to his round butt.

Slapping the door shut, Hayden groaned and flipped her around, making her face the shower wall. "That was bad, very bad, Madison."

She backed her butt into him, feeling his erection press against her. "What are you going to do about it? Spank me?"

Holding her hands above her head, he spread her legs apart with his foot and pressed his upper body into her back, pinning her to the wall. "Maybe I should spank you. I think you need a little discipline."

Her breath caught in her throat; she didn't know if he was actually being serious or going along with her joke. The grip of anxiety that swirled in her belly was both alluring and a little scary.

"I want you to keep your hands above you," he ordered in a husky voice.

He backed away from her, allowing the full spray of the shower to hit her skin. She waited as the water cascaded down her body until his fingers reached into her folds and pinched her nub, hard.

Madison arched against him, removing her hands from the wall.

Hayden put her hands back on the cool tile. "No, baby. Keep your hands on the wall and don't move."

She bit back her protests when his fingers jutted into her. Madison surrendered to him and willed herself not to move. Slowly she relaxed, and the more she let go, the deeper he went. Soon, the discomfort dissipated and she became aroused by his touch.

When he removed his fingers from her folds, she opened her eyes in time to see a red foil condom packet fall to the shower stall floor. Hayden reached between her legs, spread her folds apart, and without warning, sank all the way inside of her.

Madison grunted against the painful force of his thrust; her insides burned from his violation. "Christ, Hayden," she groaned as she stretched to accept him.

He mashed her into the wall. "Relax for me," he directed, pushing deeper. "I promise it won't hurt for long."

She surrendered to him—suppressing the urge to resist—and a strange thing happened. The discomfort of his thrusting subsided, and an unyielding yearning began to build. The heat from her loins spiraled upward, making her gasp from the unexpected intensity.

"There," he softly said, ramming into her with all his might. "You feel it now, don't you?"

She was unable to answer, and tried to steady her body against the tide of sensations threatening to knock her to the floor. Her knees buckled, and when the orgasm grabbed her, she screamed with such abandon that the sound of her voice startled her.

Limp in his arms, she had nothing left as he rammed into her. He curled into her back and groaned loudly when he came. Bracing their bodies against the wall, Hayden rested his head on her shoulder as he caught his breath.

She spun around and kissed his lips as the warm water trickled down her face. "That was incredible."

He kissed her again. "That was fucking."

"I like fucking."

He chuckled into her cheek. "So do I."

Combing her hands through his dark, wet hair, she smiled up at him. "I like this side of you."

"What side?"

"The rogue." She wiped the water from his face. "I thought you were such a cool and collected gentleman, or at least that's the way you present yourself at the office."

"At the office, I'm your boss." His smile fell and he dropped the condom outside the shower stall door. "We need to be discreet. I don't want anyone at work knowing about us. Especially not your office mate."

"I understand," she assured him, hiding her disappointment. "It wouldn't be professional."

He held her close. "I need you to remember what we're about. Let's keep it simple."

She nodded, afraid to voice any disagreement...afraid that he would go away. "Yes, Hayden."

"During the day, we must be all business," he raised his dark eyebrows, "but at night, we can play." He turned her hips slightly so that warm water pulsated against her butt. "Spread your legs and the water will take away some of the sting."

Hayden reached for a bar of soap in the corner niche and lathered it in his hands. Tenderly bathing her, he massaged the suds into her shoulders, back, and butt. Madison closed her eyes as his hands worked over every inch of her body. When he reached between her legs, gently washing her folds, she clasped his shoulder, amazed at how the gesture felt even more intimate than their night of heated lovemaking.

Suddenly, Madison didn't care anymore about what anyone thought of their being together. All that mattered was that she held on to him for as long as possible. Pleasing Hayden Parr had become her number one priority.

***

At the office, Madison was deep into her design for the Martins, working on her computer as Adam sat idly by at his desk, staring out the wide window. Since he had come to the office, she had sensed something was off with his demeanor. The usual talkative, confident man—who had liked to go on about his life, accomplishments, and countless assets—was alarmingly silent.

"What happened after I left you and Mr. Parr at the bar?" he finally uttered, breaking the chilly mood in the room.

Madison hesitated as she moved the mouse around on her pad. Remembering what Hayden had told her about Adam and his ex-wife, she carefully planned her words. "Oh, nothing. He brought me back to the building, and then I went home."

"You drove home? After drinking like we did?"

She looked up from her computer to Adam, noting the perfectly made knot on his blue tie. For a second she reflected back to fixing Hayden's tie the morning they visited the lot in Turtle Creek. "I wasn't as trashed as you."

Adam sat back in his chair, resting his hands behind his head. "Kind of surprised the boss man let you drive home, considering he was the one who encouraged us to do those shots in the first place."

"I was fine, Adam." She went back to her plans.

"Are you sure that's all that happened?"

Her hand squeezed the mouse. Did he know something? "Yes, why do you ask?"

"I just got the impression that Mr. Parr likes you…a lot."

She turned in her chair and glared at Adam. "You're joking, right?"

He stood up. "Come on, didn't you see the way he looked at you?"

"Funny, people are saying the same thing about how you look at me."

He shrugged and moved closer to her desk. "Me everyone can understand. I'm your age, and we have a lot in common. But Mr. Parr? He's too old for you."

Sitting back in her chair, she smirked up at him. "Old for me? He's what…maybe seven or eight years older than me. That's not exactly ancient, Adam."

He plopped down on the corner of her desk, grinning. "Ah ha, so you do think he's attractive?"

"Adam, what is with you? Why all these questions about Mr. Parr? He's my boss," she returned her to her computer, "and your boss, too."

"There's no rule that says you can't be interested in your boss, Madison."

"I'm not interested, Adam. He's my boss."

"What if he was interested in you? Would you go for it?"

"Go for what?" Hayden asked from the open office doorway. "Adam," he nodded to Adam as he walked in the door, "feeling better?"

Adam quickly moved away from Madison's desk. "Ah, yes, Mr. Parr."

"Glad to hear it." Hayden came into the room, his intense eyes dissecting Adam. "Garrett wants to speak with you. He has an assignment for you."

Adam's glum countenance sparked to life. "Really?"

Hayden motioned to the door. "He's waiting in his office to go over the details with you." Shifting his focus to Madison, he stated, "I came to see how the Martins' design is coming."

As Hayden approached her desk, Adam moved toward the door. After Adam had exited the office, Hayden angled closer to her.

"What was that about?"

She glanced back at the open door, checking for Adam. "He thinks you're too old for me and insisted that you have a thing for me."

"Do you think I'm too old for you?"

Her lips curled into a grin. "You weren't this morning."

Hayden backed away from her desk, took in a ragged breath, and then went to the office door. Quietly closing it, he came back to her.

"What else did Adam say?"

She leaned back in her chair. "Does it matter?"

"You need to watch out for him. He's been asking a lot of questions about me and if I'm seeing anyone." His thick brow furrowed. "It makes me wonder if Ellen sent him here to spy on me."

"Why would she do that? You're divorced."

He had a seat on the edge of her desk. "Divorced, but there is still the property settlement to get through, and if she had her way she would break me."

"I'm sure Adam is just being...Adam." She patted his arm reassuringly.

"Let's hope so." He nodded to her. "How are you feeling? Are you still sore?"

"A little, but it's not bad."

"I'll try and be gentle tonight."

She wrinkled her brow. "Is that an invitation?"

"Do you need one?"

"Yes, I do."

Madison noted a change in his features. He eyes grew a little darker, accentuating their intimidating appearance.

"We're not dating, Madison. There is no formality here." Leaning over to her computer, he pretended to study the screen. "Come by after work," he softly added.

Excited butterflies in her stomach took wing. "I should go home and pack a bag first. So I won't be late like this morning." She placed her hand on her mouse. "My boss is a real jerk when I'm late."

"Does he spank you when you're bad?"

She grinned at him. "No."

"Perhaps he should." His face remained unchanged as he pointed to her computer screen. "Now let's go over these plans."

***

Madison was leaving her apartment later that evening, her overnight bag and purse slung over her shoulder, and as she was setting her deadlock, she saw Mrs. Leder's door open down the hall. Dropping her head slightly, she sighed, wishing she could have avoided running into her landlady.

"Where are you off to?" Mrs. Leder queried, sauntering down the hall toward her.

Madison looked over her bright turquoise muumuu and matching slippers. "You look pretty tonight."

Her brown eyes behind her thick glasses inspected Madison's blue jeans and red sweatshirt. "Hot date?"

Madison pulled her blue canvas overnight bag closer. "No, I was going to the gym."

"I'm old honey, not senile. I know when a girl is off to see a man. Besides, if you were going to the gym, you wouldn't have put on lipstick and mascara." She rested her hand on her hip. "Is it the hottie boss?"

"What makes you—?"

"Your roommate told me," Mrs. Leder cut in. "She mentioned catching the two of you making out in the kitchen." She winked. "Seems that old dress of mine did the trick, eh?"

Embarrassed, Madison glanced down at the dull brown carpet in the hallway. "We weren't making out. We were talking."

"Madison, I was young once, too." Mrs. Leder placed her hand beneath Madison's chin, and gently lifted her head. "And I also had a romance with my boss, so I know a little about what you're going through." She dropped her arm to her side. "Just remember to keep it interesting. When men get bored, they move on."

Alarmed at the suggestion, Madison thought of how experienced Hayden was with sex. What if he did get bored with her?

"Exactly how do you keep a man from getting bored?" Madison innocently entreated.

Mrs. Leder's cackle reverberated about the brightly lit hallway. "Oh my God, girl, you do have a lot to learn about men." She took Madison's hand. "Come with me."

The inside of Mrs. Leder's apartment always reminded Madison of a museum. The light red walls were crowded with framed pictures of Mrs. Leder in various stages of her youth, standing next to celebrities and politicians Madison had never heard of. The furniture was antique and made of dark wood with the sofa, love seat, and dining table chairs covered with different shades of green velvet. Mrs. Leder had always bragged about it being called Gothic Chippendale, and it had a lot of pointed arches and s-designs, but to Madison it was just clunky. The air was thick with orange blossom air freshener, and the wide screen TV on the living room wall was always set to The Soap Opera Channel.

Gliding past the array of Chinese knickknacks scattered atop the oval coffee table—Mrs. Leder was obsessed with anything Chinese—and over the deep red Oriental rug, Mrs. Leder pulled Madison into a kitchen very much like her own. The cabinets were painted blue instead of white, but the white Formica countertops were identical, as was the jutting breakfast bar.

"I always keep a pair in my kitchen drawer," Mrs. Leder muttered.

"A pair of what?" Madison eyed a porcelain Chinese pug cookie jar on the countertop.

Pushing her glasses up on her nose, Mrs. Leder went to a drawer set below the breakfast bar and began rummaging around. After a few seconds, she uttered a triumphant cry and raised a pair of silver handcuffs in the air.

Madison's jaw almost dropped to the floor when she saw her diminutive, elderly landlady holding up the handcuffs.

"This should keep him interested for a while," Mrs. Leder declared as she waved the handcuffs in front of Madison.

"You're joking, right?" Madison sounded more astonished than amused.

Mrs. Leder went to Madison's side and unzipped the overnight bag. "Trust me, you'll thank me later." She dropped the handcuffs inside. "It will open up a whole new world for you."

"Mrs. Leder, I can't take those." Madison's overnight bag suddenly felt as if it weighed a hundred pounds. "I know you mean well, but I'm not—"

"Yes, you are that kind of girl, Madison. We all are. The only difference between someone who has explored their desires and someone who hasn't is fear." She patted her arm. "When you get to be my age, you discover the only thing that held you back in youth was fear. You realize that there was nothing to be afraid of in the first place. All that does matter in life are the people you share it with." She waved her hand about her cluttered living room. "All the possessions, the money, and the accolades on your wall don't mean a thing without someone to love."

"I don't know if we're that serious yet. Who can say how long we will last? It might just be a fling."

"I can tell by the way you blush whenever you speak of him that this isn't a fling. Always fight to hold on to the special ones, Madison. They don't come around all that often." She shrugged and smiled wistfully. "Sometimes just once in a lifetime. Cherish it."

Madison gave Mrs. Leder a tolerant smile, but her thoughts were on how to get out of the apartment and on her way to Hayden's. "Thank you, Mrs. Leder, and I will...." She stumbled, trying to think what was considered polite when lending bondage equipment. "I'll get the handcuffs back to you later, I guess?"

Mrs. Leder waved off the suggestion. "You keep them, honey. I've got others." She showed Madison to the door

Madison regarded her landlady with a new appreciation. "You sure are full of surprises, Mrs. Leder."

Mrs. Leder reached for her doorknob. "Everyone lives a life, Madison. We're all the same, no matter the generations in between. You have fun with that man of yours."

After Mrs. Leder had shut her front door, Madison jogged down the hallway toward the elevator. Deciding it would take too long, she darted across the hall to the stairwell and sprinted down five flights until she emerged in the lobby. Pushing through the glass doors at the building entrance, she spied the last orange spindles of the setting sun dragging across the sky.

Finally behind the wheel of her car, she tossed her bags to the passenger seat, and as she reflected on her overnight bag, she imagined Hayden naked and handcuffed to his bed.

"Thank you, Mrs. Leder," she giggled, starting the car. "This might just be a very memorable evening, after all."

Chapter 12

It was dark by the time she parked in front of Hayden's contemporary home in Highland Park. The oversized mansions up and down his street were lit from within, sending out warm beams of light into the chilly night. Lifting her overnight bag from the car, the eerie quiet blanketing the picturesque manicured lawns and pristine gardens made Madison feel even more anxious about returning to his home. It was not that she didn't want to be with him again—she did, desperately—but in the back of her mind, a little voice kept asking if she was doing the right thing. Perhaps she should have turned down his proposal, concentrated on her job, and pushed Hayden out of her life for good.

"You're overthinking things again," she grumbled, climbing up his long front steps. "You always do this when you get scared of a man."

Scared? The word rattled about in her head. Maybe that had always been her problem. When things had gotten serious with a man and should have moved to the bedroom, Madison had run. It had not been the intimacy that she had feared; it had been sharing all of those pesky little details of her life with someone. Shaking her head, Madison realized that had been the real reason why she had sought out a stranger that night to rid her of her bothersome virginity; she had simply wanted to do the deed without being weighed down by the burden of a relationship.

But now, here she stood, on the front doorstep of the very stranger she had given herself to, yearning for that long-avoided emotional relationship, but unable to pursue it. Life was more than ironic, it was downright sadistic.

"Hey, baby," Hayden greeted after he opened his front door. When he kissed her lips, all of her doubts were magically swept aside.

Putting his arm around her shoulders, he ushered her inside. After shutting the door and setting the alarm, Hayden took the overnight bag from her.

"I hope you're hungry." He put the overnight bag on the stairs in the open foyer. "I picked up a large pepperoni pizza on the way home." He glanced back at her. "You do like pepperoni, don't you?"

She nodded. "And I like mushrooms, peppers, and chicken on my pizza. But no onions, anchovies, or pineapple."

Hayden's eyes drew together soberly. "Well, that is going to be a problem, because I love onions, anchovies, and pineapple on my pizza."

She briefly grinned, but attempted to look serious. "Hmm. Yes, that could be a problem."

"Perhaps I should spend the evening getting to know your likes and dislikes so that we can avoid any future problems." He placed his hands behind his back as he took a step closer to her. "Let's start with your favorite food."

She peered up at the skylights above the foyer. "I like hamburgers the best, followed by popcorn."

He stood right before her, staring into her eyes, his face unchanged. "Least favorite food."

"Cabbage. Totally gross."

A very faint smile briefly appeared on his lips, but he stifled it. Taking another step closer to her, he lowered his head so that his mouth was positioned right in front of hers. "Have you ever fantasized about being with a woman?"

Astounded by the question, she wasn't sure how to reply. "Ah, I'm not a lesbian." She held her head up, determined to be one of those confident, sexy women he liked. "I only fantasize about men." Sounded good to her.

His eyes penetrated deep into her soul, and Madison became convinced he knew she had no idea what she was talking about. "Really? Tell me one of your fantasies." He waited, hovering inches away from her. "Do you have any fantasies?" he probed.

Shit! She remained calm, on the outside anyway. "Perhaps."

"You're lying. You don't allow yourself to have fantasies, do you, Madison?" He nodded while evaluating her reaction. "How many boyfriends have you had since me? Serious ones, ones you let touch you."

She lowered her eyes to the hardwood floor. "Only two," she softly answered.

He was so close to her that she could feel the heat from his skin coming through his white shirt. "Who were they?"

"Do you really want to talk about this?"

"I need to know everything about your experiences with men, Madison."

"Why?" she argued.

"Can you just answer the question and not debate it?"

"Fine." She cleared her throat. "Dwight was the first after you. He was in my Advanced Design class. It didn't last long."

"And the second?"

He rested his hand on her shoulder, making her jump. "Martin. We dated right after I graduated from college."

He stood behind her. "How were they with fondling you, making you come?"

"I don't know...fair, I guess," she admitted, thinking fair was being generous.

"Fair?" His chuckle was highly arousing. "Then I take it none of them made you scream...not like me."

Now she was getting flustered. No man had ever spoken to her like this. The idea of discussing her sex life with anyone, let alone the man she had already slept with, was a bit daunting. "They, ah...tried, I guess I should say."

His hand moved down her back to her butt. Pressing the fabric of her jeans into her backside, he whispered, "Tried?"

She closed her eyes. "They didn't succeed."

His hands went to the fly of her jeans. "So, back to my original question. Do you have any fantasies?" He slowly lowered the zipper on her jeans. "Things you want a man to do to you?"

She shook her head. "I haven't really…no."

He curled his body into her back. "Then we shall have to make some up for you. Play out some roles to see which one you like." Hayden pushed her jeans and silky beige underwear down her thighs, all the way to her ankles.

"What are you doing?" she questioned, looking down at her jeans.

His hands went up the back of her red sweatshirt, unclasping her bra. He then pushed the thick sweatshirt over her head. "I want you naked."

"What about the pizza?"

"You can eat it naked in front of me." He chucked her sweatshirt and bra to the stairs.

Madison become instantly self-conscious and clasped her arms about her breasts and hips.

"What is it? You weren't shy with me last night."

"That was last night," she mumbled.

"Madison, you need to feel comfortable being naked in front of me; comfortable with me doing anything I want to your body."

She wasn't sure if she'd heard him right, and suspiciously cocked her head to the side. "Anything? What exactly are we talking about?"

He kissed the tip of her nose. "Trust me, you'll love it."

She tightened her arms about her body. "I trust you, Hayden."

"Forgive me, but that's not what I see." He stood back from her, his eyes rising to her face. "If you trusted me, you would lower your arms."

Madison dropped her arms to her sides, allowing him an unencumbered view of her body. "See? I trust you."

His eyes drank in her figure. "From now on I think this should be an exclusive arrangement. Only me, no other men. Understood?"

"Like going steady?"

He grinned, appearing amused. "I was thinking of something a little more grown up than that."

Blushing, she quickly nodded. "Sorry. It just came out."

Hayden arched closer to her. "I don't like to share. I've had enough of women playing the field in order to get my attention." His gray eyes turned to two dark slits. "Like what you did with Adam the other evening at the bar. Was that to make me jealous?"

She looked away to the stairs. "You made it pretty clear that first night at my apartment that you didn't want me…he did."

"He didn't want you, Madison. He wanted to wear you like a trophy he had won at some competition." Hayden's eyes zeroed in on hers, appearing strangely menacing. "I'm not looking for a prize."

Madison was intrigued by his statement. As his stern features softened, she contemplated what he had planned for her. "What are you looking for, Hayden?"

His sexy smile returned. "Something more." Taking her hand, he announced, "Time to eat."

Hayden led her to the kitchen and motioned for her to sit at his glass breakfast table. When her naked butt hit the cold seat on her hard white chair, she flinched. As Hayden went to a large pizza box on his stainless counter, the aroma of the cheesy bread and tomato sauce concoction drifted to her nose.

"Smells good." Madison tried to find a way to be comfortable at the table, but dining in the buff was a new experience for her. Awkwardly resting her arms on the glass table, she prayed she did not look as foolish as she felt.

"There is this great little pizza place not far from here that makes the best thin crust I've ever eaten. It's small, but cozy." He grabbed a plate from one of the white cabinets overhead and slid a slice of pizza onto it.

After he put the plate in front of her, Madison glanced up at him. "Where's yours?"

He pulled another chair from around the table and set it right next to hers. "I'm not hungry, but you go ahead." He waved to her plate.

Shrugging it off, Madison snapped up her slice of pepperoni pizza and bit into it. The tomato sauce ran down her chin and she wiped it away with her hand.

"I need a napkin."

She was about to get up from her chair when Hayden took her hand. "You don't need one."

His mouth came closer, and then he licked the drizzle of sauce away from her chin. Taking the hand she had wiped her mouth with, he tasted her fingers, making sure to suck on each and every one.

Madison damn near fell out of her chair.

Seeing the flabbergasted expression on her face, Hayden pulled her index finger from his mouth and nodded to her plate. "Go on," he ordered. "Eat."

"What are you doing?"

"Being your napkin."

Warily, Madison took another bite of her pizza as Hayden looked on. When a crumb of crust fell on to her chest, Hayden rose from his chair and dutifully licked the crumb from the top of her right breast.

When he sat back down, the glint in his eyes was so seductive that Madison had to turn away. The only question she had was who was enjoying this more. Another bite led to another morsel of red sauce dripping on to her left breast.

Madison immediately glanced up from her breast to him. The smirk across his thin red lips made her smile. Within seconds he was out of his chair and kneeling next to her. His lips kissed her left breast, his tongue languishing over her left nipple. She almost dropped the pizza in her hand. This time, however, Hayden did not return to his chair. He stayed on his knees next to her, continuing to let his mouth and tongue explore her chest, neck, and breasts. Madison was convinced she would never look at pizza the same way again.

"Did you pack your office clothes in your overnight bag?" he inquired, taking her empty plate away from the breakfast table.

She sat back in her white chair and watched as his perfectly curved butt walked toward the sink. "Sure. I didn't want to have to run home in the morning to change for work and risk being late again." She shifted in her chair, her naked butt sticking to the seat.

"The Martins want to speak to you about the plans for their house," he stated. "I have a feeling they're getting cold feet about the project."

"Cold feet? But at the party they seemed so excited."

His eyes shifted to the plate in the sink and she could see the concern in them. "This evening when I pulled up, Pat came across the street to tell me they want to make a few changes to the plans."

"Changes? But I've already made so many changes."

He came back to the table. "You haven't been in this business long enough to realize the first rule of designing houses is that the client always changes their mind." He stood over her at the table. "I just hope they don't change their mind about selling me their house. I want that property."

Spying his smooth, muscular chest through his half-open white dress shirt, she tried to concentrate on the topic of conversation. "What will you do if they don't sell?"

Taking her hand, Hayden helped her from the chair. "I can't think that way. I want their land and I always get what I want." He glanced around the kitchen. "And I have to get out of here."

A chill settled about her and she rubbed her hands along her arms. "Have you made any designs for the kind of place you will build?"

"I was thinking you might be able to help me with that." He unbuttoned his shirt and slipped it from his shoulders. "I like the house you designed for the Martins, and was thinking you could draw something similar for me." He eased the shirt around her body. "Might be fun to design something together," he added, kissing her forehead.

Madison pulled his shirt closer. "I got the idea for that house from the land. I guess I would have to see the Martins' property in order to design something that could work."

"Great idea," he happily proclaimed. "You can do that tomorrow when you visit them. I told Pat you would be there in the morning to go over the changes."

Madison froze. "Me?" her voice cracked. "Aren't you going to be there?"

"No. I have meetings all day tomorrow with assorted clients and contractors."

"I don't know, Hayden." Madison was convinced standing naked in Hayden's kitchen would pale in comparison to taking on the Martins alone. "Maybe you should have someone there with me. What about Garrett or Don Worthy? What if I say something wrong or screw it up?"

He placed an arm about her shoulders, guiding her back toward his den. "I have every confidence that you can handle this on your own. Besides, there is no one else to go with you. Don is off tomorrow and Garrett will be tied up with Adam in the morning."

"Adam? What's he doing with Adam?"

They strolled beneath the archway that led to his foyer while Madison gazed up into his suddenly stoic face, waiting for an answer.

"They'll be working on that new project I told him about this morning."

Madison remembered Adam being excited and dashing from their office after Hayden had come to see her. "Yes, of course."

They came to the stairs and he picked up her overnight bag, slinging it over his left shoulder. Madison thought about the handcuffs inside, doubting she would have the courage to put them on Hayden. *Perhaps I'll save that little game for another night.*

"You'll be fine with Pat and Stevie," Hayden continued. "I really need you to get a good look at their property, so we can start planning my house." His arm went around her shoulders and they started up the stairs together.

His embrace made Madison feel safe, but something about the way he was acting was different. Maybe it was Madison's imagination, but she got the impression that tonight their relationship had changed. It was as if he was asserting his claim on her, not that she minded being his. Madison just began to consider what being his actually entailed.

In the master bedroom, he put her bag on the bed and sat down next to it. His eyes went to the dresser in the corner of the austerely decorated room. "There's an empty drawer on top for your things," he commented, motioning toward the dresser. "I've cleared out a portion of the closet for you as well."

Madison paused. She had never experienced a relationship that had been serious enough to leave things at a man's home before, let alone be assigned a designated drawer and room in his closet. It was an odd moment for her. Sort of like a rite of passage, where a relationship went from being fun to something special...but had they already reached that point?

"Ah, thanks." Stepping up to the bed, she unzipped the blue canvas bag.

Hayden sat on the bed watching as she unpacked. Feeling a little awkward as his eyes registered every item she removed, Madison kept reaching in, hoping to avoid Mrs. Leder's handcuffs. She could only imagine what he would do if he spotted them.

Taking out her black dress slacks and blouse for work the next day, she went across the room to the dresser. When she turned around, Hayden was smiling at her.

Approaching the bed, she knitted her brow. "What is it?"

He stood from the bed, held out his hand, and dropped the handcuffs on the burgundy bedspread. "Are those for me?"

A thousand and one excuses shot across her mind, but none of them would explain the handcuffs better than the truth. "My landlady gave them to me. Mrs. Leder." She gestured to the silver handcuffs. "She's eccentric, wealthy, and she gave me that dress I wore to the party last weekend."

He picked up the handcuffs and held them before her. "But why did she give you these?"

Madison hesitated, wringing her hands. "She wanted me to...keep it interesting. That's how she put it." Her shoulders sagged forward. "She thought you would get bored with me."

"I've never even met Mrs. Leder and I don't like her already." Pressing his lips together, he scrutinized her face. "Have you ever used handcuffs on a man before?"

"No, of course not."

He took a step closer to her. "Have you ever fantasized about being handcuffed?"

Before she could raise her eyes, he had positioned the handcuffs over her right wrist and snapped them closed. Alarmed, Madison tugged at the handcuffs with her left hand.

"Relax," he whispered, placing his hand over hers. "I'm not going to do anything you don't want me to do. This is about trust. If you trust me, then you know I would never hurt you." His finger traced along the supple skin on her inner right wrist. "But to do that," his finger edged along the silver bracelet, "you must give yourself to me…willingly."

Madison pushed the rising panic back down to the depths of her gut and lowered her left hand from the silver shackle. This was Hayden. A man she had been with more than once, and he had never done anything she did not enjoy. Maybe he was right; she needed to trust him. Letting out a long breath, she nodded her head.

He pressed his hands on her shoulders, pushing her down on the bed. "This is going to be a lesson in disclosure. You need to learn to open up to me. That's what lovers do, Madison."

After she was seated before him on the bedspread, he peeled his shirt from about her body; pulling the last sleeve over the handcuffs, he dropped it on the floor. Standing before her, his eyes were filled with a new kind of light Madison had never seen before. He was highly aroused, and thinking perhaps he wanted her to help him undress, she reached for the zipper of his pants.

"No," he stopped her hands, "not yet." He nodded toward the head of the low bed. "Scoot back and place your hands over your head."

Still not sure what he had in mind, Madison began to reason that maybe this was some kind of game he liked to play. She had heard of sex games—Charlie was always regaling about Nelson's newest one—but she had never experienced any. Settling her head back on the pillow, she raised her hands above her head, watching the handcuffs sparkle in the recessed lights above.

Once she was in position, Hayden came up to the side of the bed, took her hands, and secured them to the corner post of the oversized headboard. When Madison heard the click of the handcuffs, she swallowed hard.

At first he said nothing, just sat on the side of the bed, gazing up and down her naked body, as if deciding what to do first. Madison nervously shifted her legs, but he placed his hand on her left knee, pushing it back down to the bed.

"Lie still."

Slowly, his fingertips caressed the top her left thigh, tickling her flesh along the way. Madison normally would have laughed out loud, but being handcuffed to the bed—naked—made it more sexy than humorous. His hands journeyed up along her hip, over the contours of her stomach and around the full swell of her left breast. His fingers rose upward, tracing the outline of her collarbone and neck until they came to a stop right below her chin. Raising her head slightly, he admired her face, and then tenderly kissed her lips. His mouth brushed over her chin, along her throat, and down her chest, stopping only briefly to tease her right nipple. While his lips descended further, his hands crept between her knees, nudging them apart. He was kissing her stomach when his fingers roughly reached into her folds. Madison flinched, pulling against the handcuffs.

Hayden removed his hand and sat up next to her. "You're still tender. What shall I do with you?"

Perplexed, Madison stared at him, unsure of what to say. "I thought you wanted to have sex."

Clucking, he shook his head. "Sex? No, I want much more than sex." He stood from the bed and lowered the zipper on his trousers. "Sex is just the act. Like this morning in the shower. Right now, I want something else from you."

"What?" she griped, feeling completely stumped.

He lowered his trousers and briefs to the floor and stepped out of them. Reaching for the nightstand, he opened the drawer, removed a red foil package, and flung it on the bed next to her. She watched, a little mystified, as he reached back into the drawer and palmed something else; something she could not see. Coming back to the bed, he sat down next to her. While eyeing his erection, she tried to figure out what he was going to do.

He ran his left hand along her thigh and pulled her left knee closer to him. "Tell me you want me."

"I want you, Hayden." Her voice was flat and emotionless.

"Not like that." His hand careened down her inner thigh to her folds. When a low, buzzing noise filled the room, Madison's eyes widened.

"This is a small vibrator I like to use. I promise you will like it." Separating her folds with his fingers, he touched the vibrator to her sensitive nub.

Madison lurched against the handcuffs. "Oh, God," she cried out.

"Now tell me again."

Madison fought to gain control of her faculties. "I want you, Hayden," she stated, raising her voice.

"I'm not convinced."

Groaning, she arched against the bed, pulling on the handcuffs. The vibrator was stimulating her in tantalizing but intense waves. Soon, the intensity got to be too much for her. Beads of sweat broke out on her forehead, and she clenched her hands when she felt a powerful orgasm beginning to overtake her.

"What do you want me to do to you, Madison?" His voice sounded insistent and slightly dangerous.

"Make love to me," she called out, fighting against her restraints.

Just as she was reaching that dizzying height of climax, he removed the vibrator, and the buzzing noise ceased. Madison crashed against the bed, devastated.

"Don't stop," she pleaded.

He leaned over her face, grinning. "I really dislike the term making love. It glorifies a very instinctual act."

She closed her eyes, exasperated. "Then what should we call this?" she gasped between breaths.

After a few seconds passed and he had made no reply, Madison opened her eyes to see him still sitting beside her, studying her. "Tell me about your fantasies, Madison."

"I told you I don't have any—"

"You lied to me. Now tell me what you have always wanted a man to do with you." He spread her legs apart, kneeling between them, and she heard him turn the vibrator back on. "I'll make you tell me...eventually."

When he pushed the vibrator into her, she cried out, tugging hard against the handcuffs. The vibrator had her body spiraling out of control. Once again, she could feel the landslide of her orgasm building, and then he abruptly stopped.

"Ready to talk? I'll keep bringing you closer and closer until you tell me."

She whimpered and fell back against the bed. "All right, you win. I've always had this fantasy about...." She went quiet, gulping back her shame.

Hayden shoved three fingers hard into her, making her wince. "Keep talking, baby."

She gritted her teeth as he pushed farther into her. "I've dreamed about dancing naked for a man. Taking off my clothes and dancing before someone."

"That's a pretty common fantasy. Anything else?" His fingers slowly eased out of her.

"To dance for him and then...have him take me. Push me into some piece of furniture or a table, and while he holds me by the hair...you get the idea." Sagging into the bed, she felt utterly violated. She had never shared that with anyone, and knowing that Hayden was aware of her innermost thoughts made her apprehensive about what he would do with such knowledge.

"Hmmm," he murmured into her hair as his fingers once again reached into her wet folds. "Now that's what I want to hear...the truth." He turned the vibrator on and flicked it against her nub, making Madison shudder. "You like that?"

"Yes," she groaned.

His fingers roughly moved in and out of her as he held the vibrator to her nub. "Do you want more?"

She rolled her head to the side, sucking in a gasp. "Yes, more."

Desperate to relieve that awful ache inside of her, she yearned for his fingers to go deeper. Just as her orgasm was about to take over, he stopped and bit down on her left shoulder…hard.

"No," Madison cried out. "Please, Hayden."

"Tell me what to do, Madison."

She wrapped her legs about his hips. "I need you inside of me," she begged.

"That's not what I want to hear."

"What do you want from me?" Taut with need, she barely recognized her raspy voice.

"Tell me you want me to fuck you."

She stiffened next to him, unsure of what to do. She wasn't that kind of girl, or was she? Desire was a funny thing; it made you do the unthinkable. She tilted her head back and gazed into his eyes. "Fuck me, Hayden. Fuck me hard."

"That's what I needed from you…passion." Hayden pitched the small vibrator to the floor and grabbed the condom package on the bedspread beside her. After slipping it on, he reached underneath her butt and lifted her hips. With one swift movement, he entered her, hard and fast.

Relieved to feel him inside of her, Madison angled her hips upward, allowing him the deepest penetration. When he had pushed all the way into her, he stilled and sighed into her neck.

"Say you're mine, Madison."

"I'm yours, Hayden," she avowed. "I've always been yours."

Aroused by her statement, he began ramming into her, grunting into her skin, and holding her close.

Madison's arms and shoulders burned as they were stretched further with his every thrust, but she didn't mind the pain. Slapping her hips into his as he pounded into her, she hungered for him, desperate to have him go as deep as he could. When her muscles tensed and her back arched, a slow, deep moan escaped her lips. As the climax catapulted through her, her lips parted and she cried out his name.

Spurred on by her cry, Hayden hurriedly thrust into her, once and then twice more, before his whole body became rigid and he groaned. Collapsing on top of her, the weight of his body crushed her into the bed, creating more pain in her arms.

"Hayden, I can't feel my fingers," she pleaded into his chest.

Sitting up on his elbow, he reached up for the handcuffs and fumbled with the release button. After several long seconds, the silver bracelets fell away. Reclining beside her, he took her hands and tenderly massaged them, occasionally kissing her fingers.

As Madison watched him care for her, a deep fondness for him began to pervade her heart. She hesitated in thinking it could be love, but what they had just shared made her feel closer to him. Somehow more connected, as if she were truly his.

"Why did you do that?"

"Do what? Handcuff you?" he inquired, placing her hand against her chest. "You brought the handcuffs, Madison."

"Not the handcuffs. Ask me to say those things? Why did you need to hear me say that?" She rolled over to her side. "It was almost as if you weren't going to be satisfied until you got what you wanted out of me."

"I wasn't. I didn't need to hear you say you wanted me like that, Madison. You needed to say it." He rested back against the bed. "You've been almost like a spectator when we have sex. There, but not quite there, emotionally anyway. Tonight, you were there, and you wanted me."

"So handcuffing me to the bed and torturing me with a vibrator was your way of getting me to actively participate?" She let out a long sigh. "You have a hell of a way with women."

His arms came around her. "Did you like it?"

"What does that make me if I say I did like it?"

"A woman who knows what she likes." He kissed her cheek. "And you don't need any more invitations to come over."

"Is that what this was about?" Madison sat up in the bed. "You wanted to show me that I'm welcome here?"

"I wanted you to feel comfortable with me and to open up to me. You're mine now, remember that."

Madison had heard girls talk about that moment when a man wanted to commit to them; to turn dating into a relationship and a possible future. Everyone had made it sound exciting, filled with emotion and words of love. As she searched his face, Madison saw none of that. She preferred this declaration to any other. It was honest, and instead of hiding his true nature behind romance novel-like words, he had given her his raw desire; she, in turn, had given him her devotion.

She settled in next him. "I guess I'll just knock on your door, naked and waving a pair of handcuffs in the future."

"I have a very clear mental image of that."

"So will your neighbors."

He began stroking her hair. "75336."

"What's that?"

"The code. You can punch it into the keypads I have set up beside the front door or the rear door to the garage. Enter the code and the security will turn off. Then the door will pop open. When you leave, shut the door and type in the code again. That way the security will turn back on." His hand glided up and down her back. "See how simple it is?"

She sat up on her elbow, eyeing his face. "Am I supposed to give you a spare key to my place?"

He pulled her back to him. "I don't think we'll be sleeping at your place. Mrs. Leder might show up with whips and chains if I stay there."

"You never know with Mrs. Leder."

Sighing into him, Madison closed her eyes as an unfamiliar calm came over her. Never before had she felt so comfortable with a man. She wasn't second-guessing herself, wondering what he was thinking, or having that emotional turmoil clouding her thoughts. There was just peace. She wasn't sure if it was the exertion of the day, or the secure feeling of his arms about her, but within seconds, Madison fell blissfully asleep.

Chapter 13

The sound of a man's raised voice woke Madison from a dream of unicorns and green forests. Brushing aside the sleep from her eyes, she strained to get a clearer impression of the voice that she had heard. Sitting up in the king-sized bed, she listened for anything coming through the open bedroom door.

"Dammit, Ellen, I don't need this shit from you right now. So what if I have someone here?" Hayden's voice was brimming with anger. "You sent that little kiss ass to my office to keep an eye on me, didn't you? I told you before if he pulled anything I would—"

Madison sat up in the bed. Spying Hayden's shirt on the floor, she reached for it.

"Don't give me that crap," his voice was back. "You and I both know that you only want him to—"

Shrugging into his shirt, Madison snuck across the bedroom floor to the open door.

"Bullshit!" Hayden yelled.

She could hear his voice coming from a room across the narrow white hallway, where a thick oak door was partially ajar.

"I'll call Marc Collins and tell him what you've been up to. See if that helps your case any," Hayden shouted. "You can have the damned house, I told you. I just want—"

Madison crept out into the hallway, closer to the half-open door. Hoping not to be seen, she was just about to peek around the edge of the thick door when his voice rang out.

"Go to hell, Ellen, and don't call me again. Anything you want to say, send it to Marc." Then there was silence.

Madison did not know if she should forge ahead into the room to offer comfort, or sneak back to bed and pretend that she hadn't heard a thing. She was about to opt for a hasty retreat when his feet came bounding toward her.

The door flew open, and Madison almost fell backwards; his tall figure was looming over her. Wearing only his briefs, his bare muscular chest and ripped abdomen appeared even more imposing than the previous night.

"What are you doing?" Hayden snapped, and grabbed her arm.

Terrified of what he was thinking, she tugged at his hand, wanting to get away. "I heard you shouting. It woke me up." Again, she pulled at his grip. "I thought something was wrong."

His lips slammed together, and when he let her go, Madison quickly took a few steps back from him. He held up his hands, trying to allay her fear.

"It's all right." He glanced back into the room and ran his hand over his face. "I was yelling at my ex-wife. It seems one of my neighbors called her and told her I had a woman over. That set her off."

Relief pulsed through her. For a moment, she thought he would be angry with her for spying on him. Madison rubbed her hand over her right wrist and winced slightly when she found it tender.

He gently inspected her wrist. "You're bruised." He noted the thin bracelet line of bruising around her right wrist, and then checked her left one. The same light pattern of bruising covered that wrist, too.

"This is why I hate handcuffs." He turned her toward the hallway.

"You've used them before?" she asked, being ushered into the bedroom.

He went to the adjoining bathroom. "Yes," he called over his shoulder. "Many times."

She followed him into the bathroom. "With who?" came out faster than she could stifle it.

He was standing next to his double vanity, staring into a medicine cabinet behind the large mirror. "Are you asking about the women I've slept with?" He never took his eyes away from the cabinet. "Would you like to hear about them?"

Madison was not sure what to say. Hearing about his other women would only make her feel more inexperienced, but her curiosity was winning out against her reservations. Folding her arms across her chest, she boldly leaned against the countertop.

"Okay. Tell me about them."

He smiled like a proud teacher with an apt pupil. "My last lover was named Danielle. She worked as an investment banker. We met at a party and came back here. She was too aggressive in bed for me. She liked to bite and scratch a lot. It only lasted a few nights."

Madison shifted on her feet, a little uncomfortable with the topic, but determined to go on. "Before her?"

"Lydia. She was a night clerk at a grocery store. One night when I was shopping, she came on to me...then she took me into the stock room and gave me a blow job. The next night I went back, brought her in the stock room, and fucked her from behind. She was pretty, but very dull. I don't shop at that store anymore."

Madison blushed as a picture of Hayden and Lydia in a stock room came to mind. "The next one?"

He inched up to her, placing his arm about her waist. "Before Lydia there was Eve. She was into a lot of kinky things and very fun. She liked to be tied up and spanked. Eve got off on practically being raped. Real rough sex." He dropped his head into her neck, smelling her skin. "It turned me on at first, but after a while I discovered there was no challenge in that."

"Challenge?" Madison's butt hit the cold countertop.

His arms pinned her to the vanity. "No control."

Cocking her head to the side, she considered his words. "Why do you like being in control?"

"It's the way I've always liked it. When I first started having sex I was sixteen. I always felt something was lacking. In college, I met Garrett. He belonged to this fraternity...a fraternity of men who liked being in control. There I learned a great deal about sexual preferences and women."

"What exactly did you do in this fraternity?"

He rubbed his hips against hers. "I can tell you, or I can show you."

She stared assertively into his eyes, letting her lips hover in front of his. "Show me."

He easily lifted her onto the vanity, and ran his hands along her inner thighs, spreading her legs apart. "I want you to allow me to take control of your pleasure." His fingers tempted her delicate folds. "Only your pleasure."

She sucked in a delighted breath. "I think you've already done that." She opened her legs wider for him.

"Not quite, but I'm getting there." His hands gripped her hips, pulling her to the edge of the countertop. He kneeled on the floor and began kissing her inner right thigh, his lips ascending slowly to the junction between her legs.

She flushed when his mouth settled over her sensitive spot, almost crying out loud when he began sucking mercilessly on her. As she was writhing on the countertop, he positioned her legs over his shoulders, tilting her backwards. Her hands combed through his dark brown hair, pulling hard as he bit her flesh.

"Yes," she cried.

The swirling of his tongue sent her crashing into the vanity mirror, knocking her head against the glass, but she didn't feel anything. Her mind was too overcome by the roaring of her blood, the burning in between her legs, and the slow, deliberate ache rising from her gut. She wanted him to hurry, to make her scream with release, but just as she was about to tip over that cliff of unrelenting abandon, he pulled away.

The disappointment in her body was cataclysmic and she almost crashed to the floor when he stood up, removing his support from her legs.

"What is it?" she gasped, gaping into his face.

The smirk on his lips immediately told her of his intentions. He had meant to leave her aching for him, wanting her to beg for more. She sat up, feeling utterly dejected.

"What do you want, Hayden?"

He leaned over the counter, trapping her between his strong arms. His face hovered in front of her. "I need you to submit to me."

Shaking her head, Madison sighed. "I thought I was already doing that."

"Submission means giving yourself to me without question. In order to do that, you must trust me." He stood back from the vanity, keeping his sizzling eyes on her. "Get on the floor."

At this point Madison wasn't sure what to expect, but she also wasn't afraid, which intrigued her. Last night she had been apprehensive about his games, today she was just getting frustrated. Climbing from the vanity, she stood before him. "Just get on the floor?"

He eased his shirt from around her body and tossed it to the vanity. "This is going to be a lesson in trust. Get down on all fours."

The Madison Barnett she had been before meeting him would have probably bolted straight for the front door, but she knew herself a little better now, and figured no matter what he did, eventually she would enjoy it. With one last impertinent side-glance, she assumed her position on the cool, white tiled floor.

He stood over her. "I like that you didn't debate with me."

"I didn't see the point."

He kneeled behind her. "You're beginning to understand." His fingers rubbed up and down her wet folds, causing her to arch her back. "To take control of your pleasure, you must submit to my desire."

His words registered in her head, but when his fingers fondled her nub, she forgot all thoughts. The aching began again in her gut, and the harder he stroked her, the faster her hips moved against his hand.

"If I decide to withhold your pleasure...." He removed his hand. "You will accept it."

Madison's hands curled into balls and her knuckles shone white, the same color as the tile of the floor. Her body was so close to coming, and she wanted him to touch her again, but she said nothing. She rocked gently back and forth, trying to ease the vice grip of need clenching her insides.

"I have to know that I can do anything I want to you," he whispered in her ear. "Say it."

"Yes, anything you want, Hayden."

He dragged her wetness from her folds up between her butt cheeks. His finger rubbed back and forth over her anus.

"And if I want this?"

Madison's eyes snapped open and she hesitated.

"Do you trust me, Madison?"

She tensed, anticipating what was to come. "Yes, Hayden."

Silence permeated the air. She waited as the eerie quiet in the bathroom continued.

He eased over on his side, watching her. "You need to be prepared in order for me to take this prize." He rubbed his hand over her butt. "Do you want me to prepare you?"

Resting on her heels, she considered his request. "Will it hurt?"

"No, just feel different." He held up his index finger. "I'll use this, that's all for now. If you don't like how it feels, I'll stop. Are you okay with that?"

Staring into his eyes, she knew in that instant that she would never find another man who made her feel so comfortable with sex. "Yes." Madison nodded her head.

Hayden sat up from the floor and positioned her hips in front of him. His hand rubbed lightly over her ass, and when his fingers teased her wet folds, Madison closed her eyes. Stimulating her, she lost herself in the way his fingers moved rhythmically over her, but when he tracked her wetness to her anus, she sucked in a frightened gasp.

"I want to see if you like how this feels," he asserted, letting his thumb glide back and forth over her opening.

Madison tensed when she felt the pressure of his thumb pressing down.

Hayden let his hand fall away. "You need to relax for me."

Again his fingers went to her folds, but this time he rubbed her nub hard, making her groan. Her hips rocked back and forth and she relaxed as his hand awakened the heat between her legs. Then, she felt the pressure of his finger slowly entering her. He kept on stimulating, distracting her from the sensation of fullness as he pushed into her anus. At first, she did not know what to think; it felt awkward and unnatural. He began to wiggle his finger and the combined stimulation caused her insides to explode.

"Jesus!" she cried out.

"Do you like this, Madison?"

"God, Hayden, yes." Her arms gave out on her, dropping her head to the floor.

He pinched her nub harder and wiggled his finger more. "If you want me to stop, I will. You only have to say so."

"No." She pushed up on all fours. "I don't want you to stop."

"Are you sure?"

"Deeper," she implored. "Go deeper."

"Let's try something else."

Unexpectedly, Hayden removed his finger and Madison almost crashed to the floor. Kneeling behind her, he shifted her hips to him and she heard a foil package ripping open. He spread her folds open and she flinched when his fingers slipped inside her wet flesh. She was sore and wanted to reach for his hand, stopping him, but she fought against the urge. She had to submit.

"I know you're still tender after last night," he hummed in her ear, "but I need to be inside of you. Please, baby." He bit her shoulder.

She nodded her head and spread her legs apart, making ready for him.

He stood and moved away. When the heat of his body returned against her backside, she jumped as his fingers slid into her.

"This is just some lubricant. It will help reduce your discomfort."

The jelly felt good and eased the burning. When he glided the jelly toward her anus, she swallowed hard. Tenderly he entered her and Madison grimaced, but held her position beneath him. He pushed into her as his finger eased into her anus. She grunted at the discomfort, but when he pulled all the way out and drove into her again, she groaned. The delicious pressure from his finger was intensifying the sensation of him moving against her flesh. He shoved harder into her the next time, and she gasped when he reached the deepest parts of her.

"Tell me if you want me to stop." He kissed her back.

"No. More," she groaned.

He retreated from her wet flesh, and this time, he wiggled his finger in her butt as he rammed into her.

"Oh, God," she shouted.

Hayden thrust into her with an overwhelming force, pushing her forward into the floor. She lay on the white tile sprawled prone, helpless beneath him as he pounded into her. Her hands reached out to the floor, and her nails dug into the grout, holding on. When that tingling seized her, growing stronger with his every thrust, it became the most powerful sensation she had ever known. It was as if the discomfort she initially felt opened up another door, leading to absolute bliss. Her climax made her shake like a leaf in a violent wind, erasing all thought and reason. She erupted in hundreds of shooting bolts of electricity, and in the distance she could barely detect the sound of her impassioned scream.

It took a few moments for her senses to return, but she came out of it just as Hayden made one last dive into her, letting go and grunting into her back. Settling against her, he was panting into her skin, and as the seconds ticked by, Madison soon became aware of her chest and knees pressing into the cold floor.

"Now I know you trust me," he breathed in her ear.

"I never knew it could be like that. It was uncomfortable at first, but then it became…I can't describe it."

He climbed off her back and pulled her into his arms. "I know many different ways to please you."

She rolled over to him. "Where did you learn about this stuff?"

"Mostly from the women I've known. They taught me how to please them, and some things I picked up along the way." He brushed a few strands of dark brown hair away from her face.

"How come you didn't do that before?"

"Some women don't like it, and I had to know if you were receptive. If I would have tried this before, I would have probably scared you away."

"What makes you think I'm not scared away now?"

Letting out a long sigh, he looked down her body. "Because you're still here, and you still want more."

She hated to admit it, but he was right. Instead of giving her an impetus to run away, his sexual appetites only made her feel closer to him.

"You need to get in a hot shower," he advised, patting her thigh. "I can't have my favorite architect catching cold on my bathroom floor. After you've dressed, I'll make us something to eat, and I'll walk you over to the Martins' house."

"I forgot about them." She sat up, and all the tension their lovemaking had appeased instantly returned. "Are you sure about this, Hayden?"

"You mean Mr. Parr, don't you?" He stood from the floor and helped her up. "You'll be fine, baby." He gazed down at the bruised circles about her left wrist. "Make sure you put something over those bruises before you go to the Martins' place." He rolled his eyes. "The last thing I need is them wondering about you."

"Even I'm beginning to wonder about me," she admitted, stepping toward the shower stall.

"Why? Because of what we just did?"

"No," she opened the shower door and turned back to him, "because I want to do it all over again."

***

The Martins' ho-hum, natural stone house loomed before Madison like a gallows as she crossed the street, trudging behind Hayden. In the daylight, the house appeared less spectacular against the backdrop of the other million dollar mansions surrounding it. Following a path that was lined with green juniper bushes, they came to a sparse garden of pink azaleas and manicured white crape myrtle trees set before the short cement steps that led to the simple white-painted front door.

"I don't know if I can do this, Hayden."

He handed her the rolled up design. "It's part of your job, Madison. Smile, agree to whatever they want, then bring back their suggestions to the office and we'll see what we can do. Just get them to show you their property. I want you to get started on some plans for me."

Glancing over at his pressed beige suit, she almost found it a little humorous that only an hour before he had been naked with her on his bathroom floor doing things that would have terrified his neighbors and most certainly the Martins. As she took in the other houses around them, she reasoned perhaps that was what went on in every home, making the façade presented to the world the actual fantasy, and the passion pursued behind closed doors the reality. Amazing what a person could hide behind a smile.

At the entrance to the Martins' home, she peered back at his cold, contemporary dwelling across the street. Picturing a window where she was standing, her mind began to fill with ideas for different architectural designs for Hayden.

"Well, hello," Stevie Martin chirped after opening her front door. "So glad you could make it."

Her soft blonde hair hung about her shoulders and the casual, blue slacks and fitted white top she wore accentuated her very slender figure. Madison envied the woman's perfectly made up face, and wished she had taken more time to slap on a little more than lipstick and mascara.

"Come in." Stevie gave a welcoming smile, waving them inside.

"Thanks, Stevie." Hayden kissed her cheek. "Unfortunately, I have to run to the office, but I'm leaving Madison to go over the changes Pat and I discussed." He pulled Madison to his side.

"Oh, so sorry you can't stay, Hayden." Stevie's deep blue eyes turned to Madison. "It seems Pat and I will have a lot to discuss with Madison."

Madison nervously clutched the roll of paper in her hand. "I look forward to hearing your suggestions, Mrs. Martin."

"Stevie, dear. No need to call me anything but Stevie."

Hayden backed out the door. "Well, I will leave you to it, Madison." His voice was abrupt and businesslike. "Come and see me with the changes when you get back to the office."

Madison careened her head around to him. "Yes, Mr. Parr."

She noticed how he hesitated, covered his hand over his smirk, and then turned away.

"So, Madison, can I get you any coffee?" Stevie inquired while closing the front door.

Madison faced her hostess. It was then she took in the small entryway of the home. Rising up behind the short taupe-tiled foyer was a second floor balcony with black iron railings and a row of long windows behind it. The effect was dated and alluded to the homes late seventies contemporary design. Hanging before the railing was a teardrop-shaped, cascading chandelier.

"Ah, no coffee, thank you." Madison's eyes returned to Stevie. "I had a big breakfast." She briefly pictured the pile of frozen waffles with honey Hayden had served her earlier.

"All right." Stevie waved to an opening to the side of the entryway. "Why don't we go in the den and go over those changes."

Walking down a dimly lit, almost claustrophobic, hallway with framed family pictures on the darkly paneled walls, Madison began to understand why Hayden was so dead set against keeping the house when he took over the property. *My God, if this is the entrance....*

At the end of the hallway, the space opened into a large family room with a stone fireplace that rose all the way up to the top of the eighteen foot ceiling. However, that was about all Madison found redeeming. The white shag carpet, dull paneling, and row of patio doors to the left were better suited for an episode of the "Brady Bunch" rather than a modern Highland Park home.

"You can see why we want to build something new," Stevie said beside her. "It's very dated, and we moved in expecting to renovate it. But...," she threw her hands up, "one thing led to another, and now we just want to start over."

Madison took in the all glass bar in the corner of the room. "It's not bad," she admitted. "But it does need a good bit of updating."

"You should see the kitchen." Stevie grimaced, shaking her head. "The place belonged to an older widow with grown children. She apparently liked living in the seventies, because God knows she never left it."

"I understand," Madison remarked. "I have an aunt like that. Everything in her house has stayed exactly the same since I was a little girl."

"Where is your family, Madison?"

"Arlington." She took a step further into the room, and felt the lumpy shag carpet beneath her shoes.

"I'm originally from Missouri," Stevie volunteered. "Pat is from here. He has tons of family coming in and out, plus his three boys visit frequently." Her blue eyes looked Madison's figure over with interest. "In fact, he has a son, Randall. He's about your age. He's finishing up his masters in engineering at UT Austin. You two should meet."

Dread coursed through Madison's body. *That's the last thing I need.* Scrambling for a polite reply, she got out, "Ah, thank you, Stevie, but I'm kind of seeing someone right now."

The rude sneer that settled over the woman's delicate features bugged Madison. "Yes, I could not help but notice your car was parked over at Hayden's all night. Is there something going on between you two?" Her hand went up. "Not that it's any of my business, dear, of course. It's just that he was so happy with Ellen, and I think they both still want to work things out. I would hate to see you get hurt when that eventuality happens."

That cold steel rod of disbelief pierced the pit of Madison's stomach when she realized who had called Hayden's ex. She had heard about busybody neighbors—she had been dealing with Mrs. Leder for over a year now—but this was something she had never expected. A flurry of expletives came to mind, but Madison maintained her composure and came up with a more palatable solution to her predicament.

"Mr. Parr and I were working most of the evening on your design." She held up the roll of paper in her hand. "By the time we finished up, it was very late and he was worried about me making the long drive home only to have to return in the morning for our meeting. So, he kindly offered me his guest room." She smiled sweetly, gritting her teeth while crushing the paper. "I can assure you that there is nothing between me and my boss, Stevie. That would be foolish."

The taunting grin on the woman's pale face showed every one of her shiny capped white fangs. "That's so nice to hear. I was so worried for you because you seemed like such a nice girl. I know Hayden is a very attractive man, especially to a young woman like you, but he is beyond you, my dear. Ellen is who he really needs," Stevie went on. "Sophisticated, socially-connected, and she is an absolute angel of a woman." Stevie headed toward an arched opening on the other side of the bar. "She even does a great deal of volunteer work at the local homeless shelter, did Hayden mention that?"

Madison dutifully followed behind her client. "No, he never mentioned it." She swore she was going to give Hayden an earful when she saw him later that morning.

Behind the archway was an expansive kitchen with yellow linoleum floors, old yellow appliances, and green painted cabinets. Madison gawked at the décor and felt suddenly gladdened the catty woman had to cook in such a hideous kitchen. Yes, there was karma after all.

"I know." Stevie pouted her collagen-plumped lips. "It's hideous." She waved her hands about the kitchen. "But it grows on you."

Kind of like a tumor, Madison silently returned.

"There's our little design woman," Pat Martin called as he entered the kitchen from a patio door. "Stevie been showing you our retro home, eh?" he joked with a snicker.

Casually attired in a red polo shirt and jeans, the affable man with the agreeable smile and friendly brown eyes instantly made Madison feel comfortable. Some people just had that ability to fill a room with their warmth, chasing away all the negativity that lingered in the air.

"Good morning, Mr. Martin." Madison's smile widened with genuine emotion. "Yes, there's a lot of potential here," she lied.

"More like potential to end up being a money pit," he came back. "No, we need a fresh start. A new home with a new energy." Pat came up to his wife's side and clasped his arm about her tiny waist. "Took me two other tries to get it right with my Stevie. She's the salt of the earth. Kind, considerate, and would never hurt a fly." He kissed his wife's cheek and the innocent sounding giggle Stevie gave him made Madison's stomach turn. "No, she needs something wonderful, natural, and just like her."

Images of a whorehouse decorated in black and red briefly danced across Madison's mind. "Then we will have to build it for her," she proclaimed.

Going to a round breakfast table set up in the corner of the room by the patio doors, Madison began to unfurl the rolled up plans in her hand. Trying to smooth out the creases where she had crushed them, she waited patiently as her clients came up to the table, looking wide-eyed.

"This is what Mr. Parr and I have come up with." She motioned to the plans. "We've had to cut back a bit on the size of the atrium to add stability to the foundation, raised the height of the second floor to make sure the views from the second story are unencumbered by the first, and lessened the slope on your roof angles just a bit. Now this will increase the need for steel beams in the central portion of the atrium entrance, as well as along the central portion of the main walls on the first floor."

Pat eyed the drawings on the table. "Will that increase the cost?"

"A modest increase," Madison conceded, "but it will add stability to the structure."

"I wanted to open up the kitchen," Stevie joined in, pointing to the kitchen off to the right of the atrium on the plans. "I'd hoped to have it to be a part of the atrium, not have a wall dividing it."

"That's a bearing wall," Madison informed her. "To get rid of that wall, I will have to find another way to distribute the weight of the top floor."

Stevie appeared unimpressed. "Does that matter? It's what I want."

Pat kissed his wife's pale cheek once more. "If my Stevie wants it, then it must be done."

Madison's smile was getting harder and harder to maintain, but instead of driving home her point, she simply pulled a pencil from her purse and made a few notes on the plans.

"Oh, and I want a big fish pond inside of the entrance. Not one of those puny things," Stevie insisted. "A great big one. Fifteen feet wide with koi in it."

"Water is very heavy," Madison warned. "It will add a lot of weight to the lower floor."

Pat waved off her concern. "You'll figure it out." His hand once more went about his wife's slim waist. "Got to keep my Stevie happy."

Madison made some more notes on the plans, inwardly cursing Hayden as she realized why he had left her alone with the Martins. This was going to be a long morning.

***

After an hour of suggestions, a ton of notes on her plans, and the beginnings of a headache, Madison had all she needed from the Martins to design the house from hell. She was rolling up her plans as Stevie was puttering around in the kitchen, when she caught a glimpse of the property beyond the patio doors. Pausing, Madison took in the rolling woods, sloping plotline, and shining lake behind the home.

"Beautiful, isn't it?" Pat Martin spoke up beside her. "That's the real reason we bought the place. The land."

Madison walked over to the patio doors. "You don't see anything like that in Dallas these days."

Pat pushed the glass doors aside. "Come outside and get a better view."

She followed him out to a wooden deck and enjoyed the pine-scented air drifting in off the lake. The tops of the pine and oak trees descending down to the lake were visible from the deck. The sloping ground was covered with deep green brush and winding trails that could be seen beneath the canopy of trees.

"I know Hayden is real hot to get his hands on this land," Pat expressed, "and I can't blame him. I'll miss the hell out of this view."

"The new property you have is just as beautiful," Madison pointed out. "With the home we will design, you will have an even better view."

Pat's rumbling laughter encircled the open deck. "You're a salesman just like Hayden. He told me the same thing." His round, pasty face grew a little somber. "You should know I'm having second thoughts about selling this place and building on the other site."

"Mr. Parr mentioned it." Madison waited to see his reaction.

"I told Hayden if I didn't sell this place, I would sell him my Turtle Creek land." Pat Martin's friendly face turned to her. "Then you could build that great house you designed for us for him instead."

"I'm sure Mr. Parr would come up with his own design; a better design than mine."

"You're good," Pat Martin laughed. "Harry doesn't know what he has in you...or does he?" His brown eyes glided over her figure. "Forgive my bluntness, Madison, but Harry has been like a second son to me ever since he and my oldest boy, Josh, met in grade school. I want only the best for him, and I couldn't help but notice how he looked at you during the party."

Folding her arms over her chest, Madison tempered her irritation. "And you think he needs to get back together with his ex-wife, too, is that it?"

"No." Pat shook his head. "Ellen Carpenter was a grade A bitch. My wife may love her, but I never did. I'm just saying don't believe everything Stevie says."

Madison's eyes lingered on the land before her. "I appreciate the advice, Mr. Martin, but Mr. Parr is my employer, nothing more."

"I understand, Madison." She was about to turn to go when he added, "My second wife, Marg, was my secretary at the engineering firm I started. When my first wife moved out, Marg was there for me. We became friends, and then fell in love. I loved her every day until she died of cancer eight years ago."

Madison glanced back at him. "I'm sorry, I didn't know."

"Real love isn't curtailed by boundaries… it breaks them." He took a step closer to her. "Tell Harry to send over the new plans. I'll take a look at them, and give him my final decision."

"Yes, Mr. Martin."

Stepping back through the glass patio door, Madison had an odd sense of relief. The doubts that had been nagging at her about her relationship with Hayden were stilled by Mr. Martin's encouraging words. Maybe it could grow into something more, maybe not, but at least she knew he was worth the chance. Perhaps she could find with him what she had yet to find with any man; love. Only time would tell if they were meant for that. Time could be a friend or an enemy to any relationship, but love was the one constant that held time at bay. Love was timeless, and always worth fighting for.

Chapter 14

By the time Madison arrived at the offices of Parr and Associates, all hell had broken loose. People were scurrying about the halls on the thirty-third floor, and all the faces of her co-workers appeared troubled. She tried to wave down a few people she saw bustling about as she made her way to her office, but everyone appeared too busy to stop and talk.

"Madison," Garrett Hughes called as he approached her just as she was reaching her office door.

"Good morning, Garrett."

Garett came alongside her and took her elbow. Glancing about the hall, he whispered, "We need to talk."

Madison's eyes searched his face for some hint of what was going on. "Is something wrong?"

He opened her office door. "Let's talk inside."

Once they were inside of her office, Garrett shut her door. Madison gazed about for Adam and noticed that his chair was empty and his familiar blue backpack was nowhere to be seen.

"Isn't Adam in yet?" she asked, stepping over to her desk.

"That's what we need to talk about," Garrett explained as he followed her across the room.

Dropping her purse and plans on her desk, she glanced back at him. His deep brown eyes were taking in her every move, as his wide mouth and sharp features accentuated the depth of his stare. For a moment she felt as if he were analyzing her, stripping her down and studying every detail. Her eyes glided over his trim body beneath the cut of his tailored blue suit, and a flush of heat rose to her cheeks.

"So what's up, Garrett?"

"Harry fired your office mate this morning." Garrett moved closer to her, lowering his voice. "He sent me to find you and warn you."

Madison was shocked. She knew Hayden disliked Adam, but she had never imagined that he would fire the "sniveling weasel."

"There's something else you need to know," Garrett confided. "I caught Adam spreading rumors about you and Harry. He was telling several of the office staff in the conference room yesterday that you two were sleeping together. I told Harry about it this morning, and soon after he let Adam go."

Madison stood frozen to her spot by her chair. What could she say, especially to the head architect of the company?

"Not to worry." He clasped his hands behind his back, appearing indifferent. "No one believes any of it, but now my job has suddenly gotten a lot harder because of losing Adam. His absence has put a big kink in my plans."

Madison's shoulders relaxed and she let out a long breath. "What plans?"

He nodded and moved over to the window. "Harry wants to expand out of the Dallas area. He was thinking of New Orleans, especially with the rebuilding going on since Katrina. I was sending Adam back to his hometown to get us started, and also because Harry desperately wanted him out of this office." Garrett turned away from the window. "Now I will have to go instead, leaving the company short-handed and putting a lot more work on Harry's shoulders. Without a chief architect, he will have to directly supervise all of our design projects, in addition to managing the company."

A wave of guilt crushed Madison. She had been the reason Hayden had wanted to get Adam away from the office, and because of her, not only was Adam out of a job, but the entire office had been thrust into turmoil.

"Garrett, I'm sorry. I feel like this is my fault."

"No, it's Adam's fault. The little shit was always poking his nose where it didn't belong. I knew Harry disliked him, so I thought sending him back to New Orleans was a good idea."

Madison inched closer to the window. "But now you're going to be uprooted and forced to leave Dallas."

"Forced?" He raised his eyebrows. "Not at all. I'm looking forward to leaving. I've grown bored with Dallas, and New Orleans may be a bit more appealing for me."

Madison crinkled her brow. "Appealing? How so?"

"Never mind about me." Garret waved off her question. "It's Harry I'm worried about. Without me around, he'll have a lot more to do and he'll need help. I just need to know someone will be keeping an eye on him while I'm gone. Harry tends to take on too much, and needs to be reminded every now and then that he's human and not some kind of superhero."

"Why are you telling me this?"

He smiled, highlighting the curve of his wide jaw. "Because he'll listen to you."

Madison could tell by the gleam in the man's dark eyes that he knew about her and Hayden. She also wondered what else he knew. With Garrett Hughes, there was probably more going on behind his cool exterior than he let on. In many ways, he reminded her of Hayden. Both men were calculating, elusive, and controlling.

"So the official reason I'm here is to inform you of Adam's demise," Garret broke in, interrupting her thoughts. "Unofficially, I'm asking you to keep an eye on Harry."

"I'll try, Garrett. I promise."

"It's a shame we won't have time to get to know each other better before I leave for New Orleans. I would have liked to have seen some of your designs. You really are a talented architect, Madison."

"When do you leave?"

"In a few days. I'll stop in before I go."

She offered him a friendly smile, feeling a little sad to lose the one friend she had made in the office. "I'd like that."

He turned abruptly and headed for her office door. "We'll talk again."

After he strode out of the room, Madison returned to her desk and sank into her chair. The long night with Hayden and the meeting with the Martins had not only left her exhausted, but also wondering where she was going to find the strength to get through the rest of her day. Imagining a tall mug of black coffee, she was about to go in search of the needed caffeine fix when the ringing of her office phone startled her. Stretching across the corner table, she picked up the phone.

"This is Madison B—"

"Did Garrett talk to you?" Hayden's voice on the other end of the line abruptly cut her off.

"Why didn't you tell me you were going to fire Adam?"

"Because I didn't know until I came in this morning and found the little son of a bitch snooping through your desk."

Madison paused and looked to her desk. "What? When was this?"

"After I dropped you at the Martins, I came to talk to him about where we stood with New Orleans, and I found him going through the drawers of your desk." Hayden let go a long sigh into the phone. "Was there anything in your desk that could cause us problems?"

Madison's stomach curled tighter. "No, of course not. I just keep work-related supplies in my desk, nothing personal."

He sighed again, louder than before, and she could hear his frustration. "Come to my office and bring the changes the Martins made. Then we can talk."

The sound of his voice was no longer soothing and comforting as it had been the night before. The aggravation was apparent, and she feared seeing a side of Hayden Parr that she didn't want to know.

"All right," she finally said, gripping the receiver in her hand. "I'll be right down."

Grabbing her plans, she headed to her office door and went to the thirty-second floor. As Madison approached Hayden's office, she caught Emma darting out his double doors.

"Better be ready," Emma warned. "He's super grumpy this morning."

Madison nodded, holding up the plans in her hand. "Thanks for the heads up."

Easing inside the office, Madison waited while Emma shut the doors behind her before she turned to Hayden. After she was sure they were alone, she pivoted around and found him standing before his wide office window with his back to her. She edged closer to his desk, watching as he arched his back beneath his beige suit jacket and rubbed his hand behind his neck.

"You look tense."

He showed her his profile. "To say the least." He closed his eyes for a moment and then turned to her. "I'm sorry I snapped at you on the phone."

She glanced down at the rolled up plans in her hand. "You didn't snap at me. You were just a little abrupt."

"I'm sorry I was abrupt." He went around his desk to her side, and briefly rested his hand against her cheek. "How did it go at the Martins?" He stood back from her.

"Fine," she answered, but then frowned. "You should know Stevie Martin was the one who notified your ex about me staying over at your place. She saw my car parked there all night and got suspicious."

His brow furrowed, accentuating his angry scowl. "What did you tell her?"

"Only that we were working on their design plans until very late and you offered me a guest room since I had an early meeting with them."

"Quick thinking. I like that." He nodded with approval. "You can park in my garage from now on and not on the street. That should keep Ellen off my back." His gray eyes grew colder. "Did Stevie say anything else?"

"She, ah, also warned me to stay away from you. She seems to believe you and Ellen are meant to be together. Apparently, she and your ex are pretty tight."

"Tight? Hardly. Stevie Martin likes to think she's part of the in-crowd, and used to kiss Ellen's ass whenever she could." He took the plans from her. "Ellen was very much into the social scene; who to know, where to go and be seen. All that bullshit used to drive me crazy." He tossed the plans on his desk.

Madison motioned to the plans. "I thought you wanted—"

"Later. Right now I want something else from you." He came around behind her and pushed her into his large desk.

"Hayden, what about…?" She nodded to the office door.

"No one will come in." He stood behind her, running his hands up the sides of her black pants. "I told Emma I didn't want to be disturbed while I was with you."

"I thought we had to be discreet." Her hands rested on top of his as they fondled her breasts.

"I am being discreet, the doors are closed." He ran his lips along her earlobe. "But I just need to touch you right now."

She closed her eyes and tilted her head against his chest. "God, I love your hands."

"What else do you love?" he whispered into her ear.

"About you? Let me see." She backed her hips into him. "I love the way you make me feel…calm and relaxed."

"Funny, you do the same for me." His hands drifted along her shoulders, kneading into the muscles of her neck and upper back. "What else?"

"What else do I love about—?"

"Mr. Parr," Emma's voice over the phone speaker made Madison jump. "It's your attorney on three. He said it's important."

"Shit." Hayden let Madison go and went around his desk to his phone. Punching down the intercom button, he barked, "Tell Marc to hold on." He pointed to the chair in front of his desk for Madison to take a seat.

She motioned to the doors. "I should go."

"Sit!" he snapped, and again pointed to the chair.

She gave him a perturbed smirk and had a seat.

When Hayden took the call from his attorney, she watched him, intrigued by how his eyes drew together and the scowl on his lips deepened.

"What's the word, Marc? Did you talk to Ellen's attorney?"

Madison waited as Hayden sat in the black leather chair behind his desk. His eyes stayed on her as he listened intently to his attorney on the other end of the line.

"You already know my answer to that," Hayden gnarled. "No more discussion on the settlement. She's getting enough. Ellen can take the offer on the table and walk away, or let her attorney know I'll fight her for the rest. I want this over with her, Marc. I need to move on with my life, and I can't have Ellen threatening me every time she thinks I'm seeing another woman."

Madison wasn't sure how to react to his words. Instead of confronting his stern gaze, she kept her eyes on her folded hands in her lap, waiting for him to speak again.

"Since you're my attorney, then no, I'm not seeing anyone." He paused and nodded his head, listening intently. "Yes, there have been a few women since the divorce. I'm not celibate, Marc."

That made Madison's eyes fly to him. *How many women have there been?*

"No, I don't know why she thinks that. The woman staying with me last night was an employee. We were working together on a design until very late. We had an early morning meeting with some clients, so I offered her a guest room as a matter of convenience." He paused for a moment. "No, she's no one that Ellen is acquainted with." His scowl retreated and he smiled. "Yes, I remember what you told me about being discreet. I never flaunt my arrangements, Marc. You know what a private man I am."

Madison noted his grin and considered his comment. *Arrangements?* Questions like raging flood waters began to eat away at her certainty. Did he treat all of his women the same way? Was this just a game for him? Perhaps some stupid fraternity challenge he shared only with Garrett?

"Let Ellen know no more threats, or I'll get nasty." He nodded as he listened to his attorney, but his eyes never left her. "Keep me posted on what she plans next. Thanks, Marc."

After he hung up the phone, Madison held her breath, wanting him to speak first. Unable to take the silence any longer, she stood from her chair and reached for the plans on his desk. Hayden sat back in his black leather chair, carefully watching her.

"I wanted you to hear that conversation because you need to know what we're dealing with when it comes to my ex. You're important to me and I want you to know everything that's going on in my life."

She gave him a reassuring smile. "Important? Funny, I got the impression that I was one of those 'few women since the divorce' keeping you from being celibate."

He stood from his chair as she unrolled the plans over the top of his desk. "I was being discreet."

She kept her focus on the plans. "Yes, since you're such a private man."

He came around to the front of the desk. "You're angry. Why?"

"Did you tell Garrett about us?"

"No," he rubbed his hand over his chin, "but he knows how I am with women."

"'How you are with women'?" That set her off. "How many women have you been with since your divorce?"

"I already told you about—"

"How many, total?" she cut in.

He sat back on the edge of his desk, folding his arms over his chest. For several seconds he observed her, adding to Madison's unease. Sometimes his eyes could be so invasive.

"Including you, eight," he eventually disclosed in his deep voice. "However, none were serious, just flings."

"Am I a 'fling' or one of your 'arrangements'?"

He scratched his head, appearing uncomfortable with the question. "Madison, you have to understand that the only woman I've had a lasting relationship with was Ellen."

"And look how that ended," she quipped, returning her eyes to the plans.

His mouth fell slightly open and his eyes glowered at her. "Where is this coming from? I thought you understood about me...about how I am."

She gazed up at him, biting her lip to curb her anger. "I did, but maybe I'm changing my mind."

"What brought this on? Up until this morning you were fine with the way things are between us," he declared, raising his voice.

"I was, and then I heard you tell your attorney that I was just an employee. It made me think maybe you don't want to admit we're together."

"You're being ridiculous. You know why I'm doing that," he coolly replied. "We have to be careful."

"Careful? If that's the case, then perhaps we should be staying at my place, away from the prying eyes of your neighbors."

"Your place is too small, and then there is Mrs. Leder to contend with."

"Is it always going to be this way between us? Sneaking around, keeping everything we do a secret?"

His eyes transformed into two icy orbs. "You agreed to this, and you'd better start coming to terms with that. Stop expecting me to shout your name from the rooftops like some lovesick poet."

"I never asked for that, Hayden. I simply want some respect...as your lover."

"Respect? And would telling everyone we're sleeping together give you the respect you think you deserve?" He uttered a malicious chuckle. "I seriously doubt that."

She had a point, but obviously was doing a crummy job of getting it across. "That's not what I meant. I guess I would have liked a little acknowledgement. I'm not asking for any declaration of emotion, but maybe...." Befuddled, she sagged against his desk, tossing her hand in the air. "Maybe it's all happening too fast."

A few tense moments passed between them, and then Hayden inched closer to her. Placing his hands behind his back, he edged his face in front of her. "I'm sorry. I shouldn't have snapped at you like that. I think I know what you're trying to say, Madison, but you have to understand that, before I met my ex, I'd never been emotionally involved with any woman. I never liked complicated relationships, never wanted one. I just seduced a woman I wanted, and when the desire died, I moved on. In between dating, I played around…a lot, but having intense feelings for someone…that had never been me."

She pondered his confession, not quite sure of how to take it. "And I guess Ellen changed all of that for you, didn't she?"

"No, she didn't change anything." His voice was touched with bitterness. "I met someone before her who made me realize that I wanted more with a woman. Ellen was just a poor substitute for the one I did want."

Madison didn't know what was worse: suspecting he still had feelings for his ex-wife, or knowing there was another woman who had forever won his heart. Suddenly, everything made sense.

"I think I understand, Hayden." She went back to the plans.

"No, I don't think you do." His arms went about her waist. "Maybe when this mess is over with Ellen, we could talk about making some changes."

She cocked an eyebrow to him. "What kind of changes?"

"Make this something less discreet." His hand settled on her backside. "I could take you to that cozy pizza place I like, or maybe attend a party…things like that."

Inwardly Madison rejoiced, but calmly told Hayden, "That sounds promising."

"Just give me some time. Okay?" He touched his forehead to hers. "Change is difficult for me, but I would like to change for you."

Giddy with the hope, she smiled. "Take all the time you need, Mr. Parr."

"You know how much I like it when you call me Mr. Parr."

Her hand crept inside his jacket and caressed his soft brown shirt. "I know."

Hayden quickly spun her out of his arms and spanked her butt. "Any more of that, I'll have to throw you over that desk and…."

Hayden's eyes roamed over her figure. "There's always the desk at my house. We could test it tonight. I have a dinner meeting with clients, but you could go over to my place after work, since you now have my code, and wait for me."

"Maybe I need to go home and pay bills or something."

"I'd prefer you waiting for me at my place, naked, draped over my desk, and holding those handcuffs Mrs. Leder gave you. What do you think?"

Madison shifted her focus to the plans on his desk. "If that is what you desire, then I'm all yours, Mr. Parr."

***

It was after lunch when Madison finished going over the changes to the Martin home with Hayden. She was rolling up the plans as he reached for his jacket hanging behind his desk chair.

"I've got to get to a meeting, but I'll see you tonight." He slipped on his jacket. "I should be there about eight. Don't forget to pull around back and park in the garage."

Madison was about to reply to his comment when the doors to his office flew open.

Standing in the doorway, a beautiful brunette in a blue silk Alexander McQueen dress and black stiletto heels was glaring at Hayden.

"Hello, asshole!"

"God damn it, Ellen, you can't come barging in like that," Hayden loudly exclaimed.

Ellen. The name immediately registered with Madison. *So this is his ex?*

Madison immediately recognized her own slight resemblance to the slender and sensual woman with the perfectly made-up face, stunning sharp features, and piercing green eyes. As Ellen stormed in the doors, Madison lingered over the heavy amount of gold and diamond jewelry covering her neck, fingers, and wrists. The assertive sway of her hips and her blatant disregard made it appear as if she were the one in charge at Parr and Associates. Even the overpowering smell of her perfume saturating the office, reminded Madison of someone who had no concern for the welfare of others.

From her expensive designer clothes to her stiletto heels, the ex-Mrs. Parr was the epitome of a wealthy, beautiful, and very spoiled trophy wife.

"Who's that? Another little bimbo?" Ellen snarled, nodding to Madison.

Hayden's face was a deep shade of crimson. "Madison, this is my ex-wife, Ellen Carpenter."

"Still Parr, darling. I don't plan on ever going back to Carpenter." Ellen tossed her Louis Vuitton handbag on his desk, scattering several papers about. "You screwing this one, too? Does she know what twisted shit you're into?"

"Stop it, Ellen." Hayden came alongside of Madison and motioned to the door. "Get started on those changes and bring me the new plans when you're done."

Madison avoided looking over at his ex-wife. "Yes, Mr. Parr."

"She's just your type, Hayden. You always had a thing for green-eyed brunettes." Ellen moved in front of Madison, blocking her way. "Sure you aren't his newest bimbo…Madison, was it?"

"Ellen, don't start intimidating my staff!" His loud voice made Madison jump. She had never heard him speak like that to anyone.

"Staff?" Ellen moved out of the way just as Madison rushed for the office doors. "Let's talk about your staff, you son of a bitch."

"Jesus, Ellen," Hayden yelled, following Madison to the doors.

"Where in the hell do you get off firing Adam like that, you bastard?"

Madison wasn't even through the doorway when Hayden slammed the doors closed behind her. The loud thud that resounded about the hallway made Madison flinch.

"Oh shit, are you okay?" Emma came alongside Madison. "I couldn't stop her. She just pushed her way in."

"I'm fine," Madison assured her.

"That woman is such a bitch," Emma blew out between her pink lips just as more shouting erupted from Hayden's office. "Every time she comes here she sets him off." Emma waved at the plans in Madison's hand. "Take a bit of advice—"

Hayden's use of a few choice expletives came through his closed office doors, interrupting Emma.

Cringing, the buxom secretary turned back to Madison. "Stay in your office. Trust me, after a few rounds with his ex, he's looking for the first person to rip apart."

"Thanks, Emma," Madison mumbled, and started toward the elevators.

Pressing the call button, Madison stewed over the encounter. Ellen was nothing like what she had expected, and the physical similarities between the two women had been disturbing. It seemed Hayden had a preference for women who looked a certain way, making Madison wonder if he was genuinely interested in her for who she was, or for how she appeared.

Chapter 15

For the rest of the day, Madison followed Emma's advice and stayed in her office, working on her design. Well, not so much working, but thinking. Meeting Ellen had bothered her more than she cared to admit, and as she readied herself to go home, she reconsidered her rendezvous with Hayden. After his heated confrontation with his ex, and an evening with clients, she considered if the man might need to be alone. Taking the elevators to the first floor lobby of the Renaissance Tower, Madison decided that it would be best if she went straight to her apartment instead of heading to Hayden's. Perhaps a little time apart would be good for them.

During the long drive in traffic, she evaluated her time with Hayden. The man was intense, sexy, a fantastic lover, and made her feel protected, but was that it? What about emotion? Would what they had started lead to anything more permanent? As she dodged in and out of cars on the I-35, Madison contemplated if giving her his house code was more out of convenience than caring.

Her grip tightened on the steering wheel of her Rogue. "No. He does care about me. He wants to change for me."

But you don't know that. Not for sure, a devilish voice in her head countered.

That was the crux of what had been bothering her ever since she had laid eyes on his ex-wife. Did he really care about her, or was she just someone who suited his tastes for the time being? Sure, he had made her feel special, but doubts about his intentions lingered. As she headed down the off ramp, Madison carefully weighed his every word since the moment they had first laid eyes on each other in the elevator. When her blue apartment building rose on the horizon, she was no closer to an answer about her relationship with Hayden. If anything, she was more confused than ever.

On returning to her empty apartment and dropping the overnight bag on the floor, she immediately felt restless. Preoccupying her mind with bills, unpacking her overnight bag, and sorting through the mail filled in some time, but as the sun disappeared from her living room window, Madison found her edginess increasing. She kept checking her cell phone and waiting to hear from Hayden, wondering what he would say when he returned to his home and found that she was not there.

It was almost seven when she decided to change into her shorts and a T-shirt. "I can't sit around here anymore," she muttered, tying the laces on her running shoes. "I've got to get my mind off him."

Starting her slow, warm-up jog along the darkened streets, she tried to think of anything but Hayden. After repeated attempts to occupy herself with current affairs or the latest Hollywood gossip, her thoughts meandered back to her boss. Kicking her run into high gear, she gathered it was hopeless; the man was getting to her. Then, as pictures of him naked next to her in the shower earlier that morning popped into her head, Madison began to regret not going to his house. Halfway through her run, she turned for home. Maybe she could make it to his place before him, so he would never know of her reservations.

Once inside the glass doors of her building, she opted to skip the elevator and ran up the stairs to the fifth floor, invigorated by her desire. When she pushed her apartment door open, she was stunned by an unexpected visitor. Hayden was standing in the middle of her living room with his back to her, taking in the view from her window.

"What are you doing here?" she questioned, shutting her door. "How did you get in?"

He had left his beige suit jacket on her sofa and rolled up the sleeves of his light blue shirt. "Your landlady heard me knocking on your door," he replied, never turning from the window.

"Mrs. Leder let you in?"

He faced her, the fatigue evident in his eyes. "After I thanked her for the handcuffs, she let me in with her key. She said you went for a run." He waved down her running shorts and the slightly damp Dallas Cowboys T-shirt she had on. "Is that what you were doing…running away from me again?"

Madison went to her kitchen, eager for something to drink. "Actually, I was thinking…and I didn't run away."

He followed her. "Thinking about me?"

"About us," she corrected.

In the kitchen, he took Madison's arm and pulled her to him. "Is that why you weren't at my house when I got home?"

"No. I thought perhaps you might want some time alone after your day." Madison tried to back away from him. "I need to change my clothes."

He held on to her, and the intensity of his gaze shattered whatever resistance she had left. His lips moved to within inches of hers. "Talk to me."

Madison's lower lip trembled. "Hayden, do you still love your wife?"

His stern gray eyes analyzed her features. "How can you possibly think I still have feelings for Ellen? You saw how we were today."

"I know, but she does look an awful lot like me. Your sister said something about it at the party, but I was taken aback when I saw her today. It makes me wonder if I'm just your type."

"What? What is my type?"

"You know…the kind of woman you like being with. Green-eyed brunettes, like your ex-wife mentioned."

His laughter bounced about the small kitchen. "Madison, if you only knew…." He let go of her and rested his hip against the white Formica countertop. "There's a reason why Ellen made that remark." He took a moment, collecting his thoughts. "After that first night with you, I had a friend in administration at the UT Arlington Architecture School search the database for female students named Mary. I was on the verge of hiring a private detective when the same friend I asked for help announced that he had found you." He paused and sucked in a guarded breath. "He told me he was setting me up on a blind date with the woman I had hoped would be you, but it wasn't. It was Ellen."

"Did you tell her about me?"

"After we began dating, yes, I told her about Mary. I think it's always bothered her that I wanted to find you."

"What made you stop looking for me?"

"I met Ellen. I thought she could help me forget about you." He rubbed his hand over his face. "For years I've wondered if you were all right, who you were with, if you had married. And then one day you walked into my elevator, and here we are."

Madison inched closer to him. "Do you know how many times I had to stop myself from going back to your place after that night? I often daydreamed about knocking on your door and having you sweep me into your arms."

He wrapped his arms about her. "Why didn't you come back to me?"

She delighted in the way the recessed lights above shadowed the contours of his rugged face. "Because I thought you were an asshole who wouldn't remember who I was."

"Maybe I'm still that asshole." He kissed her cheek. "When you weren't at my house, I got scared; scared that you had run out on me again. Driving here, I realized I had to change things between us now, and not after I settle things with Ellen. So let's start over. Do you still need a date for your roommate's wedding?"

"What about being discreet?"

"To hell with being discreet! I don't care who knows about us anymore."

Madison felt the thrill of victory in her bones. She was making headway with her cool and elusive Mr. Parr. "Then yes, I still need a date."

"Good. I'll be your date." His hands glided over her damp T-shirt. "Now that we have settled that... how long will it take you to pack a bag so we can head to my place?"

She curled into him, running her fingertips along his soft shirt. "Let me jump in the shower and then—"

"You can shower at my place." He let her go. "Hurry and pack. I have a strange feeling we need to get out of here before Mrs. Leder returns."

"Afraid she'll stop by bearing more handcuffs?" Madison teased, exiting the kitchen.

"No, she seemed particularly interested in my plans for you." He followed her as she turned down the short hallway that led to her bedroom. "She even threatened to hire someone to kick my ass if I hurt you."

Madison stopped at her open bedroom door. "She said that?"

Hayden came up to the door and rested his shoulder on the frame. "She said it didn't matter if I was your 'hottie boss,' I still had to treat you right." He peeked into her bedroom. "Still think of me as your 'hottie boss'?"

A blush rose about her cheeks, and she slowly nodded.

He pushed away from the door and placed his hands about her waist. "Do you have a desk?"

Madison shook her head. "Sorry. Charlie had one, but she's already moved it to her fiancé's place."

Hayden's eyes took a turn of her small bedroom. "That's too bad. I have this urge to bend you over a piece of large furniture and take you from behind." He kissed the tip of her nose. "Get your things and let's get out of here. I have something I want to try with you tonight."

Her gut tingled and a rush of heat erupted between her legs. "What do you have in mind?"

He shook his head and backed away from her. "Good little girls wait for their bosses to tell them what to do. Do you understand?"

"Yes, Mr. Parr," she whispered.

"Now hurry up."

Madison dashed for her closet, and when Hayden's hand connected with her butt, she yelped, but did not protest. Madison had a strange feeling she was going to like what Hayden had in mind for her…she was going to like it a lot.

Chapter 16

It was after nine when Hayden parked his Land Rover in the black gravel driveway beside his home. Madison glanced out the passenger window to the darkened street, and when her eyes settled on the Martins' house, she grimaced. The memory of her encounter with Stevie Martin still left a bitter taste in her mouth.

"What did you think of the property?" Hayden asked, switching off the ignition.

"The house was hideous. You're right, the property was stunning, but…."

He eased back in his seat, keeping his eyes on her. "But…?"

"I honestly liked their property in Turtle Creek better. I think it has more potential than that." She thumbed out the window toward the Martins' home.

"I agree, but I doubt Pat is going to sell it to me. He seems pretty set to build on it." He opened his car door.

Madison waited as he reached into the backseat and retrieved her overnight bag. "I want you to bring a few more things next time you come over. Pack a suitcase with clothes you can keep here. I don't want you to have to keep lugging an overnight bag every time you stay with me." Slinging her bag over his shoulder, he shut the door and walked around to her car door.

"I don't mind," she asserted when he opened her door for her.

"But I do. I want you to feel comfortable in my home."

"I am."

"We'll see about that." He snickered and turned away.

Madison followed him up the gravel path toward the front glass doors. Walking behind him, she followed the curve of his butt beneath his beige suit jacket. Images of fondling that butt with her hands were distracting her when he stopped before the glass doors and pointed to the keypad.

"Punch in the code," he ordered.

"What difference does it make if—?"

"Madison, just do it."

She put her hand on keypad. "What was the code again?"

"Close your eyes and think about it. I told you several times this morning. Remember?"

She closed her eyes, recalling their conversation earlier that morning about the code. In an instant, she heard his voice in her head, repeating the numbers.

Opening her eyes, she touched the keypad and typed in 75336.

The door popped open. "Very good."

"And the point of that was what?"

"To make you think. Most people look to someone else to fill in the gaps for them. I prefer for someone to fill in the blanks for themselves. I don't like dependent people. I want you to be assertive and confident."

"You don't think I'm assertive and confident, is that what you're telling me?"

"No." He pushed the door open for her. "You don't think you're confident or assertive, but I'm going to change that."

She stepped through the door and turned back to him. "How do you plan to do that?"

He followed her in, shut the door, and pointed to the keypad. "Lock us in."

Shaking her head at his persistence, she hurriedly punched in the code. After she was done, Hayden went to the stairs in the foyer and placed her bag on the steps. As he turned back to her, his eyes grew colder and his lips spread into a lecherous grin.

"I want you to take off your clothes." His deep voice resonated about the high foyer.

"Again? What is it with you and clothes?"

"Why are you arguing with me?" Hayden removed his jacket and set it on top of her bag. "This isn't about seeing you naked. It's about you expressing your inner desires with me." He had a seat on the lowest step. "So strip."

"Is this another lesson?"

He smiled. "If you like, yes."

Shaking her head, Madison yanked at the zipper on her jeans.

"Not like that. Dance for me."

"Dance? Hayden, why do you want me—?"

"Wasn't it your fantasy to strip for a man?" He leaned forward on the step. "Well, here's your chance." She opened her mouth, but he cut her off. "I don't want you to speak. Just dance."

Madison waved her hand in the air. "But there's no music."

Shaking his head, he sighed. "This must be your difficult side." He stood from the step. "Fine, I'll get you some music."

Hayden disappeared under the arch that led to the living room and kitchen. As she stood there waiting, Madison wondered why he was doing this. What was the point? Then, strains of Michael Bublé crooning the opening to "Feelin' Good" filled the foyer. She covered her mouth with her hand, hiding her happy smile. How many times had she danced to this thinking of him?

"There's your music." Hayden came back to the steps and took his seat.

His eager eyes made her feel slightly uneasy. "Hayden, I don't—"

He placed his fingers over his lips, demanding silence. "Close your eyes and listen to the music. Seduce me, Madison. Show me with your body how much you want me."

As Madison closed her eyes, the soulful sound of the horns and straining strings came together in a crescendo. Swaying her head in time with the beat, she let the music fill her mind. At first, her shoulders shifted from side to side, then her hips began to rock back and forth. Keeping her eyes closed, she moved her feet about the smooth hardwood floor. So many times she had pictured dancing with her Harry as she listened to their song, and here she was living out that fantasy.

Her hands went to the fly of her jeans. Her clothes felt heavy now, and were weighing down her movements; she needed to be free of them. Easing the thick denim down her hips, the cool rush of air against her naked legs added to the tingle building in her stomach. With a kick, she did away with her jeans, and her hands went to her long-sleeved T-shirt. Shaking her hips, she dropped the shirt to the floor and quickly unsnapped her bra.

The steady rhythm was taking over her senses. Madison felt sexy, empowered…and then she remembered Hayden. Opening her eyes, she saw him. With his elbows resting on his knees and his hands clasped together, he was focused intently on her. She stared at him, but instead of feeling nervous, the way his eyes were watching her hips set her on fire. She wanted him, to feel him naked with her, inside of her, taking every part of her. Madison inched forward, swinging her hips, and when she saw him hungrily wipe his hand over his mouth, she felt triumphant. He wasn't laughing at her; he was turned on, really turned on. Doing a small spin on her toes, Madison grinded her hips as her fingers hooked the waistband of her silky beige panties. His eyes burned with desire, and she had never felt more wanted by a man.

As she drew closer, Madison ached to show him how he made her feel. Arriving at the stairway, she lowered her panties to her ankles and then set her hand on his shoulder. Pushing him back on the steps, the finale of the song echoed about the foyer. Her fingers worked the buttons of his shirt until the fabric gave way, exposing his wide chest. She swayed as her fingernails raked down his ripped abs. Climbing the bottom step, she straddled his hips. Hayden sat back, watching her every move but never touching her. He waited as she lowered her hips onto his lap. Only when the song ended and she was nestled against him did he raise his hands. Pushing her brown hair away from her face, he let go a long, happy sigh.

"There she is, the confident woman I dreamed you could be." He kissed her lips. "Do you want me, Madison?"

"Yes, Hayden."

"Mr. Parr." His hand gripped her hair, pulling her head back. "Say I want you, Mr. Parr."

The gesture made the warmth between her legs balloon into an undeniable inferno. "I want you...Mr. Parr."

She tossed her arms about his neck, fiercely kissing him. Her hunger was insatiable, and her hands went to the zipper of his trousers, almost clawing at them. With Hayden covering her chest and neck with kisses, she pushed his pants below his hips. Hayden clutched her hips and spun her around in his arms, pinning her on all fours to the bottom step.

Madison gripped the edge of the step in front of her, fighting against his weight. He pushed her head down and she raised her hips higher, waiting for him. She heard the familiar sound of a foil package ripping open, and knew he was preparing to take her.

He spread her folds apart and rammed into her, propelling her forward. "Tell me you like this." He pulled out and slammed into her flesh.

"God, yes," she whimpered, her insides burning.

His hands gripped her hips as he shoved into her again. "You like it when I'm in charge, don't you, Madison?"

"Yes, Mr. Parr."

Her words excited him. Hayden began driving into her with all of his might again and again. Madison cried out as he forced her flesh apart, penetrating her to the deepest depths. She clawed the wooden step as he rutted behind her, rocking her forward and obliterating all thought.

"That's it," he moaned, pounding into her even harder than before. "You're gonna take every inch of me."

Her body became weak, and her mind spun out of control as she was besieged by his intense thrusting. It felt as if he were splitting her apart. When her orgasm gained momentum, sapping every ounce of her strength, his arms came around her, holding her in place. Her body tensed as his relentless assault brought her closer to climax. When the tension inside of her finally snapped, she arched her back, opened her mouth, and screamed.

Everything became lost behind a veil of fog as she collapsed on the step. She could hear Hayden grunting, feel him slamming into her, she even noted the tickle of the beads of sweat rolling down her forehead, but she could not move as that blissful ripple of satisfaction pervaded her muscles.

With one final long groan, he fell on top of her, panting into the back of her neck. Letting go of the edge of the step, Madison flexed her fingers, waiting for the stiffness to go away.

Throwing his arms about her, he pulled her to him. Curled up on her side and satiated beyond belief, Madison had never felt like this. Suddenly, she wanted him to take her in any way he desired. She loved the idea of handing her body over to him. What was happening to her?

He kissed the back of her neck. "Don't ever run away from me again."

"I'm not going anywhere, Hayden."

"Did your fantasy live up to your expectations?"

"It was much better than I imagined." A thought occurred to her and she tilted her head to the side. "What about you? Do you have any fantasies?"

He rolled back on the step. "We might have to work up to those."

Interested, she sat up. "Why? Are they weird or something?"

He stood from the step and removed the condom. "No, just different. There are things I want you to do to me. Ways I want you to tie me up and take control. But you're not ready for that yet." He tied a knot in the condom and dropped it to the step.

She waited as he zipped up his trousers. "Will you teach me…teach me to be the kind of experienced lover you fantasize about?"

Hayden cupped his hands about her face. "Is that what you want?"

"Yes. I want to please you, Hayden."

His smile melted her heart. "You already have, Madison."

***

The following Friday afternoon, Madison left work early to meet Charlie for her final dress fitting before the wedding. The Mockingbird Bridal Boutique was not far from their apartment, but by the time Madison fought the traffic from the city and parked her car outside of the upscale store, she knew she was going to get an earful from her friend for being late.

Rushing to the glass entrance, she peered inside, hoping to spot a familiar face. After she smoothed the wrinkles in her black skirt and white silk blouse, she pushed the door open and was greeted by the soft strains of a harp. Looking up, she spotted the small speaker by the door, and then her eyes traveled to the sweeping pleated gold drapes and crystal chandeliers strewn about the ceiling. Positioned about the gold carpet were headless, black mannequins donning an array of fitted and beaded white wedding gowns. The air was thick with rose air-freshener, and when Madison turned to her right, racks of white wedding dresses housed in thick clear plastic bags could be seen lining each of the three walls in the long showroom. In the distance, she thought she heard the sound of women's laughter, but she could not see a doorway or entrance to the rear of the shop.

"Are you here for the Tonti-Peevy nuptials?" an older woman with blonde hair and big brown eyes inquired as she emerged from behind a mirrored door hidden by the rack of dresses.

Madison nodded. "Ah, yes, I'm one of the bridesmaids."

"Then you're just in time." The attendant gestured to the mirrored door. "The bride is trying on her gown. Follow me."

After being ushered to the rear fitting area, decorated with gold velvet sofas and white plastic flower arrangements, Madison was confronted by three severe looking women with sour faces. All three were middle-aged, had sallow-complexions, thick twists of black hair pulled behind their heads, and large dark circles beneath their black eyes. They were dressed in similar dowdy dark pantsuits that far from flattered their stout figures.

Swallowing back a rush of nerves, Madison smiled and held out her hand. "I'm Madison Barnett, one of Charlie's bridesmaids."

The tallest of the women came forward, attempting a slight smile. "Yes, Charlie mentioned you were coming. I'm Nelson's mother, Caroline Peevy." Taking her hand, Caroline Peevy nodded to the other two women. "These are my sisters. We've been waiting to see—"

A barrage of curse words cut off the mother of the groom.

"Charlie is not very happy with the dress I helped her pick out." Caroline Peevy leaned over to Madison, and lowering her voice she added, "I think the stress of everything is getting to her." She pointed to a line of dark green shutter doors to the side of the fitting room. "She's in the first dressing room and won't listen to anything I have to say, but she might listen to you." The woman's lower lip determinedly flattened out, reminding Madison of Nelson. He always got the same stubborn look when Charlie was insisting on having her way.

"Let me talk to her," Madison offered, tugging at the black strap of her purse.

Stepping away from Caroline Peevy, Madison went to the first door she came to.

"Charlie, it's Mads…you okay?"

"No." Charlie's voice was faint and childlike, hardly the Charlie she knew and loved.

"Can I come in?"

The door crept open, and when Madison saw Charlie's tearstained blue eyes, she dashed inside the dressing room and pulled the door shut behind her.

"What is it?"

Charlie pouted and waved her hand down her long white dress. "It's hideous!"

Madison's eyes settled on the off-the-shoulder, crystal-beaded gown. A tight bodice cinched around Charlie's slender waist, and the shiny, silky fabric flared out into a wide skirt with a short train tapering behind. Round crystals were sewn into the bodice in a teardrop design, and then scattered intermittently along the skirt. The overall impression was far from hideous…if anything, Madison believed her friend looked like a princess.

"Charlie, you look absolutely breathtaking."

"Really?" Charlie's lips curled into the smallest, hope-filled smile. "You don't think it's too much?" She rolled her blue eyes. "Caroline insisted on it and I went along because Nelson said I should, but now I'm afraid I made a huge mistake."

"No, Charlie, it's really beautiful. It's not a mistake. Nelson's gonna hit the floor when he sees you coming down the aisle in that."

"Yeah?" Charlie sniffled.

"Yeah!" Madison assertively replied.

Taking in a deep breath, Charlie nodded and then wiped her hands over her face, smudging away her tears. "Okay, I can do this."

"Of course you can," Madison encouraged.

"You met Caroline?" Charlie motioned to the shutter door. "What did you think? Monster-in-law?"

"She's nice, Charlie. You need to cut her some slack." She waved her hand down the dress. "The woman's got taste. You look stunning in that dress."

"Yeah, well," Charlie turned to the mirrored wall behind her, "I'm not entirely convinced." She ran her hands over the fabric in the skirt as she glanced back through the mirror at Madison. "I thought you were going to take off work early."

"I did. I got held up in traffic." Madison dropped her black purse on the small wooden bench built into the wall next to her.

"How's the hottie boss? You two still an item?"

"Things are good, but...." Madison sunk down on the bench, sighing. "Is it supposed to be this exhausting?"

Charlie rested her hands on her hips. "What do you mean?"

"I don't know." Madison sat back against the wall. "I spend all day at work, working on these damned plans for the Martins. After that I race home, grab some clothes, and head over to Hayden's. Then at night...well, I haven't been getting a whole lot of sleep."

"Girl," Charlie clucked, "look at you! A regular slut like me."

Madison laughed. "I know relationships are hard work, but this is like another full-time job."

Nodding, Charlie turned around. "I know what you mean. That first year with Nelson wore me out. If we hadn't spent so much time dining out, I might have actually lost weight and not gained it."

"At least you get to go out. Hayden and I always stay in. Dinner is usually take out, and even then I never get to finish my meal, if you know what I mean."

Charlie's blue eyes clouded over with concern. "He never takes you out?"

"He just wants to keep it low-key for now. His ex is trying to go after him for a chunk of his assets, and he doesn't want to anger her by flaunting our relationship—"

"Horseshit!" Charlie shouted. "He's divorced. He can see whomever he wants, and his ex can't say squat. He knows that."

Madison scrambled to come up with something in Hayden's defense. "You don't know his ex, Charlie."

"No, but I know the law, Madison, and the law says once they are legally divorced he's free to see other people. Being with you has no bearing whatsoever on his division of assets."

"Yes, but it has a bearing on his business. I'm an employee, and if any of his other staff knew—"

"Aw, come on, Mads…you don't buy that, do you? The guy never struck me as someone who gave a shit what anyone thinks. He seemed like he always got what he wanted, no matter the consequences." She paused and eyed her friend thoughtfully. "Do you like being with him?"

Madison slowly nodded. "Yeah, I really do. I don't know how to describe it, but when I'm with him I feel…good. He makes me feel safe and protected."

"And the sex? Still hot?"

Madison blushed. "It's satisfying."

Charlie frowned and gathered up the skirt of her dress. "So is this just for the sex, or are you hoping for more?"

"We haven't really talked about the future, but he makes me feel like he wants one."

"Feel like?" Charlie went back to the mirror. "Start insisting you two go out. A man who is crazy about a woman wants to show her off. If he cares, he won't treat you like some kind of sex toy."

"He's going to be my date at the wedding, Charlie, so it's not like we aren't going out. We just haven't done it yet. We're taking time to build a solid foundation."

The dubious smirk on Charlie's lips concerned Madison. "It's a relationship, not a building, Mads." She sighed, sounding fed-up with the topic of Hayden Parr. "I guess if he's stepping up to the plate and being your date for my wedding, he might have some good intentions."

Madison stood from the bench, refusing to accept Charlie's dire warnings about Hayden. "Enough about me and Hayden; today is about you." She began fluffing up the skirt of the dress. "Are you ready to go out there and face your mother-in-law to be?"

"Do I have to?" Charlie whined.

"Play nice, Charlie. Remember, she's going to be grandmother to your children one day."

"Gee, thanks, Mads. Now I really want to call the whole thing off."

Madison reached for the handle on the dressing room door. "Just keep thinking of Nelson. You're doing this for him."

Charlie gathered up her short train. "I know, I know." She headed toward the dressing room door. "If this is the wedding, can you imagine the holidays I'll have to endure? Thank God for vodka!"

Holding the door as Charlie paraded out of the dressing room, carrying the yards of shiny white fabric in her hands, Madison grinned. Like most things with Charlie, she knew a lot of the animosity towards her future mother-in-law was more for show than genuine. That Caroline Peevy was having such an influence on the wedding boded well for the two women building a lasting relationship.

And what about you and Hayden? her inner voice taunted. *Are you two building a lasting relationship?*

"God, I hope so," Madison muttered under her breath. "I really hope so."

In her short time with Hayden, hope had become her aphrodisiac; because nothing turned her on more than the possibility of a future with the man who had conquered her heart.

Chapter 17

The afternoon before the rehearsal dinner, Madison was in her office, checking over the latest specs the engineers had given her for the foundation on the Martins' Turtle Creek home. She had been rushing for days to finish the plans and line up the necessary drafts for the house to move out of the planning stage and into construction.

While sitting at her computer, making some last minute adjustments to the main beam along the atrium ceiling, she heard a gentle knocking on her open office door.

"Yeah," she hollered, never looking up from her computer screen.

"Is that any way to talk to the boss?" his silky voice answered right before she heard her office door close.

Madison spun around in her chair. Despite the hours she had spent in his arms and in his bed, she still got a jolt when she saw him before her. At times it was hard to believe that her Harry had found his way back to her.

"I was just finishing up the engineering plans on the foundation." She motioned to the computer screen. "Seems you were right about that center beam in the atrium. The engineers want steel beams and not wood to support the weight."

Hayden came up to her desk and leaned over to her computer screen. "That will significantly increase our cost estimates. Do they think we need it throughout the first floor?"

She peered over at his profile. "Yes. I know, not what we expected, but necessary."

When he turned his head, placing his lips within inches of hers, Madison's toes curled. "Did you tell the Martins yet?" he questioned.

Madison blushed. *How does he do that?* "Ah no. Not yet."

He knelt beside her chair. "I'll tell them tonight when we meet with the contractor to go over your plans."

"Maybe you should cancel with the Martins and come with me to the rehearsal dinner. Might be more fun."

"Wish I could, baby, but I've got to settle this deal tonight. Once they have signed with the contractor, I'm going to firm up a deal with Pat on his house. We can get together at my place later to celebrate." He playfully bobbed his eyebrows up and down.

She chuckled at his display. "You're lucky I'm such an understanding girlfriend."

He placed his face right in front of hers. "You're much more, Madison. A girlfriend implies a half-assed relationship bereft of commitment. To me you are simply…mine."

"That's something a sailor tattoos on his ass, Hayden, and not what a woman wants to hear from a man who has been preoccupying her every thought."

Dismayed, he stood up. "I preoccupy your every thought?"

Her eyes dropped to her desk. Perhaps she had said too much. Charlie had always warned her to play hard to get when it came to her emotions, but with Hayden that was impossible.

As the seconds ticked by, Madison became more apprehensive by his lack of reply and she squirmed in her chair.

"I was beginning to wonder what I meant to you," he finally voiced. "That I have become your preoccupation means we're finally even."

She gazed up at him. "Even? I don't understand."

"You have been my preoccupation since I first saw you in that bar. 'Bout time you started to get a little of your own back at you."

"I was your preoccupation? I find that hard to believe."

He tilted his head to the side and casually tucked his hand in his trouser pocket, appearing coy. "I'll admit I'm not the most forthcoming of men with my emotions, but I thought all the time we've spent together, giving you access to my home and my life, would have at least let you know how I feel."

Madison was confused. Sure he had done those things, but he had never actually mentioned anything about feelings. Didn't it only count when he actually said something?

A knock at her office door interrupted them, and Hayden backed away from her chair. The icy look that overtook his features was more than a bit disconcerting to Madison. He always seemed to run hot and cold.

"Yes," he called to the door.

"Sorry, Mr. Parr." Emma smiled sheepishly as she came into the office. "You told me to come and get you when your two o'clock showed up."

"I'm coming, Emma." Hayden pointed to Madison's computer. "We'll need the engineering specs to go over tonight."

Madison's eyes went to the door where Emma was still waiting. "Yes, Mr. Parr."

She thought she saw a slight smirk cross his thin lips, but then it was gone. He was always so difficult to read. As Madison considered the curve of his square jaw, his carved cheekbones, and thick brow, she suddenly became aware that there was a great deal about Hayden Parr that she did not know.

"Looks good, Madison," Hayden commented. "Bring them by my office before you head out," he added, and dashed for her office door.

She listened to his heavy footfalls as he headed along the hallway toward the elevators. He laughed briefly with Emma, but the sound faded. Tucking her chair into her desk, Madison tried to refocus on her design, but that nagging voice in her head would not let up. Instead of working, she began to go over every detail of Hayden: his smile, his laugh, the way he slept, the way he liked his coffee, and even the shampoo he used. All the things she had come to know about him. And as she tallied up his idiosyncrasies, preferences, and dislikes, Madison realized that she did not know a lot about the man...emotionally, anyway. Some people she could read, some she couldn't, and Hayden Parr was starting to feel a lot like someone who was very good at keeping secrets.

"It's time to get to the bottom of Hayden Parr," she murmured, returning to her plans. "I need to find out where this is going."

***

When Madison punched the code into the keypad outside of Hayden's front door, she was fuming. Not only had Charlie grilled her about Hayden's absence during the rehearsal dinner, she had been seated next to Mrs. Leder, and had put up with even more questions about her relationship with the man.

"You need to insist he take you out to nice places," Mrs. Leder had suggested, waving her fork filled with prime rib in front of Madison. "Charlie told me he never takes you out, just keeps you at his house all night, counting ceiling tiles."

"It's not like that, Mrs. L," Madison had argued, reaching for her glass of wine. "We're being discreet."

Mrs. Leder had shoved the piece of prime rib in her mouth. "And you believe that? He's just using you for sex. I've seen it a million times before, Madison. I knew he was too good-looking for his own good."

As the glass door to Hayden's home popped open, Mrs. Leder's words repeated in her head. Incensed, Madison shoved her shoulder into the door. Once inside, she had to steady herself against the doorframe. The three glasses of wine she had consumed with her dinner were beginning to hit her. Pushing away from the door, she was about to go in search of Hayden when she remembered she needed to input the code on the other keypad. As she punched in the code, footfalls came from the foyer steps.

"I wasn't expecting you home so early, baby."

Unsteadily, she whirled around and watched as he descended the stairs. Dressed only in a pair of jeans with his bare, muscular chest gleaming beneath the bright lights in the entrance, Madison was momentarily distracted from her irritation.

"When did you get back from your meeting?"

"About an hour ago." Clearing the bottom step, he moved toward her. "After Pat and Stevie signed the contracts, we discussed the sale of their property."

"Did you make an offer?"

He nodded as he came to a stop before her. "In about a year, nine months if I'm lucky, we'll close the deal and I will be the new owner of that piece of shit across the street."

She patted his chest and wavered slightly. "That's great, Hayden."

He put his arms about her waist, his eyes intently exploring her face. "What is it? Was the rehearsal dinner a disaster?"

"No, the dinner went fine. Charlie seemed really happy and was even getting along with her future mother-in-law."

"That'll be short lived," Hayden snorted, and eased the strap of her purse from her shoulder. "Ellen and my mother fought like cats and dogs."

"Your mother?" Madison paused. "You never talk about your parents. Where are they?"

"Three blocks over on Deer Run Road. Why?" He took her purse to the stairs. "And I talk about my parents. I told you about my old man."

"I know you took over the company from your father, but that's about it. You've never mentioned your mother."

Shrugging, he placed her purse on the bottom step. "Nothing to say. She's a housewife, active at her local church, and has put up with my father's bullshit for thirty-six years."

"What's she like, your mother?"

He came back to her side. "Why? You've met Mike; she's a lot like our mother, except for the obnoxious personality. Mom is more easygoing than my sister. Don't worry, you'll find that out when you meet her."

"You want me to meet your parents?"

"Yes, of course I do."

"When?" she demanded in a harsh tone.

He stood before her, his eyes drawn together in a perplexed scowl. "What's wrong?"

She held up her head, appearing confident, but on the inside she was swimming in self-doubt. "I guess I'm starting to wonder if I'm the kind of girl you bring home to Mom, or just the kind of girl you sleep with and get rid of."

"'Get rid of'?" His booming voice echoed about the foyer. "What are you talking about? I don't want to get rid of you."

"That's not the impression...forget it." She was about to stumble past him when he clasped her arm.

"What happened at the rehearsal dinner? You were fine when we talked in my office earlier this evening. And now you come back from that dinner...drunk and upset."

She shirked off his hand and went to the stairs. "I'm going back to my apartment," she proclaimed after collecting her purse.

"You're not driving home." He took her elbow and urged her up the stairs. "We're going to go upstairs and you're—"

She pushed him away and halted on the first step. "If we go upstairs, we'll just have sex, like we do every night. You are just out to screw me."

"'Screw you'?" He gripped her arm. "We're going to have a little chat." He took her purse and pitched it to the bottom step before pulling her toward the archway that led to his den.

"Where are we going?"

"Kitchen. I think you could do with some coffee while we have that chat."

When they reached the kitchen, Hayden seated her at the glass breakfast table. She hadn't wanted to admit it before, but she was more than a little tipsy. In retrospect, driving to Hayden's had been a stupid idea, but her anger had fueled her stupidity.

"Charlie sends her regards." Madison smirked at him. "She asked me a lot of questions about where you were tonight."

"Is she the one who told you I was just out to screw you?"

She shook her head, feeling the wine sloshing about in her system. "That was Mrs. Leder."

"Mrs. Leder. Yes, she would be the expert on men." He went to the chair next to her. "What did she say?"

Madison drooped forward in her seat. "Does it matter?"

He lifted her chin, raising her eyes to him. "Mrs. Leder is a silly old woman who I think enjoys putting her nose into other people's business. What did she tell you?"

The way his eyes were burning into her, Madison figured it would be best to disclose everything. "That you were out to screw me and then dump me."

He dropped his hand. "And you believe that?"

She put her elbows on the table and then hung her head in her hands. "I don't know what to believe."

"Come on." He scooped her up in his arms. "I'm taking you to bed."

"Taking me to bed to have sex with me, you mean."

He carried her out of the kitchen. "I'm taking you to bed because you're drunk."

"I am not drunk."

He climbed the back stairs that rose from the den to the second floor. "You're drunk, angry, and lashing out at me. If I don't put you to bed, we will both say things we're going to regret in the morning."

"You can't just put me to bed like I'm a child, Hayden."

"Well, you're acting like one." He turned the corner upstairs, heading down the short hall to his bedroom.

"Why, because I'm beginning to wonder if I'm just your sex toy and not your…girlfriend?" she replied, raising her voice.

He stopped at the bedroom door and deposited her on the thick Berber carpet. "Did Mrs. Leder say that?"

"No, Charlie. She thinks you're using me for sex, too."

He hesitated for a moment, and when he wiped his face with his hand, his expression calmed. "Madison, you need to stop listening to your friends. I know they have good intentions, but they don't know mine."

"What are your intentions, Hayden?"

"Are you sure you want to discuss this when you're drunk?"

"I told you, I'm not drunk."

He put his hands on her shoulders and ushered her into the bedroom. When they came to the edge of his low platform bed, he pushed her down onto the burgundy comforter. "Sit."

She grudgingly sat down and, with his hands clasped behind him, Hayden began to pace back and forth in front of her. After a few turns before the bed, he stopped and stared at her.

"What do you need to hear from me to convince you that I'm not just in this for the sex?"

"Tell me how you feel about me."

"How I feel?" He sucked in a pensive breath. "That's not so easy for me."

"Why?"

He came up to the bed and had a seat next to her. "Look, Madison, I care about you, make no mistake, but asking me to put all that into words is...well, impossible for me. I'm not a writer; I'm an architect, and if you ask me to draw up a plan of where I see us heading, that would be a hell of a lot easier for me to—"

"Then tell me of your plan, Hayden. Describe what you see for us. Put into words the pictures you see in your head."

"Words, huh? It would be a hell of a lot easier for me to show you how I feel."

Disgusted, she stood from the bed. "Show me? I knew it. I am a sex toy to you."

He held her hand, keeping her from walking away. "I don't have to have sex with you to show you what you mean to me."

She stopped and peered down at him. "You don't?"

"No. You make it sound like having sex is something only meant to please me." He stood up and traced his fingertips over the outline of her finely carved cheekbone. "Pleasing you is the goal for me."

His touch made that familiar tingle come to life. *Damn him!* "Well, you sure seem to enjoy it a hell of a lot."

He shifted her long brown hair away from her shoulders. "Then perhaps you should give me the opportunity to prove to you that my pleasure does not matter...only yours."

"What are you going to do, give me another lesson?"

He grinned, amused by her comment. "No more lessons." Moving behind her, he rolled his hands along her shoulders. Then his fingers gently nudged down the zipper on the back of her light blue, tea-length dress.

"Hayden, this isn't going to—"

"Shh." He eased the delicate fabric down her body. "Hand yourself over to me; don't resist."

"But I—"

He covered her mouth with his fingers. "Let me show you how I feel, Madison. Just for tonight, let go of your doubt."

She figured debating his intentions would be a waste of time, and in her heart Madison knew where this was headed. Without further objection, she let him remove the rest of her clothes.

Setting her on the bed, he flipped her over on her stomach. "Now relax," he whispered as his fingertips stroked her back.

He began pressing his palms into the muscles along her spine, massaging away her tension. After gently kneading the sore muscles in the back of her neck, he moved down to her bottom, lingering over the curve of her butt as his fingers prodded deep into the tissue.

Madison concluded if a massage was his way of showing her how he felt, then she wouldn't argue. For the most part, his hands were magical, but when they dug a little too hard into her stiff muscles, Madison would wince and stiffen.

"Stop working against me. Let go, baby," he urged as he honed in on a big knot in her neck.

He determinedly reduced the tightness in her shoulders and lower back. Feeling utterly relaxed, the warm rush brought on by the wine and massage began to make her nod off.

He patted her behind. "Turn over for me."

Groggily, she lay on her back and Hayden straddled her hips. His hands worked on her right shoulder and then her left. He lightly raked his fingernail down her chest, and Madison found the sensation strangely arousing. When his hands cupped her breasts, he gently stroked them and scraped his thumbs over her nipples. Madison's breath quickened and her skin flushed. He purposefully concentrated his attention on her breasts for several minutes, sparking to life her desire. He scooted down her legs while his hands moved lower, caressing her abdomen and settling over her hips. Hayden kneaded the flesh along the sides of her hips, manipulating the thick muscles, and when his hands edged underneath to her butt, he squeezed her cheeks.

He eased off her legs and pulled her knees apart, causing Madison's eyes to fly open. She raised her head to look up at him.

"What are you doing?"

He never uttered a word while his fingers rubbed slowly up and down, fondling her folds and making Madison rock her head back against the bed. His fingers were methodical and relentless, and when his thumb started drawing circles over her sensitive nub, she reached out and balled the comforter up in her hands.

It did not take long for her orgasm to come barreling upward. Gasping, she arched her back when the fire exploded in her. A long moan escaped her lips as the trembling began, and by the time she slammed back on the bed, she felt spent.

Instead of stopping, Hayden slid his fingers inside of her, massaging her slowly and rhythmically.

"Hayden, please," she begged, running her hand over her face.

He ignored her protests and kept moving his fingers in and out. A damp sweat broke out on her brow and her muscles twitched when the second climax rose up her spine. She clawed at the comforter, gathering it about her body. As the white surge of electricity bounded upward, she rolled her head back and bit down on her lip, suppressing her cry.

Again she fell against the bed, but Hayden never stopped. His fingers probed deeper. The sensation was overpowering as his fingers stimulated the deepest parts of her. The third orgasm was even more intense and came faster than the other two. This time she did not hold back and cried out with wild abandon as her body shook.

Hayden's lips began their assault on her inner thigh; his teeth nipping at her skin. When his mouth settled over her very sensitive flesh, she gasped as the rush of heat overwhelmed her.

"Oh my God."

He kept sucking on her, tantalizing her with his tongue until she was drenched in sweat. Madison crashed into the bed—shrieking so loud, she was sure that someone would hear—but just as she was catching her breath, his mouth attacked her all over again.

"I can't." Madison grabbed at his hair. "No more."

Her begging only seemed to spur him onward. Realizing what he had in mind, Madison was helpless to stop him. She was his willing captive, wanting him to stop, but also desperately wanting him to continue. Closing her eyes, she reached her arms up to the bedpost above her head and held on. When the next orgasm took hold, she was shattered. Weak and unable to move, she wanted to shout with thanks when his mouth moved away from her throbbing folds and up her stomach.

Hayden bit down hard on her right nipple, and as his lips worked their way up her neck, he mumbled, "I'm just getting warmed up, baby. I've got hundreds of ways to show you how I feel. I'm going to make you understand how much you mean to me."

When he slinked back down her chest and over her hips, Madison willed the strength to object, but as his mouth clamped down again on her tender nub, she surrendered to him. The last thing she remembered was the scream coming from her as his tongue began to mercilessly tease her back to that limitless cavern of bliss.

***

When Madison awoke, every muscle in her body ached. She was sprawled on her stomach, her thick brown hair half in her face, blocking her vision. In the background, she heard the sound of running water and wasn't sure if she was still dreaming. When a hand ran up her spine and settled behind her neck, her eyes flew open.

"Time to get up, baby."

She groaned. "No, God no. I can't move."

He brushed her hair away from her face. "I've got a hot shower waiting for you."

She sat up, wincing slightly as she felt an ache between her legs. "What did you do to me last night?"

"Showed you what you mean to me. Wasn't that the point?"

She pulled her legs up beneath her, sitting up. "Yeah but…ten times?"

He scooped her up in his arms, lifting her from the bed. "I think there might have been one or two extra in there." He carried her into the bathroom. "I'll do it all over again tonight when we get home from the wedding."

"The wedding. That's today, isn't it?"

"That's right." He placed her next to the shower. The steam from the hot water inside was collecting on the clear door, blocking the view into the wide stall. "You have exactly one hour before you have to join the bride." He opened the shower door. "Get in and I'll start the coffee."

Before she turned to the shower, she gazed over his wrinkled jeans and bare chest. "I guess you showed me last night, didn't you?"

"I'm glad you're convinced."

She stared into his small gray eyes and tried to fathom the depth of emotion she saw there. "You are coming to the wedding, right? I think you need to prove to Mrs. Leder and Charlie that you're serious about me."

"I'll be there. And I'll even dance with Mrs. Leder at the reception to show what a forgiving guy I am."

"I think Mrs. Leder will enjoy that."

Slipping under the shower, Madison let the pulsating water work away her stiffness. Wiping the water from her face, she glimpsed the closed shower door. Hayden may have tried to convince her of his feelings, but she believed he was the one who actually needed convincing. It was almost as if he were going through the motions with her; acting like the attentive lover, but somewhere the emotional commitment fell far short of the physical one. Why was there such a disparity with him? As the hot water massaged away her aches, she pondered why he was the way he was. Perhaps that was his appeal for her. The mystery of what

Hayden Parr was thinking was becoming her most perplexing dilemma.

THAT NIGHT WITH YOU

Chapter 18

"Christ, I'm sweating like a pig," Charlie complained as she tugged at the bosom of her wedding gown. "I didn't think it would be this hot."

Waiting in a small room by the entrance to the Highland Park Presbyterian Church, Madison was fanning Charlie with her bouquet of blue hydrangea and chocolate sunflowers intermixed with white baby's breath.

"That stinks, Mads." Charlie pointed to the bouquet. "I'm gonna be sick."

"Maybe we should get her some water," Lizzie offered, pulling at her tea-length, drape-cut silk dress. With alternating flowing layers of tie-dyed teal and chocolate fabric hanging loosely about the front and back of the dress, she reminded Madison of a colorblind hippie who had created the monstrosity during a drug-induced designing rampage.

Madison cringed as she recalled her own image in the mirror when she had prepared for the event at Caroline Peevy's posh Highland Park home. She could not wait to hear the barrage of acerbic comments she was sure Hayden was going to inflict at the reception.

Pushing a daydreaming Madison aside, Carolyn Peevy came up to Charlie. "She'll be fine," she asserted, and patted Charlie's neck with a damp paper towel. "Linney, get the candy from my handbag," Caroline called to her daughter, another of the fashion challenged bridesmaids in the room.

Nelson's sister, the renowned high school gymnast, dashed to a dark pink handbag that perfectly matched the mother of the groom's chic, pink crepe Chanel dress. For a split second Madison could have sworn that Caroline Peevy purposefully dressed the three bridesmaids in the unattractive frocks to make herself look good.

Caroline took a piece of hard candy from her daughter. "You need to eat this. You haven't touched a thing all day, and with all of this excitement, your blood sugar is low." She unwrapped the candy and placed it in the palm of Charlie's shaking hand.

All eyes watched with mounting anxiety as the bride sucked on the candy, and even Madison sagged with relief when Charlie's color returned.

"I'm feeling better."

"You're sure?" Madison pressed.

"I'm fine." Charlie laughed, sounding like her old self. "It's not like I can cancel, Mads."

"Okay, crisis averted." Caroline Peevy began fluffing out the skirt of Charlie's wedding gown. "Girls, take your places at the back of the aisle." She motioned to Madison. "Get them lined up, while I get her ready."

Heading out of the room, Madison approached the alcove that opened to the nave. Built of white stone arches on either side, the church floor was filled with dark wooden pews crammed with guests and adorned in pale blue and chocolate bows. A red carpet had been placed down the center aisle to guide the wedding party to the altar. Gazing ahead, Madison's eyes rose to the grand oak-covered chancel at the far end of the church, where the altar stood covered with white linen and decorated with a simple gold cross. Above it, rising up to the vaulted walnut ceiling, were the seventy-seven silver pipes of the massive organ encased in matching oak woodwork. The horizontal *Trompette en chamade* dominated the center of the façade. In the air, the sweet strains of organ music entertained the guests as they waited for the wedding to begin.

Madison strained to look down the row of pews, searching for Hayden's thick, brown wavy hair and rugged features, but as she snuck from one side of the alcove to the other, trying to get a better view of the packed church, she could not find him.

Suddenly, a hand grabbed her arm. "Come on, girl," Caroline Peevy chided. "Take your place. It's time." She dragged Madison back to the alcove that opened to the center aisle. "Now remember, go slow and don't rush. You're first, and set the tone for the rest of the bridal party."

Figuring resistance was futile at this point, Madison just nodded.

While stepping over to take the arm of a dashing gray-haired man in a black suit waiting for her at the start of the aisle, Caroline instructed, "Go slow and remember to smile."

The handsome gentleman next to Caroline winked at Madison. "You'll do just fine, Madison, not to worry."

"Thanks, Dr. Peevy."

She waited as the famed Dallas cardiac surgeon escorted his wife to their pew at the front of the church. Once the Peevys were seated, Madison clutched her smelly bouquet, sucked in a deep breath, and headed down the aisle.

Smiling sweetly, just as Caroline had insisted at the rehearsal, Madison slowly marched along. Her eyes volleyed back and forth between the pews, and as one face after another turned out not to be Hayden's, a sinking feeling came over her. Determined not to let it show, Madison kept up her smile until she reached the end of the aisle. Frantically searching those front pews as she turned to the left of the altar, Madison wondered if she had missed him. Perhaps he had been further to the side and out of her line of sight.

Passing Nelson, she winked. Decked out in his rented tuxedo, he looked pale, but happy. The slender man—with the unruly, frizzy black hair and soft brown eyes—had always held a soft spot in Madison's heart because of his easygoing nature and deep love for Charlie.

Waiting for Lizzie to join her at the altar, Madison took in the unencumbered view of all the guests and her happiness wilted as her hope disappeared into the cold stone floor. He was not there.

The organ music instantly changed and Felix Mendelssohn's "Wedding March" reverberated throughout the church. All the guests stood as the bride slowly came down the aisle to her groom.

But Madison's eyes were not on the bride, they were on the guests, searching for Hayden. *He didn't come.* The thought repeated over and over again in her head until it was interrupted by the words of another.

"Dearly beloved, we are gathered here today...."

***

"Did you try his cell phone?" Lizzie asked.

Madison raised her cell phone in her hand. "I tried it. Goes right to voice mail." She put the phone on the black onyx and gold bar next to her and retrieved her flute of champagne. "Now how in the hell am I to get home?"

"Barry and I will bring you home," Lizzie told her. "Maybe he was in an accident. Have you tried the hospitals?" Lizzie's innocent brown eyes made Madison want to hug her for not doubting Hayden.

She searched the white and gold-painted ballroom of Arlington Hall, noting that some of the wedding guests were seated at white linen-covered tables eating their food, while others were still standing in the long line that snaked around the grand hall, waiting for the buffet. At the front, between two large white Corinthian columns, was a stage where a band was setting up to play.

"I don't think he's in the hospital, Lizzie." Madison gulped back more of the bubbly gold liquid in her glass.

"I'm sure he didn't stand you up without a damned good reason, Madison," Lizzie loudly proposed to be heard over the din of the crowd.

"Oh, I'm sure he has a reason." Madison cast her eyes to her drink. "I just don't want to hazard a guess at what it is."

Charlie came up to them. "You two disappeared right after the pictures; what's up?"

Her veil was gone and on her left hand, the shiny three-carat diamond was now partnered with a diamond-clad wedding band.

"Where's your groom?" Madison questioned, glancing behind her.

"I left him talking to his friend, Jimmie, from law school. They were going on about some case Nelson has." Charlie's blue eyes worriedly scanned Madison's face. "Is he still a no show?"

Madison held up her champagne flute and nodded.

Charlie gave Lizzie a worried frown. "Maybe he got in an accident?"

"I already said that," Lizzie affirmed.

"Look, Mads, perhaps something came up and—"

Madison held up her hand. "Forget it, Charlie. You were right about him. He was using me and had no intention of ever getting serious. Tonight proves it."

Charlie took the champagne from her hand. "You don't know that, Madison, and you certainly don't believe it. If you ask me, you're crazy about this guy, and it's killing you that he treats you this way. Hell, it's killing me." She banged the glass down on the bar next to her.

"There she is." Charlie was picked up and twirled around by a tall, lanky man in a black tux and disheveled thick black hair. When her feet returned to the floor, Charlie kissed her new husband's lips. "What are you girls talking about?" Nelson inquired in his unusually deep voice.

Madison looked over his hooked nose, full, wide mouth, and high forehead...and for a moment envied her friend. For the rest of her life, Charlie had someone to be there for her, making Madison wonder if she would ever know such contentment.

"Madison's date never showed," Charlie told Nelson.

Nelson's dark brown eyes narrowed with concern. "Isn't he your boss?"

Madison nodded.

Nelson gave Madison an encouraging smile. "Screw him. You don't need that kind of man, Madison. There are lots of men here tonight who would do a lot better by you than your boss."

Madison felt guilty. She didn't want to be talking about such a depressing subject as her love life at her friend's wedding. It was a happy occasion, and no matter how devastated she felt, she could never let it show.

"Never mind about me, Nelson. I'll be fine." She put on a brave smile.

"I know you will. You just need to find someone new to forget about him." Nelson turned to his wife. "You ready to take our first dance together? The band's waiting for us to dance before they start their set."

Beaming, Charlie let Nelson lead her away. Lizzie and Madison watched as Nelson slipped his arm about Charlie's shoulder as he guided her to the white-tiled dance floor set up in front of the stage.

"I need to find Barry. He left ten minutes ago to get me something to eat," Lizzie stated as she scanned the room. "Are you going to be all right, Madison?"

She patted Lizzie's hand. "Go and find your date. I'm just going to stay here and watch their first dance."

Lizzie took off in the direction of the buffet tables as Madison checked her phone once more.

"Damn things," a man spoke up behind her. "Always got to keep checking them to see if you've missed anything."

Madison was about to turn to the voice when a handsome man in a black suit appeared in front of her. He was of medium height with a wide set of shoulders and lots of blond, curly hair.

"Yeah, technology," she remarked with a shrug. "What are you going to do?"

He pulled his cell phone from his pocket. "My addiction is email. I'm always checking to see if I got any. What's yours?"

Madison put her phone back down on the bar, uncomfortable with his piercing blue eyes and how they were examining her face and figure. "I was, ah, just waiting for a phone call."

"At a wedding?" He laughed, and the sound took Madison by surprise. It was a jovial chortle that instantly made her stop and look at the man with a renewed interest.

"I was waiting to hear from a friend." She picked up her champagne.

He held out his hand to her. "I'm Jimmie by the way, Jimmie Kirkland. I went to law school with Nelson. You're Madison, right?"

Madison shook his hand, recalling Charlie just mentioning Nelson's friend. "Are you looking for Nelson?"

"Actually, he told me to come over here and talk to you."

Madison suddenly felt foolish. "I see."

A booming voice came over the speakers at the front by the stage, announcing the first dance of Mr. and Mrs. Nelson Peevy. Madison peered through the crowd, wanting to catch a glimpse of the important moment.

"So this friend you're waiting to hear from," Jimmie moved next to her at the bar, "is he a boyfriend?"

"No. He's just a friend." A twinge of sorrow meandered through Madison's heart.

Jimmie's blue eyes perked up. "Glad to hear it."

The strains of a famous rock ballad from the eighties blared across the ballroom as the lights dimmed. Madison stood by the bar, not sure of what to say or do, when Jimmie edged closer to her.

"You're drinking champagne?"

She nodded.

He waved down a bartender dressed all in black. "Another champagne, and a scotch and soda." When the bartender hurried to get their drinks, Jimmie returned his unsettling eyes to her. "Nelson told me you're an architect; where do you work?"

"Parr and Associates."

"Never heard of them," Jimmie confessed. "What do you build there?"

Madison told him about her design for the Martins as they waited for their drinks. She thought she would have a hard time talking to a stranger, but somehow Jimmie made her feel at ease as he asked her questions about architectural design.

Soon they were talking about more than houses, and as Madison became comfortable with the attractive lawyer, she began to relax. She found that she was laughing at his jokes and liked the way his eyes crinkled around the edges every time he smiled. When he talked he waved his slender hands about in the air, and Madison was captivated by his long, supple fingers.

A long ago disco classic was making the walls of the ballroom thump as the dance floor crowded with everyone trying to "shake their booty." Madison gawked at the couples running to the dance floor to share in the excitement.

Jimmie reached for the champagne flute in her hand. "Come on. Let's go dance." He plonked her glass on the bar and held out his hand.

Madison's stomach twisted into a knot and her eyes darted about the faces of the guests, nervous about what everyone would think if she danced with the handsome attorney. She needed to be cautious and not draw attention to....

Christ, I sound just like Hayden.

The weeks she had spent with Hayden came into focus in that instant. She had been living sequestered away with him for so long that she had forgotten what it was like to just be carefree, uninhibited, and...normal. The realization sent a shockwave through her. Was that what had been missing from her life, being normal? Madison knew what she shared with Hayden wasn't exactly ordinary, but she had never understood how much their secretive affair had affected her. Perhaps it was time to embrace a new way of thinking.

Madison reconsidered Jimmie's outstretched hand. "I would love to dance with you."

As he escorted her across the ballroom, placing his hand about her waist, she thought of Hayden and how she wished it had been him taking her to the dance floor instead of Jimmie.

But he's not here, Madison, the voice in her head reminded her.

A catchy Latin song was heating up the dance floor when she set foot on the white tiles. Emboldened by the beat, Madison started to sway her hips, laughing as she got caught up in the music. For the first time in what seemed like forever, she was having fun, kicking up her heels and living. Surveying the dance floor, she spotted Charlie with her new husband and Lizzie clinging to a lanky redhead. When her eyes returned to Jimmie, awkwardly gyrating to the music, Madison made a solemn promise: never again would she be left in such an awkward situation by a man. She was going to have to make some changes in her life…big changes. Otherwise, she would never find the kind of happiness she now knew she deserved.

***

It was around eleven when Jimmie escorted Madison to her apartment building after giving her a ride in his new black Lexus GX.

"Thanks again for bringing me home," she told Jimmie as they rode up in the elevator to the fifth floor.

"It's the least I can do for stepping all over your toes."

Madison softly giggled, tucking her hair behind her ear. "Don't worry about it. It was fun."

He rolled his blue eyes. "Fun until you told me you were a dancer in high school. Then I felt like a total geek."

That made her laugh out loud. "No, please. I only dabbled in dancing. You make it sound like I was a professional, but it was nothing like that."

The elevator doors opened on the fifth floor. "But you're a really good dancer. If I promise to try very hard not to step on your toes, would you let me take you dancing again? What do you say?"

Madison followed him out into the hallway, searching her purse for her keys. "I'm tempted to give you another try. I think…." Her voice faltered as a figure moved out from the shadows by her apartment door.

He was wearing the black suit she had selected from his closet earlier that day, but he had not put on the yellow tie she had picked out, and his white shirt was open at the top. His dark, wavy hair was disheveled, as if he had been running his hands through it again and again.

"Madison," Hayden calmly said as he came closer, his eyes riveted on Jimmie.

"Hayden, what are you doing here?"

"I went to the reception hall to collect you and was told by Mrs. Leder that you had already gotten a ride home." He came right up to her, his gaze never leaving Jimmie.

"Ah, yes." Madison motioned to an uncomfortable-looking Jimmie. "Jimmie Kirkland, this is my boss, Hayden Parr."

Jimmie shoved his hands into the trouser pockets of his black suit. "I guess I should go." His eyes shifted to Madison, and suddenly she felt like shit. "Thanks again for the dance."

"Thank you for the ride."

Jimmie spun around and headed back toward the elevators. Madison stood in the hallway and waited to hear the elevator doors close before she directed her gaze to Hayden.

"I can't believe Mrs. Leder told you I got a ride home." She went to her door and he came up behind her as she worked the lock.

"You danced with him?"

Madison glared back at him. "Well, you weren't there."

"Was he my replacement?"

The deadbolt gave way on her front door. "He's a friend of Nelson's. We talked and danced a bit. When he found out my ride stood me up, he offered to take me home."

"I didn't stand you up, I was late." She felt his breath on the back of her neck. "I have to wonder what would have happened if I hadn't been here. Were you going to let him in?"

"Drop it, Hayden," she sharply warned, pushing her apartment door open.

He followed her inside. "I'm a little late to the party and already you're picking up strange men." His voice was peppered with anger. "Makes me wonder what I mean to you after all."

"I could be asking you the same question!" She hurled her purse at the sofa. "The ceremony was three hours ago, Hayden. Where were you?"

"I got held up."

"Held up where?" she bellowed, wrenching off one of her high-heeled, chocolate and light blue tie-dyed shoes.

He contemplatively pursed his lips together before casually strolling to her side. "I was getting ready to leave for the wedding when Pat Martin knocked on my door. He wanted to talk about the house in Turtle Creek. I've spent the better part of the ceremony and reception trying to talk Pat out of backing out of the deal."

She dropped the shoe in her hand to the floor and reached for the other. "What happened?"

"He and Stevie have reconsidered the build. Seems they want to renovate the place they're in."

"Son of a bitch!" Madison shouted, and threw her shoe to the floor. "After all the hours I've put in on their design?"

"My sentiments exactly, but that's the business, baby. Some build, some don't."

"Why didn't you at least call me, and leave a message…a text, anything?" She went over to the sofa and plopped down on the cushy material. "It was humiliating, Hayden, standing there, waiting for you to show up. Meanwhile, I had to listen to my friends go on and on about what an undeserving shit you are."

"'Undeserving shit'? Really?" He grimaced. "Then I'm sorry. Truly, Madison, but I couldn't get away from Pat and Stevie to phone you. I couldn't chance Stevie listening in. She would have run right back to Ellen with that, and then where would we be?"

She sat back on the couch with a thud. The entire evening she had felt rejected by Hayden and humiliated in front of her friends, but all he had been concerned about was his ex finding out about his plans.

"Where are we exactly, Hayden?"

He took a seat next to her. "What do you mean?"

"Hayden, how do you feel about me?"

"I thought we cleared this up last night."

"No, we didn't." Madison shook her head, her disgust rising in the back of her throat. "You just avoided the question."

"What will it take to convince you, Madison?"

She sat up and faced him. "The words, Hayden. I need to hear the words."

"You're…important to me," he begrudgingly answered.

She glared at him, trying to find an inkling of emotion in his frigid eyes. "Important? After tonight, I'm not convinced of that."

He leaned in to kiss her. "Then let me remind you."

She arched away from him. "Stop it, Hayden. That's not what I want from you right now."

"Come on, Madison." He stood from the sofa. "You're mine, what else do you need to hear?"

She stood up next to him. "In all the time we've spent together, I don't remember you mentioning anything about your emotions. You keep telling me I'm yours, but that is possession, not emotion, Hayden. There's a difference."

"I know that!" Stepping away from the couch, he raked his hand through his hair. "Jesus, what more do you want from me?"

His eyes changed, and in an instant he was like a cornered animal. Was this the real Hayden Parr?

"Shit!" His stern features softened. "I didn't mean that. I'm just saying…. When I married Ellen, I thought I had found the woman I wanted. Afterwards, I realized I'd made a mistake. I regret ever telling her how I felt because she used it as a weapon against me time and time again. I want you in my life, Madison, but I'm a cautious man where my feelings are concerned."

He went to embrace her, but she backed away. "This isn't about being cautious."

"Are you going to run away from me again?"

"I'm not running, Hayden. I'm just figuring out where I stand with you."

"Where you stand? Dammit, Madison, you know where you stand. Stop acting like a child."

Like a brick through a plate glass window, Madison was jarred by his comment. He was right; she had been acting like a child. She had handed herself over to Hayden and forgotten about her wants and desires in order to please him. Suddenly, something inside of her snapped. She was done with being his to control. It was time to get her life, and her future, back on track.

"Tonight at that wedding, when I was dancing with Jimmie, I realized something." She eased back from him, wrapping her arms about her body. "I don't want to hide behind closed doors anymore. I want to do all of those boring dating things you've avoided: go to the movies, dine out with friends, and be just like every other couple. I'm sick of worrying what people will think or what they will say. I've been pleasing everyone else but me lately and I can't go on like that. I guess that's what I discovered tonight. What we have doesn't feel real...at least not to me."

His small eyes became wide with astonishment. "Real? How can you—?"

"If it was real, you could say the words I need to hear."

Combing both hands through his hair, he blew out a frustrated breath. "Look, Madison, I know how hard it has been for you, and I'm sorry—"

"I don't want any more apologies, Hayden. I want you to go."

"Go?" He eased closer, and dipping his head in front of her, he growled, "Don't do this. Don't push me away. You're upset."

"I'm not upset. I need more; more than just an arrangement. That's what this has been. That's all it has been."

The flash of anger in his eyes quickly gave way to pain. She had hurt him, and that more than anything only added to her misery. Part of her wanted to fling her arms about him and take back her words, but the realist inside of her knew that could never happen. She would never have the kind of life she wanted if she continued with him.

Turning away, Hayden went to the apartment door and paused, eyeing his hand on the doorknob. "You take some time and think about this, Madison. You must know that I want you, more than I've ever wanted any woman, and I'm willing to wait for you...for as long as it takes."

Slipping out the door, he slammed it closed.

The overwhelming anxiety to chase after him flooded through her like a crushing torrent over a high dam. She wanted him to hold her, to tell her what she meant to him, and make all the apprehension inside of her go away. Shutting out her emotions, Madison vowed that it was for the best. A man that could not give all of himself would never be completely there for her. She had seen what true happiness was with another; Charlie and Nelson had shown her the right kind of relationship to make her want to avoid continuing with the wrong kind. It was time to move on.

Chapter 19

After a weekend of contemplation, Madison decided on a plan of action for her life. In order to break clean with Hayden and start anew, she had to do more than leave him behind…she had to leave her job, too. The decision made her anxious, but after going through her finances, she figured she had three solid months to find a new job before all hell broke loose.

Monday morning she marched into her office and sat down at her computer. She had been writing and re-writing her resignation letter in her head all weekend, and as she typed out her planned explanation for her hasty departure, she prayed Hayden would let her go and not put up a fight. She didn't think she had the strength to fight him. No, Madison knew she didn't have the strength, which scared her more than the possibility of being destitute.

A knock at her open office door made her hands come to a halt on the keyboard. Swallowing back her apprehension, she slowly pivoted around in her chair, fully expecting to see Hayden standing in her office doorway. Fortunately, a happy surprise awaited her when she beheld the intense brown eyes of Garrett Hughes.

"I just wanted to stop by and say good-bye." Garrett closed her office door. "I'll be leaving for New Orleans tomorrow."

"Tomorrow? So soon?"

Garrett nodded as he approached her desk. "Harry wants me to get rolling on the new office. He came in this morning pretty adamant I get down there as quickly as possible." He halted at the corner of her desk. "He's also in a real bad mood. Any idea why?"

Madison returned her eyes to her computer screen. "Maybe he fought with his ex again?"

Garrett snickered. "Not his ex. I was thinking more along the lines of you."

"You're mistaken," she shot back in a dismissive tone.

He shifted his hip on the desk. "I may not know a lot of things that go on inside of Harry's head, but I do know how he feels about you...how he has always felt."

Madison sat back in her chair, eyeing the handsome man with the dark, brooding features. "What do you know, Garrett?"

He glanced about the office. "When we were at UT together, I remember a time when he became obsessed with finding a certain undergrad architecture student. I worked in the administration building at the time and tried to help him find her, but instead I found Ellen." He folded his arms over his wide chest. "I always thought she was the one he wanted...that was until I saw how he was with you. Ellen was a poor substitute for you, wasn't she, Mary?"

Madison shook her head, smiling. *So much for secrets.* "How long have you known?" she gently challenged.

"Since the day he saw you in the elevator. He told me he had found Mary. Then, when you began working here...well, I can't remember the last time I saw him so happy. Now, he's back to the man I knew before your arrival; grumpy, snapping at everyone, and ornery as hell." His uncanny eyes patiently explored her face, making Madison shift uncomfortably in her chair. "Do you mind if I ask what happened?"

She stood up, unable to take his piercing gaze any longer. "Nothing to tell. We rekindled an old flame, but it was only a fling." Madison moved away from her desk and went to the picture window overlooking downtown.

Several seconds of silence ticked by, making her wonder what he was thinking.

"So why are you typing a resignation letter?" Garrett probed as he came alongside her. "Seems a bit much if it was only a fling."

"It's better if I leave."

Garrett laughed, filling the office with an alluring sound. "You may be a great architect in the making, Madison, but you're a crummy liar."

She turned to him, frowning. "I'm not lying. I can't work with him anymore."

"You can't work with him because you're in love with him, just as much as he's in love with you."

The comment floored her. "Hayden Parr isn't the kind of man to fall in love."

Garrett placed his hands behind his back and his eyes cut into her. "You're wrong. He may never want to admit it to you, or even to himself, but he is. He's been in love with you since that first night you two met. You changed him then just as you have changed him now." He paused and a smile curled his thin lips, adding an uncharacteristic warmth to his features. "And he has changed you, Madison. You're not the same timid girl who came into this office on that first day. You've grown; you've become a woman to be reckoned with. I would hate for Parr and Associates to lose such a valuable employee."

Madison went back to her desk chair. "It's no use, Garrett. I have to go."

"Quitting won't deter him, Madison. Harry won't give up on you. He's the most determined man I know."

Madison took her chair. "I can be pretty determined, too."

"So I've noticed." Garrett came around her desk. "Any idea where you'll go after you leave here?"

"I've called my former boss at Pellerin, Everly, and Walters. He's offered me a position in his firm."

"I guess you've got it all figured out then."

He moved toward the door, and Madison's eyes followed him across the room. "Good luck in New Orleans, Garrett. I hope you're happy there."

Stopping at the door, he turned back around and faced her. "You know, it doesn't matter whether we call them marriages, relationships, or arrangements; in the end it's how two people make each other feel that's important. How did Harry make you feel?" Garrett opened the office door. "Think about it, Madison."

Sitting back in her chair, Madison mulled over Garret's question. How Hayden made her feel didn't matter anymore. That was the past and she needed to refocus her sights on her future, despite the protests of her crumbling heart.

"Life is filled with tough choices," her mother had always told her. For the first time in her life, Madison was beginning to comprehend how tough those choices really were.

***

After several minutes of pacing in her office, Madison headed to the elevators with the envelope containing her letter of resignation gripped firmly in her hand. She had planned on leaving it with Emma, hoping to avoid a confrontation with Hayden, but when the elevator doors opened, Hayden stood before her.

"We're going to talk," he growled, exiting the elevator.

Staring into his eyes, she saw the anger simmering just below the surface. "There's nothing to say. Here." She handed him the envelope.

"What's this?"

"My resignation."

His eyes scanned the empty waiting area of Parr and Associates. Taking her elbow, he ushered her toward the dark-paneled doors. Practically dragging her along the empty hallway, he reached her office, shoved her inside, and slammed her door closed.

"You're not leaving, Madison."

"I can't stay. We can't work together anymore."

"Bullshit. I stayed away all weekend believing you needed time to think. You've had time. Now you want to quit, just like that, without discussing it with me."

"Do you honestly think I could stay? After everything...." She turned away and headed to her desk.

"Everything we had, we still have. Nothing has changed." He came up to her desk, his eyes blazing. "I know you're angry about the wedding, and I told you I was sorry. What is it going to take for you to forgive me?"

She was dumbstruck by his question. What was it going to take for her to forgive him? Or was backing out of their relationship and leaving her job what she really wanted? Sure she had been thrilled he had chosen her, but in the back of her mind she'd wondered why a man like Hayden Parr desired someone like her.

"Why did you pick me up in that bar? I know you were looking for a one-night stand, and I'm sure any woman in that bar would have done, but why me? What made you want me?"

He tossed up his hand, still holding the letter. "What difference does that make?"

"Tell me, Hayden."

He went to her desk and dropped the envelope in his hand on her keyboard. "It wasn't how you looked, it was more about how you acted. Like you needed to be taken care of. I found the quality very attractive."

"But I didn't need to be taken care of, and I still don't. I can take care of myself."

"I disagree, Madison. I feel you need to be taken care of, and by a man who knows how." He sat on the edge of her desk. "I want to be that man."

"Jesus, you just don't get it, Hayden," she exclaimed, raising her voice. "You can't keep me locked away because you want to take care of me or control me. That's not how relationships work. You were always asking me if I trusted you, but did you trust me? In relationships, you have to trust each other."

"Then what do I have to do? Take you to fancy parties, dine in nice restaurants? We'll do all of it. Anything you want." His lips pressed tightly together, accentuating the irritation in his eyes. "Just reconsider your resignation."

She slowly walked up to her desk, noting how the anger instantly vanished from his gray eyes only to be quickly replaced by lust. "I have to go. If I stay, I'll always wonder if I'm getting assignments in this firm because I'm a good architect or because of our arrangement."

His lips stretched into a disarming smile. "It's not an arrangement anymore, Madison. It hasn't been for quite a while."

She held up her head, determined to resist his charm. "You've always kept me from knowing how you feel, from telling me what you're thinking. If it were more than an arrangement, Hayden, we would have shared so much more than our bodies."

He sat on the edge of her desk, staring into her eyes, as if making up his mind. "I'm sorry you feel that way. I had hoped...." He abruptly stood from the desk and adjusted the sleeves of his suit jacket. When he raised his eyes to the office door, his face was like stone. "If you need to go, I won't stop you." He strode across the office to the door and stopped, but never faced her. "You can return to your job with Parr and Associates at any time. The door is always open to you."

After he had left the office, Madison picked up the envelope containing her resignation letter. Fighting back the tears, she began to rub her hand across the envelope, smoothing out the wrinkles Hayden had made. "I have to walk away, because if I don't do it now, I never will, and I'll be his forever."

Chapter 20

Sitting in her cramped office behind her oak desk, Madison tried to think of some way to change the design staring back at her on her computer monitor. The French provincial exterior she was hoping to incorporate into the strip mall she was drawing was going nowhere, and the more she tweaked her plans, the worse it became.

Pushing her high backed chair away from her desk, she made her way to the corner scenic window that overlooked the children's playground next door. This was the best part of her job at Pellerin, Everly, and Walters: being able to stare out her office window and watch the children running amuck on the grassy playground. There were days, like today, when she itched to join them.

"You keep staring out that window and you'll never get any work done, Madison."

When Madison wheeled around, she was greeted by the dull brown eyes and wrinkled countenance of her boss, Curtis Pellerin. No one really knew how old he was, but by the way he shuffled into her office—slightly hunched over with his loose-fitting, brown suit hanging from his bony frame, and with a smattering of white hair on his head—Madison guessed he was well into his seventies.

"Sorry, Mr. Pellerin. The kids just help me think."

Curtis Pellerin cackled loudly, betraying his frail exterior. "Something I would expect a woman to say. Ever think of having any of your own?" He slowly came up to her side, taking up a position beside her at the window.

Madison wistfully shrugged. "Someday."

"Well, be careful who you have them with. My daughter married an idiot and now she has three idiot children to show for fifteen years of marriage." He held up his hand. "Yes, I know. I'm supposed to love the little heathens, but my grandchildren often give me indigestion." He motioned to her desk. "Show me what you have on that strip mall. The contractor wants to get started soon."

"Actually, I still have a bit more to do." She went to her desk and hit the space bar on her keyboard, pulling up the design on her computer screen.

Curtis Pellerin eyed the plans, lifting the thick, wire-rimmed glasses slightly higher on his face. Madison stood by her desk, intently studying his craggy features as he perused the computer screen.

"Perhaps strip malls aren't your thing," he reasoned with a half-smile. "I know it's boring as hell, but it's what we do here at Pellerin, Everly, and Walters. However, you knew that before when you interned for me, which makes me wonder why you returned to us last month."

"I told you I wasn't a good fit with Parr and Associates. Mr. Parr was very kind, but I think my designs weren't what he was looking for."

"Uh huh," the older man said with a slight nod of his head. "So Hayden told me."

"I'll get better, Mr. Pellerin. I'm just...a little distracted these days."

"Seems to me you've been distracted for quite a while now, Madison." He examined her through the lenses of his thick glasses. "You're not the same young lady I knew before you went to work for Parr and Associates. You've changed."

"I grew up, Mr. Pellerin."

"No, that's not it." He stood back from her desk, shaking his head. "Since you've come back to work for me, you've been withdrawn, sullen, and, I dare say, almost teary-eyed." He waited for her reaction, but she kept her eyes glued to the linoleum floor. "Is there anything you would like to talk about, Madison?"

Her gut twisted into a dozen small knots at the idea of sharing her personal troubles with her boss. It was bad enough she spent her days wandering around in a virtual fog, and her nights longing for Hayden, but to disclose her relationship with Hayden Parr to her current employer would have surely been the death knell for her job.

"I think I'm just adjusting to living alone. I miss my roommate. It's been kind of lonely without her around," she offered to the older gentleman, hoping it sounded reassuring.

"Perhaps a new assignment might help snap you out of your doldrums." He motioned to the computer screen. "A different type of challenge might spark your creative juices. What I have is out of the ordinary for my firm, but I think right up your alley." He paused and grinned at her. "I was contacted by a client about building a home. He has recently acquired a nice lot of land and wants to build something that will blend in with the woods covering his lot." Curtis Pellerin arched an eyebrow at her. "Interested?"

A ripple of enthusiasm tempted her belly. "Yes, absolutely, but I don't have a lot of experience with house construction, Mr. Pellerin. Even less than I have with strip malls."

He removed a slip of paper from his brown suit jacket pocket. "Not to worry, the client understands and is still willing to take you on." After he handed her the paper, he checked the stainless Rolex on his right wrist. "You have exactly thirty minutes to meet him at this address."

Madison's jaw slackened. "What? You want me to meet the client today? I haven't seen the lot, let alone—"

Mr. Pellerin waved a gnarled hand at her. "Madison, just go. The rest will work itself out, trust me."

***

Exactly thirty minutes later, Madison eased her blue Rogue in front of a spacious wooded lot with thick oaks, a few crape myrtle trees, and trails that cut through the high grass and light brush. While gazing at the familiar terrain, she spied the black Land Rover on the opposite side of the street. As she stared at the car, the driver's side door opened and Hayden stepped out.

It had been over a month since she had seen him. He was wearing a form-fitting dark brown suit that accentuated his toned body, and Madison felt that old flurry of tingles she got whenever he was near come roaring back to life.

"What is this, Hayden?" she demanded, climbing from her car. "Did you put Mr. Pellerin up to this?"

He raised his hands, assuaging her anger. "Before you fly off the handle, let me explain." He motioned to the property. "After the Martins refused to sell, I bought this lot from them. I figured I could build my new place here, and I need an architect to come up with a design that blends the house with the property. Kind of like the design you came up, but with some changes."

"What about your house? I thought you didn't—"

"I've settled things with Ellen. I decided I needed a fresh start. Some place new. Some place special."

Madison folded her arms, trying as hard as hell not to grin. "So, it's all over with your ex?"

"Yes, it is. After you left, I realized that I needed to get on with my life."

"I'm glad for you," she gazed into the lot, "but why am I here?"

He moved closer to her. "Because you drew a house once for this property; a house I fell in love with. I would very much like to hire you as my architect to help me design the home of my dreams. You're the best I know at making dreams into reality, Madison."

"The best at daydreaming, you mean." She waved off his attempt at flattery. "You don't need me. You have an office full of architects who can build your dream home."

"But none of them are you," he purred in his deliciously deep voice.

Her resolve wavered, and she shifted uncomfortably on her feet. "Nothing has changed, Hayden. You still want to control me, but I can't be that way with you anymore."

"I know. I guess I never acknowledged the confident woman you've become until you left me. I realized then I'd been wrong to keep you hidden away from the world. I still saw you as that innocent girl I'd met in the bar, and I thought I was protecting you, but I was really protecting me." He diverted his attention to the property. "I told you once that there was a woman who changed me, changed everything I wanted in my life. The woman who made me want more than emotionless arrangements." He sighed, lowering his gaze to the street. "That woman was you. You wanted to know why I picked you up in that bar, and the real reason is from the moment I saw you sitting on that bar stool, I was in awe of you. You were wearing a little blue dress with white flowers and looking so terrified that I...." He shook his head and returned his eyes to her. "I could never admit that to anyone before because I thought there was something wrong with me for feeling that way about a total stranger. The next morning, when you were gone, I knew I had to find you; and when I couldn't, I married the next woman that came along. But when I did find you again, I was desperate to make sure you never left me. So desperate that I got scared."

The shock of his confession caused the walls around her heart to give way, and all the feelings she thought she had successfully put behind her came crashing back. "Why are you telling me this now?"

Hayden came right up to her, his eyes pleading with her. "Because I want another chance with you, Madison. A chance to make up for all of my shortcomings. If I promise to change, can you promise to give me that chance?"

"You think hiring me as your architect will fix everything? It's not that simple, Hayden."

"No, I'm hiring you because you know what I want in a home. You know me better than anyone. You know my tastes, preferences, and desires. There is no one else who could design this house for me." He shrugged his wide shoulders. "As for the rest, I'm willing to do whatever it takes to prove to you that I'm sincere."

Her eyes darted about the property as she tried to make up her mind.

"Why don't we discuss this over dinner?" he softly suggested. "I know the best little pizza place, not far from here. It's cozy and quiet, and very good for long talks."

"Are you asking me to dinner?"

"No, I'm asking you to pizza." He slowly grinned. "Tomorrow night we could go someplace nice for dinner on an official date. What do you say?"

Her stomach trembled with excited butterflies. "An official date? I'll think about it, Mr. Parr."

He chuckled and ushered her toward his car. "Perhaps you should start calling me Harry."

"I'll think about that, too."

He opened the passenger side door of his car. "Does this mean you're warming up to the idea of being my architect?"

Stopping at the car door, she sucked in an apprehensive breath. "If I agree to be your architect, I think we need to set some ground rules."

"Ground rules?" Hayden knitted his brow. "You're joking, right?"

"No, I'm not." After Madison had climbed into his car, she gazed back at him. "I'm looking at this as a new kind of arrangement for us, one that starts out as friends. The rest...we'll see."

He smashed his lips together, looking like the stubborn man she had come to know. "Not sure if I like the sound of that."

She grinned at his displeasure. "A wise architect once told me that 'the only part of a building that matters is its foundation. The rest is just for fun.' I think we need to work on our foundation...for now."

He nodded with understanding, giving her a hint of a smile. "In that case, I guess it's a start."

"It's a very good start, Harry." She admired his handsome face. "It's our new beginning."

Epilogue

The long frame of a two-story house with a stunning view of Turtle Creek sat embedded into the side of a ridge at the rear of the wooded property. All around the construction area men were scurrying about wearing hardhats, while heavy moving equipment transported needed building supplies about the site. In the air, the essence of freshly cut pine trees—intermixed with the stench of diesel from the machinery—added a surreal touch to the organized chaos. As Madison slogged through the thick muddy ruts in the ground, she spied the jutting rear porch of the expansive home that looked out toward the creek. Taking a moment to survey her creation, she felt a surge of satisfaction. For the first time in her career, she was watching her design come to life, and in that instant she realized that it didn't matter if it was a thirty-story skyscraper or a single family home, the effect would have been the same. Size didn't matter, the achievement did.

"Madison," a velvety voice called from the rear of the home.

When she careened her head around, she saw him. Standing by a work table set up near the rear porch, he had removed his suit jacket and rolled up his white shirt sleeves. Madison sighed, surprised that he still had the ability to take her breath away. Trudging through the muddy terrain, she nodded at Hayden.

"Hey, baby." Hayden wrapped his arm about her waist and pulled her close. "We've got to go over the interior color scheme sometime today. My decorator needs to know what we want."

Placing her leather purse on the worktable, she coyly smiled. "It's your house, Harry. You don't need me to help you decorate it."

His eyes came together in a vain attempt at a scowl. "I disagree. I already told you numerous times that your opinion is invaluable to me."

Madison felt that kick of reservation floating around in her gut. "We talked about this. I know we've been spending a lot of time together with dinners and meetings about the house, but my feelings haven't changed."

"I'll wear you down yet. By the time I move into this place, I expect you to feel quite differently about us."

"I'm better as your architect, rather than your girlfriend."

"My mother would disagree with you. She keeps asking when I'm bringing my 'girlfriend' to dinner again. She likes you."

Madison smiled, tucking a strand of brown hair behind her ear. "I don't think you should be bringing me to your parents' house for dinner anymore. I only agreed to it that one time last month because you practically forced me into it. If we do it again, it will give them the wrong impression about us."

"Wrong impression? You're killing me, Madison." He tossed something on the table. "You'd better take a look at that."

Atop the copies of the house plans was a small, square white box. There was no wrapping or bow, just the plain box.

"What's this?"

"My back-up plan, in case you continue pushing me away. I have been apologizing profusely for four months now, and decided this is what I needed to do to allay your fears about me."

"What back-up plan?"

He pointed to the box. "Open it."

Carefully removing the top of the box, Madison noticed something gold shining back at her. On further inspection, she discovered the gold object was a key chain with a circular gold disc attached to it. Fingering the key chain, she lifted it from the box.

"It's a key chain."

"It's an invitation," he told her, inching closer. "I figured I could get the electronic lock combination carved into it once we move in."

"We?" She gripped the key chain in her hand. "Hayden, I agreed to be your architect on the condition that we would not—"

"Turn it over," he interjected, pointing to the key chain. "I think you'll find what you're looking for on the other side."

Flipping over the round disc, she spied an engraving.

I love you, Madison.

Madison was at a loss for words. This was not what she had expected.

He motioned to the key chain. "I thought putting the words on something permanent would show you how I really feel."

"You love me?"

He gazed into her eyes. "I always have. I was just too afraid tell you, and I didn't want to risk losing you in case you didn't feel the same way about me."

She wanted desperately to believe him, but the pain of their past break-up still smarted, tempering her willingness to take him back. "Hayden, how can I trust you not to shut me out like you did before?"

"This time will be different because I have a plan. You asked me once to describe my plans for us, as an architect." He gestured to the key chain. "This is our foundation. The rest," he shrugged, "we'll just draw as we go."

Madison's toes tingled. This was more than she had ever hoped for. "That's quite a plan."

"But it won't work without you, Madison." He took in a nervous breath, keeping his eyes on her. "So am I forgiven?"

Gripping the key chain in her hand, her heart caved. She couldn't resist him any longer. Perhaps it was time to give him a second chance. Nodding her head, she declared, "Yeah, you're forgiven."

"Took you long enough." He clasped her left hand and started guiding her toward a long white trailer set up to the side of the construction site. "I'm glad that's settled, because there is something else we need to do right away."

"Where are we going?" Madison halted, and waited as Hayden came back to her.

He motioned to the white trailer up ahead. "I had an office set up close to the site because the condo I'm leasing is too damn small. I've even had my big desk moved out here. Interested?" He bobbed his eyebrows up and down.

"I don't know." She eased up to him with a Cheshire cat grin curling her deep red lips. "Maybe I should be the one tossing you over the desk. I think I might want to take control for a while."

"I definitely like the sound of that." His arms went about her. "Is this the start of a new kind of arrangement?"

"No more arrangements." She edged her lips closer to his. "And, Hayden…call me Ms. Barnett."

Frowning, he let her go and took a step back. "No, that doesn't work for me. Not quite the fantasy I had in mind." He paused, and tipped his head thoughtfully to the side. "How does Mrs. Parr sound?"

Madison's heart skipped a beat. "You're serious?"

"I wanted to put it on the back of that key chain," he nodded to the key chain still in her hand, "but it wouldn't fit."

"Are you sure, Hayden? Are you sure you want me?"

With a spectacular smile, he inched right in front of her. "Marry me, Madison. You've been the only woman for me ever since our first night together." He put his hands about her face. "Be mine, utterly and completely, forever."

"Wow," she whispered, her eyes filling with tears. "For a man who isn't good with words, you sure found the perfect ones."

His thumb wiped away the single tear that had begun trickling down her left cheek. "Is that a yes?"

Nodding, she took his hand in hers and pulled him toward the trailer. "Come on, Mr. Parr. Let's go and break in that desk."

The End

Alexandrea Weis is an advanced practice registered nurse who was born and raised in New Orleans. Having been brought up in the motion picture industry, she learned to tell stories from a different perspective and began writing at the age of eight. Infusing the rich tapestry of her hometown into her award-winning novels, she believes that creating vivid characters makes a story moving and memorable. A permitted/certified wildlife rehabber with the Louisiana Wildlife and Fisheries, Weis rescues orphaned and injured wildlife. She lives with her husband and pets in New Orleans.

To read more about Alexandrea Weis or her books, you can go to the following sites:

Website: http://www.alexandreaweis.com/
Amazon page: http://amzn.to/1orDPLT
Facebook: http://www.facebook.com/authoralexandreaweis
Twitter: https://twitter.com/alexandreaweis
Goodreads:
http://www.goodreads.com/author/show/1211671.Alexandrea_Weis

Made in the USA
Middletown, DE
18 November 2015